THE TRISKELION SERIES

IF TOMORROW NEVER COMES

LUNA EVERLY

For those of you who fall a little too hard,
a little too quickly,
a little too deeply.

This one's for you.

Especially if the ones you fall for are the sexy, morally gray rulers
of the underworld...

TRIGGER WARNINGS

This book contains dark elements such as crime, violence, death, grief, drug use, drinking, cheating, abduction, scenes, and vivid talk of abuse/torture, infertility, menstruation, light bondage, and explicit sexual content. Intended for those 18+

The Kennedy brothers are desperate to get their women back after being captured the night of Madison's graduation dinner.
With the help of their connections in Miami, they track their captors down.

But that's the easy part.

Getting them back is becoming more and more challenging as secrets begin to rise to the surface.

Tension builds between the brothers. Liam finds himself arguing with Killian over just about everything—especially when it comes down to Madison.
Meanwhile, Killian faces an impossible decision. A decision that leaves Madison's fate dangling in the hands of the *Bone Breaker.*

A man so feared he has the criminal underworld speaking in whispers.

He is lethal.
He is calculated.
And he takes what he wants.

Except the one thing he wants—he can't have.
Madison.

CHAPTER 1

MADISON

A PERSISTENT BUZZING radiates throughout my skull. *Over and over and over again.* It's a unique melody, horrendous and torturous. At this point, I can't be sure of its origin. Pain and dehydration? The obnoxious flickering of the fluorescent lights? Caffeine and nicotine withdrawal?

Or maybe it's my lovely cell mates—the flies and mosquitoes.

Welts and bruises scatter my body so extensively that with one look, you'd think I came down with the plague.

Heavy, languid footsteps approach my door, encouraging my heart to thrash against my bruised rib cage. That nightmarish sound can only indicate two things—*pain or food.* Sometimes both.

The sound of my racing pulse whooshing in my ears temporarily replaces the buzzing. I can't tell which I prefer:

Whooshing or buzzing?

Buzzing or whooshing?

"Haha," I laugh out loud to myself. My hand slaps across my mouth as another hysterical giggle rises and bubbles in my throat, threatening to slip out. A testament to my slipping sanity.

How is this my life right now? *You just had to fall in love with*

—not one—but two mobsters, didn't you? Didn't you, Maddy? God. Even my mind is turning against me.

"I thought we were supposed to be friends, *bitch*," I retort, the words just a whisper as they leave my mouth.

Just like my poor lips, I'm starting to crack. My tongue darts out, running over the peeling flesh in an attempt to soothe them. *What I wouldn't give for some chapstick.* A metallic taste awakens my taste buds as the cuts reopen from the abrasive contact. My mouth is so dry it feels like I ate an entire sleeve of saltine crackers.

Oh wait, I did. That was my breakfast.

Stale saltine crackers, I might add.

When the bland little squares are one of the only forms of sustenance you get, you become rather fond of them.

At least I get three meals a day.

Every morning I wake to a sleeve of saltines, followed by one tiny piece of grilled chicken—if you would even call it that—for lunch. The quality is so bad, I wouldn't even feed it to the stray dogs. A majority of the time, it isn't even fully cooked. But you do what you gotta do to survive. Like eating around the raw pieces and praying you won't be on your knees vomiting your guts out in a few hours—which has happened a few times now. The rancid evidence of that resides in a five-gallon plastic bucket in the corner of my cell.

Last but not least, the final meal of the day: a meager bowl of questionable fruit. Yesterday was exciting...pineapple. *Mmm. Wonder what today will bring?* I always love a good surprise.

A tray slides into the small opening in the door. I waste no time at all, guzzling down the bottle of water placed on it. *Slow down, Madison.* I really should save some for later. I'm sure I'll need it. There's a high probability I'll vomit again from the pain of today's torture...or this game of chicken roulette I'm playing.

"Talking to the walls again, Madison?" The smooth rich baritone voice of Selena's older brother floats through the small

2

window in the cell door. A boisterous laugh follows along with the jingle of keys engaging the lock. He usually brings me my food, slides it through the window, and sits against the outside of the door to talk to me.

But not today. *What's changed?*

My heart rate works up to a gallop as the metal door scrapes against the concrete floor and opens.

He's much taller than I had imagined. Very tall actually, considering my own height of 5'6. For some reason, I was expecting the male version of Selena. Of course, he's not as tall as...

I can't bring myself to mention their names.

If I do, I'll surely break for good.

A sliver of hope is all I have left. Without that, I doubt I'll make it through my upcoming meeting with *El Rompe Huesos —The Bone Breaker*. I haven't met him yet, but the name alone makes me want to curl up into a ball and scream. I was convinced (those who shall not be mentioned) would have been here by now. But it's already been three weeks.

How do I know that?

The man now standing in my personal space leaves me a Post-It note each morning with the date and a random inspirational quote scribbled across it. Reminds me of when my mom would leave little notes in our lunch boxes. *Except, instead of bringing joy, it brings dread.* The cheerful neon memo is a cruel reminder that another day has passed without being saved.

Nervously, I gaze up at him. I doubt he's *that* much older than me. Maybe late twenties or early thirties. Older than... *Never mind.* Espresso-brown, windblown curls hang over his forehead. He looks like he just got back from surfing all day. Striped board shorts grip his toned thighs while thick bands of muscle strain against a light blue Billabong tank top.

The color brings out the intensity of his topaz-blue eyes, making them pop and contrast beautifully against his sun-kissed

3

skin. Those exquisite eyes bore into mine as his lips form a thin line.

"I brought you another bottle of water." He pushes the bottle into my trembling hands and takes a step forward. Warm and surprisingly gentle fingers grip my elbows as he peers down at me. A small gasp escapes my lips. I wasn't expecting— *gentle*.

Not in this cell. Not as a prisoner.

Nothing in this place has been *gentle* or *soft*.

His touch is the exact *opposite* of his Uncle Geraldo's. That fucker may be old, but he still has enough energy left in his ancient ass to beat the living shit out of me. All for information.

Information I don't have a clue about.

He keeps asking about the death of Selena's father. How the fuck am I supposed to know?

During my visit last night with the vile man, I was told I would be seeing the *Bone Breaker* for my next *session*—as he'd call it. A threat I didn't take lightly. A threat that has been running wild in my mind, keeping me from any ounce of sleep.

Geraldo sent me back to my cell—conscious this time. The feel of his hands around my throat still lingers from the days before. Our meetings always end with me blacking out under the talons of that monster.

Most nights I don't remember much of anything. Sometimes in my haze, I imagine Liam holding me, cradling me close to his body. Keeping me alive another day.

I break out of the memory reel I've been stuck in all day and focus on the man before me. *Ocean Eyes* finishes his perusal of my body as his blue orbs meet mine again, inducing a wave of anxiety that crashes into me like a tidal wave. The scent of salt, coconut, and mint drifts across my nose, temporarily ridding it of the rancid smell of my cell. Somehow that calms the storm brewing beneath my skin and the fight or flight mode threatening to resurface.

"You ready to meet *El Rompe Huesos*?" His eyes drop to my

bruised throat, lingering there a second too long, and making me squirm.

"I told your uncle, and I'll tell you as well... I truly don't know what happened to your father," I say, putting as much confidence into my voice as possible. It strains and withers, too abused by the screaming and asphyxiation.

"I don't believe that, *Madison*. You know something. It's there, deep inside that pretty little head of yours." He taps his index finger twice against my temple. Footsteps sound in the hall, warning me we aren't alone.

I take a healthy step away from him. The last thing I need is him taunting me. Disapproval flashes across his eyes as they narrow at my sudden movement. Gripping the back of my head, he pulls me even closer, before lowering his face to mine so that the sturdy bridge of his nose presses against my own. The mint dancing on his breath brushes over my face as he begins to talk.

"I'll throw you a *bone*," he smirks at his little pun. "I'm sure *The Bone Breaker* would enjoy breaking the wings off of a clean *little butterfly* over a filthy one. Nothing thrills him more than to watch fresh blood splatter a clean canvas."

Ice snakes its way up my spine, making me shiver underneath the heat of his palm. His lips curl and a cryptic smile forms at my response.

"Let's go." Grabbing me by the arm, he tugs me out of the room and leads me down a damp, dark hallway. His hand shifts to grip the back of my neck, guiding me towards a staircase. As we ascend, he leans in and pushes a strand of my dirty knotted hair behind my ear.

"Don't even think about running, *Mariposita*. We are on a private island. The only way in or out is by boat. And trust me, you won't be finding the keys." He shrugs. "Feel free to try and swim. If the tide doesn't take you first, the sharks will." A dark eyebrow raises in an *I dare you*, kind of way.

I throw my hand over my eyes, shielding them, as he pushes

the door open at the top of the staircase. Sunlight filters through the windows in what looks to be a beautiful living room. It's difficult to *see* anything other than blurry furniture while my vision adjusts.

Ocean Eyes rolls his eyes at me, then hands me the pair of black sunglasses he has tucked into his shirt.

My eyes are able to focus better now that there's a polarized barrier—and I'm silently grateful for it. The shades are dark enough to hide my wandering eyes as I take in the space...and a little more of *him*.

The living room is airy and beachy. Wicker furniture, wide-planked wood floors, glass decor, and rope accents create an atmosphere that's incredibly inviting. *Beats the hell out of the dark, dank dungeon below it.*

I can feel him watching me. *Analyzing me.* So I turn my head a fraction. From the corner of my eye, I swear I see a hint of a smile. It's then he releases his hold on my neck, clearly realizing his threat struck home. *I won't run.*

Beige leather flip-flops start clicking down the hall. My body is slow to register that the fading sound indicates the need to follow. I start scrambling to catch up, tripping over my own feet and falling to my knees behind him.

Son of a—

"You learn quickly...already on your knees for me." He smirks down at me before lifting me up under the arms like a doll. My bare feet find their place back on the smooth hardwood before we are moving down the hall again.

We climb yet another set of stairs. The muscles in my legs scream, threatening to give out on me again. *Ocean Eyes* wraps a supportive arm around my waist, bearing my weight, and guiding me the remainder of the way. After shuffling me down another long hallway, he stops and opens the door to a bedroom just as airy and stylish as the living room.

I don't get the opportunity this time to take in the decor. I'm immediately ushered into the en suite, his presence lingering just inches behind me, so close I can feel the heat radiating off his chest. Irrationally, I think about leaning back to absorb it all. *Maybe I truly have lost my mind.*

"Everything you need for a shower is there." He points to the vanity. "Make it quick. You don't want to keep *El Rompe Huesos* waiting long."

Diego De La Cruz winks at me while crossing his arms over his chest and leans against the door. Not showing any signs of leaving me here alone.

Hell no.

"I'm not undressing in front of you," I say between clenched teeth.

"Would you rather tío Geraldo be here to supervise you?" One of his dark eyebrows lifts in a challenge.

My brow arches in response to his, getting ready to argue. Before I get the chance, he opens the door and leaves. His head pops between the small opening he left, a stern look sweeping across his face. "I'll be back in fifteen minutes to collect you. Be dressed and ready. There are clean clothes on the bed."

And then he's gone.

I turn and look at myself in the mirror, horrified by my reflection. The clothes from my graduation dinner are torn and filthy. Caked blood and grime coat my body along with a constellation of bug bites. Dark rings are carved beneath my red-rimmed eyes. My gaze travels down to my neck—which looks worse than it feels. Purple, blue, and green bruises are scattered around it like a necklace. The outline of Geraldo's fingertips is imprinted on each side of my neck. Thumbprint markings stain the column of my throat.

Tears build behind my eyes as I strip my dress over my head and drop it to the floor. I reach into the shower behind me and turn it on. When the temperature becomes scalding, my fingers push into my underwear and yank them off. I toss both garments in the trash and try not to focus on the reminder of my graduation ceremony. *What is my family thinking right now? There is no way Lexi bought anything the guys have told her.*

Pulling the enormous glass door back, I step into the steaming shower. Immediately, the hot water makes contact with my skin, eliciting a high-pitched yelp from me. *Agh, does that burn.* I settle into the scalding water, letting the pain numb my thoughts.

Moving as quickly as possible, I grab the shampoo and start massaging it into my strands. *Even my hands are weak.* My fingers tingle and ache just washing my hair. Conditioner is next, followed by a good scrubbing of my entire body.

Holy. Fuck. A fresh razor is sitting in the shower niche. I make quick work of shaving my legs and underarms before rinsing and getting out. White fluffy towels are neatly stacked next to the shower. Collecting two, I wrap one around myself and another around my hair, then walk straight into the bedroom and bypass another glance in the mirror. If I look at myself again, I'll just end up taking more inventory of my body.

And I really don't have time to waste. I still need to get dressed. Plus, my body is about to change again anyway.

That is...if I even make it out of my meeting with *The Bone Breaker.*

I've used up ten minutes already. The remaining five I use to dress into the lace thong, black capri leggings, and gray sports bra laid out for me. With haste, I toss my hair up in a messy bun. Generously enough—there was a hair scrunchie provided.

A pair of black socks and sneakers are at the foot of the bed —*which is gorgeous by the way.* A king-sized bed takes up a large portion of the room. The headboard and footboard are made of driftwood that continues upward to create a delicate canopy, enhanced by sheer white curtains. Distressed white end tables are next to each side with blue nautical lamps sitting on top.

Even the comforter goes along with the theme. Little starfish and coral embellish the sea green material.

What the fuck is wrong with me?

I'm taking in the decor when I should be looking for a phone or... I don't know... a weapon, maybe. My eyes scan the room. *Nothing.* I guess I could use this lamp, but I'd probably miss and just end up getting punished. But if I was successful... then what? How am I getting off this island? I release a frustrated breath.

Hopefully Lia—I just hope *he* finds me soon.

I pull the knot taut on the laces of my shoe as the door swings open.

"Time's up, *Mariposita*."

CHAPTER 2

LIAM

MADISON'S SISTER *Mikayla and I are doing some sickly sweet Green Tea shots at the bar. All I heard was Jameson. I don't know how they drink these damn things. I'd rather drink my own piss. But considering it was a peace offering, I just grin and bear it, letting the liquid slide down my throat. Madison and Selena are out front smoking and chatting. They really should have someone with them. I'm glad those two are getting along for Killian's sake, but there is still something I can't put my finger on with her.*

Something that makes me question if she is back here for the right reasons.

"I think you and Maddy are a better fit, to be honest. Don't tell your brother that though..." Mikayla's voice is muffled over my thoughts—which are loud as hell right now. Something's not right. I can feel it.

Before I can respond, an old rusted black van comes screeching to a halt by the curb. The door slides open and two men in black ski masks get out, grabbing my girl and Selena. My heart drops into my stomach at the scene unfolding before me. Mikayla's back is turned from the window—thank God.

Madison cries out my name, terror lacing her voice. Her attempts at escaping do nothing besides piss off the men who are abducting her. The man with Madison in his grasp is becoming more aggressive with each move of resistance. She's thrashing and clawing, kicking and punching. He pulls her flush against him, securing her in the van.

It's shaking me to my fucking core seeing her like that. Those bastards will regret the day they laid a hand on my woman. I bolt past a questioning Mikayla but it's too late.

It's too fucking late.

Madison's screams die behind the slamming of the van's door. Her beautiful eyes, wide with panic as a needle slides into her neck. The van speeds away without anyone at the party noticing.

FUCK! I tug on my hair violently.

I keep fucking failing her. I'm so sorry, baby. I will find you. I promise you. I promise you, I prom—

"Liam," Killian's voice jolts me awake. I haven't slept much. Every time I do, I relive that moment over and over again. His hand lands on my shoulder, gripping it firmly. "We are landing in a few minutes."

I wipe the sleep from my eyes and sit up straight in my chair. We are on the jet heading to Miami. Our connections in the Miami Syndicate have been in touch with Killian this past week.

It's been two long torturous weeks of not knowing any information.

Until now.

There was always the possibility this could have been retaliation from the Cuban-Miami Syndicate. For killing Selena's father. Our Miami allies received visual confirmation. The footage shows Selena and another woman being escorted off the private airfield and into a helicopter idling nearby.

The part that really got my blood boiling was the fact that they observed Selena awake and walking on her own accord. Madison—or we assume this to be her—was hauled over a man's shoulders, seemingly unconscious.

Killian had a hard time believing Selena could have played

him this way. Honestly, my gut kept telling me she set this whole goddamn thing up. I should have listened to it when she first came to the house crying for help. *Alan just so happened to be in our home the same day she begs her ex-lover for refuge? Trojan horse, remember?*

"Fuck." I let out a shaky breath, running my hand through my hair. A nervous habit of mine that Madison finds sexy and loves to point out. The Cubans are ruthless. Their forms of torture make *even me* want to vomit.

I remember being witness to Selena's father torturing a young boy. The lad was barely a day over seventeen.

He had been caught stealing from one of the grocery store registers in downtown Miami. His mum was severely sick and his infant sister had run out of formula. I don't think the boy knew who he was stealing from or that it was from the mafia. Perhaps if he had known, he would have found another way to get what he needed. *Perhaps not.* He was willing to do anything just to feed his sister.

Selena's father Basilio blindfolded Killian and I, got us on a boat waiting at the dock of his Miami mansion, and brought us to some exclusive island. Our blindfolds weren't removed until we reached a dungeon below the property.

All kinds of torture devices were laid out on a stainless steel table. Devices, as a young lad, I had *never* seen before in my life. And quite frankly—never want to see again. All sorts of twisted shit.

The boy had been strung up by heavy rusted chains attached to the ceiling. His head was slumped forward, eyes swollen shut, barely able to keep conscious after his initial beating.

And here I was thinking Jack Kennedy was merciless. Basilio was downright evil. Evil to his fucking *pathetic* core. I'm so glad I got to be the one who ended his life. Although, my bullet was far too kind for the way he deserved to leave this Earth.

Needless to say, the boy was left bloodied and missing a few fingers. His face was slashed so horribly you could see right down to the bone. Basilio let him go back to his sister and mum. But he made sure to send him home with a 'goody bag' of formula and his fingers taped to the top of the box. *Like I said... pure evil.*

The jet begins to make its descent. I look out the window at Miami's coast below, admiring the beauty of the ocean and all the little islands surrounding it. Wait a fucking minute...that's it. *The island.* That could be the key to what we've been trying to figure out.

"Kil, I think I know where they are," I smile. For the first time, I feel like we are one step closer to getting my girl back.

It's the first time I feel a shred of hope.

I quickly run Killian through my idea as we are landing.

DECLAN, the head of the Irish Miami Syndicate, greets us as we take a seat in the back of his blacked-out Suburban.

"I'm sorry to hear about all this, Killian. I'm sure having yer woman taken by your ex-fiancée has not been easy." His eyebrows come together in sympathy as he turns in the passenger seat to look at him. "I can't begin to imagine what I'd feel right now if they took Maeve."

A low growl escapes past my lips as my fingers clench into fists. Killian notices. A brief moment of indecision forms on his face. He nods, silently granting me permission to disclose the truth to Declan.

"About that, Dec. It's a long fucking story. One I will get into when we have more time. All you need to know right now is that Madison is *mine.*"

Declan's eyebrows practically smash into his hairline before a low whistle leaves his lips. "All the women in the world and the lot of you fall for the same lass," he chuckles, shaking his head.

"As I said, the situation is *complicated*—"

Killian intervenes, sensing my emotional instability and knowing I'm on the very edge of snapping at anyone or anything. "He knew her years before me, Dec. I just got wrapped up in it, not knowing it was who Liam had his heart set on. Long story short, Madison and Liam had a falling out. Liam attempted to shield her from this life. She had no idea that he's my brother, let alone that we were involved in the same organization. We worked through it all over the last few months. Selena and I reconnected...but now I'm not certain I can trust her." He releases a shaky breath and pinches the bridge of his nose.

Sighing, he says, "I love her. I really do. I need to know *for a fact* that she is responsible. No one lays a finger on her unless I say."

"I understand. As for Selena, brother, I can't find a reason to trust her right now. She walked off the tarmac like she just had the most relaxing flight. Not a care in the world for the unconscious girl slung over the shoulder of her lackey.

Killian leans over, looking like he's been punched in the gut. He scrubs his hands over his face, then through his unruly hair. I pat his back, letting him know that the signs don't necessarily indicate one hundred percent fact yet. This, however, should give him the strength he needs to get our girl back.

Our girl.

That's what she is, isn't she? She may be mine in every sense of the word. Romantically, emotionally, and spiritually she's exclusively mine. But we both know Madison still holds space in Killian's heart—a fact I can't deny or ignore. He may not love her the way he used to, but he *does* love her.

"Let's just focus on getting *our* girl back, shall we?" Killian lifts his head at my admission and his eyes narrow in determination.

Lethal. He looks absolutely lethal.

"I'll do whatever it takes," he declares, grabbing the back of my neck, and giving it a firm squeeze. "Dec, when we get to the compound, I need every ounce of information you can get on all the private islands off the coast. Especially ones with helicopter access."

WE REACH the compound a half hour later. There are a handful of men surrounding the gates of the property. Some faces I know, others I haven't met before. Declan leads us into his home where we are greeted by Maeve. She's stunning as always. Her beautiful red hair is pulled back into a low ponytail, a few wisps falling loose around her ivory skin. She looks between me and Killian before pulling us both into a hug.

"I'm so sorry to hear about your sweet girl Madison. Why don't we head into the kitchen and I can whip you both up some comfort food."

Declan wraps his arm around his wife and chuckles. "Or... perhaps they prefer to drink, love." He places a kiss on top of her head as she smacks his chest playfully.

"They need to keep their wits about them, Declan. Food *first.*" Her stern green eyes pierce mine before shifting over to Killian. *This lioness is not to be fucked with.*

Declan and Maeve are in their forties. Not much older than us, yet, the motherly instincts Maeve is giving off is oddly comforting.

"The rest of my men should be joining us soon," Declan announces as we all take a seat at the oversized dining table. Maeve leaves us, heading off to the kitchen. Cabinet doors start to slam, and pots and pans clink together as she works on dinner.

"I heard you have one of the best hackers in the country on your payroll." I take a sip of the double of whiskey Declan placed on the coaster in front of me.

He chuckles and brings his rock glass to his lips, hiding his smile. "Who told you that?"

"Guilty," Killian smirks.

Dec folds his hands on the table. "I do. His name is Sebastian. We call him Seb for short. And he's *really* fucking good at his job. I already brought him up to speed on the way here. The two of us have a secure line to text back and forth on."

The sphere-shaped ice clinks against the glass as I finish off my drink. Helping myself to the bottle in the middle of the table, I pour another. My mind goes to Maddy. *What possible hell could she be enduring over there?* I slam the second drink back. Fire coats my throat, burning its way down my esophagus. The glass almost shatters as I return it to the stone coaster.

Basilio may be dead, but his brother Geraldo—the current leader—is just as corrupt. And he isn't even *the worst* of them.

Rumor has it, they have a man in their arsenal so deadly, so unworldly, that they nicknamed him *The Bone Breaker*—AKA —*El Rompe Huesos*. One of the hushed rumors swirling around describes the barbaric surgery he endured where surgical metal was placed over the bones of his knuckles. If that were to be true, his right hook must be lethal.

I swear I am going to have TMJ by the end of all of this. My jaw clenches at the thought of this psychopath being anywhere near Madison. Bile surges in my throat before slipping back into my uneasy stomach.

If *The Bone Breaker* gets his hands on *my woman...*

I need to stop. *We will get her back.* But...even when we do, what kind of trauma will she have had to endure? Will Maddy even be the same after all of this is over?

CHAPTER 3

MADISON

OCEAN EYES LEADS me to an office in the same hallway as this bedroom. *I wasn't expecting that.* An office? My mind conjured up something *way* scarier than even my cell in the dungeon. He takes a seat at the desk, kicking his legs up and leaning back in the office chair. I stand there wondering what the hell I should be doing.

"Take a seat, *Mariposita*," his lips purse together like he's holding back some sort of inside joke. One I am most likely the butt of. He points to the turquoise leather chair in front of the desk.

With a sigh, I cross my arms over my chest and sit. "Where is Selena? I'm sure your sister feels *accomplished*...now that she's managed to fool the entire Tri-State Syndicate... and *me.*" My voice cracks on the last part. I was naive to think Selena was my friend. Guess my mother was right—I am too trusting of people, always seeing the good in them. It's just who I am. I don't know if that will ever change, even after all of this.

That is...if there *is* an after.

"Oh, she's pleased with herself alright." Diego brings his index fingers together like he is holding a gun, or praying, and taps his lips. I can't decipher if he's happy about that or not. It almost sounds like he is being sarcastic. Those intense eyes of his survey me again.

"You clean up nice." He shoots me a wink.

I scowl, bearing my teeth at him like a wild animal.

"Settle down, *Mariposita*. I like my women willing and acquiescent. It's only a matter of time before you'll be begging me to kiss you. Then to *touch* you, relieving that ache between your legs. The ache that you're confused about feeling right now. Eventually, I'll have you under me, screaming my name so loudly you'll forget all about your man. About your old life. The only thing that will matter to you anymore will be that you experience the kind of pleasure you deserve. *Every. Fucking. Night.* With the kind of man who can give it to you. I'll show you pleasure you never knew existed...in my bed, on this desk—" he glides a finger across it "—and on every surface of this island I can find to claim you on. Until then, I won't touch you."

"Pig," I shout, my voice finding its strength. Heat swarms my cheeks. How dare he! I will *never* fuck him. He's delusional.

An egotistical. Self-righteous. Smug. *Asshole.*

He's out of his chair so fast, I almost forget to breathe. Then he's in my face. Solid arms wrapped in cords of tendons and veins rest on the arms of my chair. The leather groans between my legs under the weight of his knee pressing into it. His frame towers over me as he leans in to whisper. My heart pumps faster at the tingle of his minty breath fanning across the shell of my ear. Goosebumps start sprouting up across my battered skin.

"Hmm...I don't think that's the name you'll be crying out in my bed. Maybe *God*...but that's not the one either...try again. I'll give you a hint—it's something a little *longer*. Some would say it's a nickname. Any ideas?"

The words sit heavily on the edge of my tongue. *No. It can't be.*

He's goading me.

Taunting me.

"My name is *El Rompe Huesos*." He pulls away just enough to watch the fear cloud my eyes.

"But you can call me Diego, *Mariposita.*" *Jesus Christ.* Diego's smile turns menacing. Yet for some reason, I don't feel threatened.

Scared? *Yes.* Fearing for my life? *No.*

I refuse to bow down to this man. He wants me to submit, to break me. Well, guess what? *I fucking refuse.* I'm done being incapable of taking care of myself. Of needing to be saved. I'll save my damn self. My eyes raise to meet his in disobedience and challenge.

Now that the lighting is better, I notice the complexity and uniqueness of his eyes. They are even more beautiful up close. Swirls of sapphire and blue topaz fight for dominance in his irises. There's an explosion of cobalt fireworks surrounding his pupils. *Stunning.* They remind me of the view of the Caribbean Ocean. The depths of them, so clear, I can see my reflection.

Instead of horror—*which should be written across my face*—there's curiosity and awe of the man in my personal space. Diego drops his gaze to my lips, and whether he realizes it or not, he licks his own.

"You aren't going to touch me." It wasn't a question—rather, confirmation.

"As much as I would love to get a taste of you right now...I won't touch you. Not until you ask me."

"Trust me, Diego. *I never will.* You'll be as good as dead by the time Liam gets here." His pupils flare at my threat and his hands grip the armrests tighter.

"Here's the deal. I need you to do something for me. Don't ask questions. If you listen, you will be rewarded. You no longer have to stay down in your cell. You will also have access to a bed, shower, regular meals, and some freedom to enjoy the island as well as the pool."

"And if I don't do as you ask?" The muscle in his jaw pulses.

I'm not sure how much more I should poke the grizzly bear. He got the nickname *The Bone Breaker* for a reason. I'm lucky that he's infatuated with me or I'm certain my defiance would have gotten me killed already. He needs me alive for something.

"If you don't...then maybe I'll let Geraldo get his wish." Diego's eyebrow raises, daring me to question what that wish is. My stomach somersaults, knowing *exactly* what that vile man desires. Either my death or my pussy. *I'd gladly give him the first before I ever give him the latter.*

"That's what I thought, *Mariposita*." Releasing the chair, he steps back and offers me his hand.

A warm bed, real food, and a shower sound amazing. Especially now that I had a small taste of life outside my cage. I accept his outstretched hand. He tugs hard, pulling me flush against him, making his desire apparent. An impressive length nudges firmly against my stomach. Before I get the chance to say something snarky, he leads me out of the office and back down the staircase. We keep moving until we reach the door to the dungeon.

I don't understand.

I don't ask questions, either.

The foul smell of laundry left in a washing machine for too long assaults my nostrils. *Ugh.* I don't want to be back down here again. He opens a door a few over from my cell. The heavy metal screams against the concrete as he ushers me in and closes it.

What the fuck is this place? There are massive, thick chains attached to the ceiling. Something you'd find at a construction site. Leather cuffs hang from each of them. A stainless steel chair sits in the corner next to a table of the most horrific instruments. An array of saws and different kinds of blades are lined up along it. My throat begins to constrict.

The air in here is too damp.

Too heavy for me to breathe.

I try, yet my lungs refuse to respond. Diego comes up behind me and rubs his hand along my back. His touch spooks something inside me, making me jump and inhale sharply.

"Good girl," he praises, pulling my hair out of my bun, and running his fingers through it until it becomes messy. Damp, jet-black waves curtain over my face, partially obscuring my view of him. "I told you I won't hurt you—*and I won't*. I just need it to *look* like I did. Or that I will."

What. The. Actual. Fuck?

The door screeches open, making me jump again. A chill runs down my spine in anticipation. Selena comes prancing in, not a care in the world. Geraldo is right behind her carrying a tripod and video camera. The bitch has the audacity to wear a sunflower print sundress and platform cork heels. Designer sunglasses sit like a tiara atop her perfectly styled hair. A full face of makeup completes the look. She struts closer and grabs my face between her perfectly manicured fingernails.

"Hey, Maddy. *Sooo* sorry about all this. It's nothing personal. Just business. This is how it is. But how would you know? You are just an *outsider*. An outsider who should have never gotten herself involved with the likes of Killian and Liam Kennedy. Tío Geraldo seems to be under the impression that Killian ordered the hit on my papá. Which means you, *unfortunately*, are just collateral damage in this war." She winks at me, plastering on a fake ass smile.

Diego splays his hand along my waist and guides me toward the chains hanging from the ceiling. I spin around and face him. My voice drops to just a whisper, "You said you wouldn't-" Diego places his index finger over my lips to silence me. His back is to the others, concealing me from them.

"I won't. I *promise* you, I won't." His voice has dropped to a whisper. "No one here will lay a hand on you ever *again*. Just please, *please*, *Mariposita*—follow along. It will all make sense soon. You have to trust me." His eyes gleam with that promise.

Trust him? The Bone Breaker?! Why should I? Something swirls in my gut that I can't place.

And it's not chicken roulette.

I just know—in this moment—I can trust him. With a nod of my head, I let him chain me up.

The leather cuffs are tight and nip angrily against my wrists. Luckily, my feet are still planted firmly on the ground. The stretching of duct tape echoes in the tense silence. Diego tears it from the roll with his teeth and places it over my mouth. He rubs his thumb over my lips, almost seductively, securing it even further. Amusement and a bit of curiosity is written all over his face.

His eyes are the deepest shade of blue right now. I focus on them, distracting myself temporarily with thoughts of the ocean.

The calmness I always feel when I'm around it.

The rhythmic melody the waves create when they crash against the shore.

The serenity lasts only a minute before a rush of panic takes over me. I'm then reminded of how *powerful* the ocean is.

The utter destruction it can cause.

The ferocity of it during a storm.

The danger that lurks beneath its surface.

Geraldo awkwardly steps behind the camera and Selena takes her place next to me. As if on cue, she cries into her hands.

"3. 2. 1." Diego counts down dryly.

Selena wails so loudly it echoes off the concrete walls. "Kil, baby! I need you to listen carefully to what I am about to say. As you already are aware, we were taken by my family. Word got out that you and I were back together. They know you ordered the hit on my papá. Killing Alan and sending his head in a box tested the last of their patience." She sniffles for added effect. "Tío Geraldo wants retribution. He said if I cooperate, he won't kill Madison. He'll let you and I be together. But I'm not sure she'll last much longer. You have to hurry. *The Bone Breaker* is here for her. Tío Geraldo agreed to take Liam prisoner, in exchange for our freedom. They will send you the details for the swap tomorrow night." She covers her face again and starts crying and trembling. "If you refuse, they will kill us both." Her theatrics are almost believable, her tears beginning to look justified.

Diego walks over to the wall and pulls down a lever. The grating sound of *clinking* drowns out Selena's sobbing. My feet leave the floor as my arms become suspended higher. A sharp pang zips through me. My shoulders strain like they are ready to pop out of their sockets any second. I scream out behind the tape. Diego runs his hands over the collection of barbaric tools, lingering over a large blade before retrieving it. He spins the handle around in his hand. I shake my head furiously.

God, why am I so easily trusting of people? I should have learned this lesson with Selena. *Yet, here we are.* My biggest downfall will always be that I try to see the good in everyone. Even the damn *Bone Breaker. Yeah... that was dumb, Maddy.*

"Don't. Don't touch her!" Selena jumps up. Diego pushes her back until she falls on her ass. Geraldo runs over to restrain her out of the camera's view.

Diego circles me twice before the cool metal of the blade feathers across my chest, and then over my sports bra. Surprisingly, there is no trail of blood. My chest heaves and my heart feels ready to explode out it. Beads of sweat cling to my forehead and collect at the base of my throat.

The thin nylon material of my bra begins to separate, revealing the swell of my breasts. My nipples harden to peaks as the knife continues its descent. Diego's hand is steady as the knife whispers down over my stomach and navel, before hitting the waistband of my leggings. The blade slices through it like butter.

Outrage builds inside of me as he guides the tip through the seam of the crotch and up the back, dividing the pants in two.

How many times has this man done this? Is he always this precise? Or is he just toying with his prey?

I tug at my restraints to no avail. It's only making them bite into my wrist more. Not to mention, the movement is revealing more and more of my breasts. And *dangerously* close to revealing my nipples.

Selena keeps screaming. "Stop this! Leave her alone. You *promised*. You promised me!" *What the hell is she talking about? Who promised her what? Did Diego promise her he wouldn't touch me?*

"Then you are a stupid little girl for believing me," Diego directs his attention to Selena, pointing the knife at her. "Keep your mouth *shut*, Sel."

He drops the knife. It clatters to the floor, making me jerk and squirm like a fish on a hook. Diego squats down to remove each of my shoes, followed by my socks. Moving to stand in front of me, he admires his handiwork. Covetous eyes zipline down my exposed body. The bastard even has the nerve to smile at me, flashing me a set of perfectly straight white teeth. Even his canines are sharp, making him appear even more sinister.

Bold hands grip the two pieces of my leggings, maneuvering them down my legs. I'm left in nothing but a split-open sports bra and a black lace thong. That fucker knew what he would be doing. Of course, he would lay out a black lace thong.

Liam is going to lose his shit. But I'll be damned if he thinks he is sacrificing himself for me. I just have to figure out how to change our fate at the exchange.

Diego walks over, grabs the camera off the tripod, and begins recording himself. "I'm going to have so much fun breaking your little *princesa*, gentlemen. Be quick about getting to the meeting spot. If you're even a second late, Selena and Madison are dead. And the both of you will be next."

He slams the camera screen shut and tosses it to Geraldo, who fumbles it before securing it to his chest. "Get this uploaded and sent to them *immediately*. And take my sister with you. She's good at that tech shit."

Diego turns to face me while they leave us. "I still have my work *cut out* for me." His gaze becomes dark and ominous. Gone are those beautiful blue ocean eyes. I am now staring into the eyes of a hunter—and I happen to be his favorite kind of prey.

CHAPTER 4

DIEGO

MY SISTER and Geraldo leave us in silence. The room is thick with sexual tension and fear. Metal clangs against metal as the door aggressively slams shut behind them. I've *royally* pissed off my sister, but she'll have to get over it. I promised her I would only make it *look* like I was going to torture Madison. Hell, we agreed I wouldn't even be picking up a knife. It was never in the plan to cut open her clothes and strip her of them.

I can't say I didn't enjoy watching her pupils dilate and her breathing intensify. She was turned on the same way I was. *Fuck, that was hot.*

This was the way it had to be done to prevent my uncle from catching on to our plan. I saw the look on Geraldo's face. He knew the chains alone wouldn't be enough to get Killian and Liam to agree to the exchange. In his eyes, women are disposable. Believing no man would risk their empire or loyal soldiers for a slut. *His words—not mine.*

He's wrong. Those two would die for her.

That's their Queen.

One thing is certain. Geraldo is riding on borrowed time. He's about to have a reunion in Hell with his brother. Ending up right alongside the rest of the like-minded, corrupt men of this organization.

As the next leader of this syndicate, I'll be damned if we don't rid ourselves of the disease plaguing it first.

I make a beeline to the lever and release it slowly. Madison inches lower until her bare feet touch the ground. Her eyes widen as I approach her. They hold fear again.

Fear of me.

That shouldn't bother me, but it does. Finally, we have the video. And now that we do, I can fill Madison in on our plan.

You see, Sel and I had to have Madison's terror appear real. We needed tangible proof for Killian and Liam. This video will be the fuel required to fire up their hatred and anger. To encourage them to go beyond just retrieving Madison.

They will be bloodthirsty.

Their devotion to her is *exactly* what is necessary for the rest of this plan to be successful.

"You did good, *Mariposita*," I whisper, gently pulling the tape from her lips. Part of her lower lip starts bleeding where it has cracked open too many times. I grind down on my molars and take in a soothing breath. Not a drop of blood should have been spilled from this sassy little creature in front of me. Her eyes blaze with an inferno that could melt you on the spot.

Worth it, if you ask me.

"You. *Bastard.* You promised me you wouldn't tou—touch me." She kicks her legs out aiming for my dick. I already anticipated it, grabbing her thighs and wrapping them around me before they got the chance to connect. The pressure of my body molded against hers breaks through her anger.

"I *technically* didn't touch you." I bite my lip, holding back a laugh. *She's fucking cute when she's angry.* "Hold on to me with these sexy thighs while I open these restraints." Like a good girl, she obeys, squeezing her thighs tight around my waist.

When both her hands are free, I take a second to admire the

exquisite woman in my arms. She doesn't attempt to move from my hold right away. Warm brown eyes search mine for any sign of the monster that was present a few moments ago.

"What did you mean before? The part about 'I just need it to *look* like I did. Or that I will'."

Regretfully, I place her back down and strip my shirt off, sliding it over her head. Her brows come together in confusion before she slips her arms through the openings. My tank top is long enough to look like a dress on her. It lands at the tops of her thighs. *And damn if she doesn't look sexy as sin wearing it.* I bite down on my lip, preventing a moan from slipping past them. *Get it together, Diego. Sheesh.*

She has a man. She has a man. She has a man. It's been my mantra since I met her.

Who am I kidding? She would never want a monster like me, even if she didn't.

And after tomorrow night, if we don't get the chance to fill her man in, he's going to kill me. *Or try to, at least.* I really don't want to have to kill him first. I may be named *El Rompe Huesos,* but that name was designed for those who truly deserve it.

Liam does not. That doesn't mean I think he's *right* for Madison. He may not remember me. But I definitely remember him.

Before Selena's engagement was called off, we had dinners and events with them frequently. Liam was such a shithead. So hot and cold. So irritable. *What the fuck does Madison see in that guy anyway?*

"I have one last request from you, and then we will go back upstairs. I will fill you in on *everything*. Nothing is as it seems. I'm not your enemy, *Mariposita*. Neither is Selena."

"A request? *Ha.* That's rich coming from you. You get off on submission and obedience," she glares at me, crossing her arms over her chest.

Mmm...she's a feisty one. It makes my cock pulse with a

31

desire stronger than I've ever felt. Never have I felt this drawn to a woman. *And I've fucked plenty.* She isn't wrong. I do get off on obedience and submission. With her it's different. These last few weeks have given me a taste of something rare, something I didn't know I'd enjoy so much.

The fire she throws my way is what I've been craving all along. Threatening her to submit gets my blood flowing south. But having her throw it back in my face? *Fuuuck.* Has my balls aching for release.

I'm not sure that I would ever truly want her to become obedient. I want her fire, her stubbornness, her sharp tongue.

She has a man.

"Yes. A request. I need you to scream your pretty little heart out... So much so, it will make Geraldo think I am torturing you."

Her full lips pop open, dumbfounded.

"That's great. Good form." I lift her jaw with the knuckle of my index finger and press my thumb to her chin.

"Now I need you to *actually* scream."

She stares at me all of two seconds before screaming like a banshee.

"Feels good doesn't it? Let it out. Let everything you've been feeling these last few weeks out."

After a minute or so, I cup my hand over her mouth and silence her. She bites the inside of my palm. Not hard enough to draw blood, but hard enough to leave teeth marks. I'm tempted to get them tattooed there. A constant reminder of the sacrifice she is unknowingly making for me and Selena. As well as every innocent person she will save from my uncle's wrath.

"That's for cutting up my fucking clothes in front of your creepy...sadistic...*vile* uncle."

"Ahh, so you didn't mind that I got a look? Or that I sliced through your clothes like they were butter? I think you liked it, *Mariposita.*" She hesitates for a moment.

32

"That was...fear, you asshole."

"I'm going to have you watch that video one day. Then you'll see yourself through my eyes." Pink creeps into her cheeks as she lowers her gaze from mine.

"You won't get the chance to because you'll be dead."

I ignore her comment. "You trusted me to chain you up. Even after seeing those tools." I nod my head to the table. A shiver races up her body. "That was lust, Madison. If my fingers slipped under that black lace right now, I would find my fingers soaked and gleaming. Which would make you a *liar*."

"Can we get out of here? *Please.*" Her voice has dimmed, becoming small and sheepish.

I bend down, scooping her up in my arms. Bridal style. She hesitates for a second before lacing her arms around my neck. When we reach the top of the stairs, I glance down at her. She's gnawing on her lower lip, seemingly lost in thought.

Damn, her eyes are so fucking gorgeous.

Everything about her is gorgeous.

There's not a stitch of makeup on her—not that she needs it. That right there is natural fucking beauty. *Perfection.*

"Pretend to be knocked out. Go slack in my arms as I carry you upstairs," I whisper.

Her eyebrow raises in a form of dramatic defiance. Then she throws a hand over her head, sighs theatrically, and flops backward. Raven-colored waves of hair cascade over my arm as her eyes flutter closed. My pulse spikes seeing that bruise on her neck. Instinctively, I pull her body closer to mine, shielding her with it.

Fucking Geraldo. He deserves every ounce of pain coming for him.

I make my way through the first floor and up the next set of stairs to the bedrooms. Bringing her to my room, I kick the door shut behind us and place her down on the bed.

"You are a *terrible* actress," I chuckle.

Madison sits up on her elbows and looks around. "Who's room is this?"

"Mine. This whole island is my private residence. It *was* Basilio's. I inherited it when he was killed."

Tucking a strand of hair behind her ears, she looks around, taking in the room. A slight blush stains her cheeks as she realizes she's on my bed. I close the space between us and take a seat next to her. I expect her to flinch or at least back away. Instead, she lays down, laces her hands behind her head, and closes her eyes.

Such a brave little butterfly. *She trusts me.*

"Tell me *everything*."

"Yes, ma'am." Her lips go up in the tiniest of smiles.

"When Killian executed the hit out on my sper—*father*, there was outrage amongst my syndicate. They couldn't believe their perfect, sadistic leader was dead. They called for immediate retaliation. My uncle included. I suggested they wait to attack until the Tri-State Syndicate least expected it. They agreed— which held them off for a while, buying us some time. Selena and I met in secret after she and Killian got back together. We had to figure out a way to take out every last one of the men like my father. There are a handful of them. All perfectly content torturing innocents, women, and children." I take a calming breath before continuing. Madison's eyes are open now and laser-focused on me.

"My sister was one of them." I clench my jaw at the cruel memories resurfacing.

"She suffered at the hands of that asshole one too many times. My sperm donor would send me out on assignments on the nights he needed to let off steam. Being *The Bone Breaker* and all, I needed to uphold our reputation. Either follow orders or wake up to the barrel of a gun pressed to my head and a bullet in my skull. I couldn't let that happen. I had to protect my mamá and sister. Mamá would take the beatings he dished out on the nights I wasn't home to intervene. One night I arrived home from an assignment to Selena waiting for me on the front steps. Tears streamed down her face. My sorry excuse of a father had become belligerent drunk and was too rough on my mamá. He took it too far and killed her."

Madison gasps and her eyes go wide. "Diego..."

I pat her bare leg before resting my hand there. *She doesn't seem to mind.*

"It was that day I swore to my sister that I would *never* be anything like my father and that I would find a way to end his reign of terror. That's when I contacted Killian. Telling him if he killed my father, I would find a way to get Selena back to him. They could reconnect. And he could once again take her as his bride. It would keep Selena safe and happy in New York—and away from the rest of my father's men. My sister is so fucking in love with him, I knew she would easily agree to this. I could only hope to experience that kind of love one day." I chance a quick look at Madison before continuing.

"The plan has always been for me to take over after his death. This syndicate was going to get a much-needed deep cleaning. I was going to rid it of all the darkness and turn over a new leaf. Geraldo wasn't having it. Neither were the rest of his followers. They felt he deserved to continue my father's legacy."

Madison sits up and places her delicate hand over mine. "Why didn't you just kill them yourself?"

I look down, basking in the softness of her touch. "I couldn't risk it. If anyone found out that it was me, I'd be killed. And so would Selena for collaborating against our syndicate."

"So...you waged a war with the Tri-State Syndicate so they will carry it out for you."

"Does that make me the biggest pussy of all time? Not being the one to end their pathetic lives myself. Having other men do my dirty work."

"No, it doesn't. It makes sense. Killian and Liam *will* kill the men involved because Geraldo took me. That will rid your syndicate of the vermin and leave an opening for you to take over. Then you can lead the rest in a new direction, all while protecting your sister." I nod, hoping that she understands now.

"So, Selena was just acting before?" Her teeth clamp over her bottom lip and her brows come together.

A deep laugh escapes me. "She's a better actress than you."

She slaps me across my bicep, her eyes lingering on the scars that cover my body. Most are from Basilio. The rest are from my encounters as *El Rompe Huesos*. I may be the best at my job, but that doesn't mean I don't receive resistance.

"Why wouldn't you just ask Killian to help you again? Why risk so many lives, including your own? You know Killian and Liam won't hesitate to kill you for your involvement."

"Because he swore if he killed my father, it would be a one-time deal. A week after our arrangement, he called me back. Told me that the plans had changed. He agreed to still end Basilio, but he had met someone and couldn't honor the Selena part of the deal."

The beautiful little butterfly on my bed is processing everything I just said.

"So...you had Selena participate the night your men took me. You knew that I still meant something to Killian. That he would go to the ends of the world to get both Selena and me back."

"Precisely."

"And Liam? What about him?"

I sigh. I don't want to talk about her man, but we have to. "Liam is going to try and swap places with you. Killian won't tolerate that. He'll fight to keep you both. That will be the catalyst for the gunfight at the meeting spot. All of the people in this organization that need to be executed will be there."

"This all sounds...chaotic and crazy. I don't want anyone I care about to get hurt."

"People do crazy things for love." I shrug.

She pulls her knees to her chest and rests her head on them. Her face is angled my way. A lone tear slips down her cheek.

I swipe it away with my thumb. "What's wrong, *Mariposita*?"

"You are not what I expected. You are doing anything you can to protect the people you love and care for. Even for the ones you don't know—innocent lives." She starts to whisper, so I lean in closer.

"Why did you let your uncle beat me when I first got here? You let me stay in that dungeon for weeks. You let him wrap his hands around my throat, each and every night until I passed out."

Her tears pour more freely now.

My heart palpates wildly in my chest. Anguish claws through my body until my hands shake with the desire to change the past. I never meant for that to happen. My uncle wasn't supposed to be here.

"It was never meant to happen that way. As the leader, Geraldo would bring you into that room, and his lackeys would guard the door. If I showed up..if I questioned..if they saw any other side of me besides *El Rompe Huesos,* they would figure out our plan." I drop my head in shame. It's a fucking terrible excuse. I should have stopped him from hurting her. I could have done so much more to prevent all of that pain. She will never understand how much she sacrificed for my family.

"My sister was inconsolable. So was I for that matter. I destroyed so many guest rooms in this house. Trashing the place to shreds. I would take local assignments just to be able to break some bones and do to them what I couldn't do to my uncle. Hearing your screams and having to pick you up off that filthy floor and carry you back to your cell was pure agony. I would stay with you, holding you in my arms on that tiny little cot until my uncle went back to his home in South Beach. I needed to know he wouldn't come in and do anything further. That he wouldn't...." I can't even say the last few words.

37

My sweet little butterfly crawls over and hugs me. Her body shakes as she sobs into my shoulder. "You did what you had to do. To protect Selena. I would have done the same thing for my sisters. Thank you for," she hiccups, "for staying with me at night —even when I didn't know it. Thank you for defending the innocent."

"I'm not a saint, Madison. I'm still very much a monster," I sigh. "I'd like to think that one day I can be...somewhat redeemable."

She swivels her head, which is resting on my shoulder and looks at me. Her glossy indecisive eyes drop down to my lips before she pulls away.

I'm about to say *fuck it*, break my promise to her, and get a taste of those luscious lips when an explosion rocks the entire house.

Madison grips my shoulders, her eyes going wide. Gunfire goes off in all different directions.

Coño.

I pull her off the bed, dragging her to my walk-in closet. There's a hidden room in the back. I shove the clothes aside, unlatch the door, and nudge her in.

"Stay here, *Mariposita*. I'll be back for you."

CHAPTER 5

KILLIAN

IT'S JUST shy of three weeks. *Three. Fucking. Weeks.* Without our women. I hate that we are sitting here waiting for the call to get Madison back...and possibly Selena. *If she's still the woman I believe her to be.*

Seb was able to find the island the same evening we arrived at the compound. It was owned by Selena's father and was gifted to her brother Diego. *Fucking Diego.* I gave him my word and killed his father and *this* is how he *repays* me? Taking Madison hostage?

It doesn't add up.

Less than a year ago we had an agreement that if I killed his father, he would find a way to get Selena back to me. I was desperate for it, clinging on to every shred of hope that we would get the chance to try again. Her father would be dead and his horrific reign would be over. That was right around the same time I had met Madison. So I declined the offer to have Selena sent to New York and still kept good on my promise.

Even if Selena found out that I had Liam kill Basilio, why would she care? Her father was a monster. He killed her mother with his bare hands and beat his two kids almost daily. *Does this have to do with Madison? Perhaps she found out that I had chosen*

Madison over her and resented me for it? She could have set me up this whole time, pretending to still be in love with me. Maybe her brother helped her, seeking out his revenge on me for fucking over his sister.

Seb delivered us the number of Geraldo's burner phone shortly after finding the island. Dec, Liam and I called him, demanding to meet that night. We would avoid more bloodshed if we worked out a deal. Geraldo just laughed and told us if we even stepped foot on his island, he would kill both girls. He even sent a picture of Madison in a disgusting cell. Filthy and scared shitless.

As of right now, Selena is being well cared for. Geraldo threatened for that to change if we attempt to play any games. The last words he said before hanging up was that he would reach out when he was ready for a deal to be made.

After hearing that, Liam was ready to steal one of Declan's boats and set of coordinates and go there himself. Dec and I had to hold him down long enough for him to cool off. As much as that's what I want to do as well—we can't. Geraldo is a sick son of a bitch who would make good on his threat. If it was Basilio, everyone would have already been dead.

We need a plan—and a solid one at that.

Painfully, we decided to give them a few more days to contact us. If they do not—we will split up. Half our men will go to Geraldo's house in Miami. The other group, including myself, Declan, and Liam, will head to the island.

TIME'S UP, *fuckers.* My men and Declan's are ready and have their orders. Half are stationed outside of Geraldo's home as we speak. The rest of them are with us.

We are on a military-grade helicopter heading over to the island when a text from an unknown number comes in.

Attached is a video. Liam and Declan lean over their seats. With trembling fingers I hit play.

A rush of profanities collectively leaves our mouths as the video progresses. Madison is chained to restraints attached to the ceiling. She hangs there, feet dangling. Panic written all over her beautiful face. Her arms and neck are thoroughly bruised. Duct tape covers her smart mouth. Diego—as in Selena's brother—has his back turned to us as he slices Madison's clothes off her.

"I am going to fucking slaughter all of them. There won't be a Cuban-Miami Syndicate left when I'm done with them. Fuck!" Liam bellows from beside me.

The video wraps up and Selena is screaming something in the background at her brother—the fucking *Bone Breaker.*

El Rompe Huesos.

I have this sickening feeling that once we go in, not all of us will be making it out. *It doesn't matter.* That's the cost of war. No one touches our women and gets away with it.

"Diego is the fucking *Bone Breaker*?!" Liam booms. He's pacing the small space now.

Declan is pinching the bridge of his nose and shaking his head in disbelief.

This is becoming a goddamn nightmare.

WE'RE HOVERING over the estate. A decoy explosion was dropped at the front entrance, giving us an opening to head through the back. Geraldo's men start shooting at us and we return fire killing off a good amount of them.

Liam was supposed to wait for my signal to propel down, but that thick-headed eejit decided to move. He slides down the rope, shooting every fucker in his path.

Landing on the upper deck of the estate, he runs stealthily towards a glass sliding door. With the butt of the gun slung around his chest, he shatters the glass. I lose sight of him as he disappears behind it. *Damn it, Liam.*

Declan and I propel down at the same time. We land a level lower, near the beach, at the back entrance of the home. Gunshots erupt from all over. Another helicopter approaches the front of the house.

Our backup.

There are two men stationed at the back door. Dec and I look at each other and nod, silently communicating. Dec takes out the guy on the right and I do the same to the one on the left. I reach for the handle of the sliding door, and by some miracle, it's unlocked. Quietly, we creep inside...it's empty. *Good.*

"I'll let the guys in through the front. Find Liam before you start destroying the place." Declan points upstairs.

"Be careful. Maeve will have my balls if we don't bring you home."

"Aye." I can hear his quiet laughter as I ascend the staircase.

I make my way to the landing. The hairs on the back of my neck stand up at what's before me. There in the middle of the hallway is Selena. Geraldo has a gun pressed to her head. I raise mine and take a hesitant step forward.

"Kil. Don't. He *will* kill me," she sobs. Tears are streaming down her face. "I never betrayed you, Kil. I love you more than anything."

"Shut your mouth, *sobrina.*" Geraldo's wrinkled, leathery hand covers her mouth. Turning to me he raises his voice, "I told you not to come here, Killian. And yet you have the *cajones* to stand in front of me right now." Selena's eyes are screaming a silent plea to go. *Fuck that.* I'm not leaving until she and Madison are with us, and Geraldo and the rest of his men are dead.

"Selena is coming with me. We can have a peaceful alliance again, Geraldo. It doesn't have to be this way. Just let her go. Let *them* go."

"I'm not a forgiving man, Killian. But in my old age, I find myself giving out a few rare second chances. I am changing my offer. You can take Selena with you to do as you please with her. I will be keeping Madison and whoever else my men have captured in your little ambush. Madison will no longer be staying in the dungeon. I think she would warm my bed well or perhaps I'll gift her to my nephew—*El Rompe Huesos*. She will do well pumping out a bunch of his heirs. I won't be around forever."

He shrugs like he doesn't give a fuck about his niece or that an innocent woman will become a slave to one of the most vile men in the history of the mafia. His name is whispered around the underworld. Stories so grueling, you can't tell what is real and what is fabricated.

I still can't believe it is Diego.

It's as if my thoughts summon the devil himself. At the mention of his name, he steps out of the shadows and into the hallway holding a gun to Madison's head. *Jesus Christ*. There are bloody handprints on her face and blood smeared across her lips.

"Take the deal, Killian. Liam is already dead. Madison has nothing left to live for. She's already agreed to stay here if you take Selena and go." Diego plays with her hair, "I happen to like this one. I think she would make a great little pet. Thank you, tío."

Liam's...dead? No. *No.* That can't be true. I told that bastard to just wait. He's bluffing.

I look between Selena and Madison. An impossible decision.

"Just fucking do it, Killian. Take Selena and get the fuck out of here." Madison's head nods ever so slightly. *What the hell is going on? And why isn't she crying?* That woman tried beating the shit out of me when she thought I was leaving Liam dead on the side of the road. This response is *so* not like her.

"Trust me," Madison mouths. Diego shoots me a wink, his lips curving into an arrogant smile.

"Okay. But I am taking the men that are left with me. My brother's body *will* also be coming with us."

"I will deliver him to you myself. Can't promise he'll be in one piece," Diego taunts. Bile rises in my throat.

Fuck, Liam. Fuck you for not listening to me! It should have been me.

I promise you I will get Madison back home.

I swear it.

"You're just like your father." Geraldo shakes his head, releasing Selena and shoving her toward me. "Deal."

CHAPTER 6

LIAM

BLOOD TRICKLES down my hand from smashing the sliding door. I clawed at the double-layer tempered glass to access the lock. My automatic rifle is raised as I enter the room. It's a master bedroom—possibly Diego's. I survey the room before clearing the en suite.

Empty. Everything but the ...

Rustling in the closet catches my attention. Glass crunches under my feet as I make my approach. With my gun raised, finger hovering over the trigger, I push open the door.

It takes a second for my eyes to adjust to the darkness before my brain registers what—rather— *who* is at the end of my barrel.

"Liam?" Madison's sweet voice fills my ears.

Swinging the rifle around so it sits at my back, I drop to my knees in front of her and pull her into my arms. She is shaking like a leaf. And *so* fucking frail. Her ribcage protrudes beneath my fingers. Her olive skin, angry and irritated, is covered in welts and bumps that blanket her entire body.

"Liam, it's *really* you," she weeps. "You're here. You're really here." An endless supply of tears pour over the rims of her eyes. Trembling fingers clasp my face as she pulls my lips to hers. I do the same, locking my hands around her face and devouring her mouth. The need to be gentle with her hits me. I loosen my grip, cradling her head instead. Madison's lips continue to mold around mine, refusing to let me move an inch.

Her kiss is my salvation. A drug far more effective than nicotine. Her taste instantly calms the storm raging inside of me.

She moans as I slip my tongue between her lips. "I knew you would come for me." Her voice is just a whisper. I lean back on my heels and help her up, securing my arm around her waist.

"I would go to the ends of the Earth to find you. Even death itself couldn't stop me from getting to you. I would fight tooth and nail, dragging my sorry arse out of the depths of Hell, just to have you back in my arms. You are *mine*, Madison. Anyone who has touched what's mine will no longer be breathing by the end of tonight."

We need to move. The boats should be here by now. We just need to make it down to the beach. I grab her hand and lead her out of the closet. Something hard slams into me, knocking me back a step.

Diego.

Dropping Madison's hand, I grip Diego's throat. His fist comes up as he swings at my face, getting a solid punch in. *Shit.* Now I know why they call him *The Bone Breaker.* I don't think he broke my jaw—but *fuck*—if that wasn't the hardest hit I've ever taken.

A mixture of adrenaline and loathing heats my blood. I ram into him, pounding my fist into his ribs over and over again. I grab his throat with both hands, ready to watch the light leave his eyes. Diego's right hook connects with my lip, splitting it and sending me reeling back.

"Stop!" Madison shouts over us.

"Get back, Madison." I whirl around and push her behind me while swinging the rifle around. Diego is quick—already having his Glock out and aimed at me.

My woman steps directly in the middle of our cocked guns. I automatically lowered mine the second she stepped foot in front of it.

What the hell is she doing?

"Madison, baby. Move." Tilting my head a fraction, I stare at her.

Move, baby. What are you doing?

"Dale, *Mariposita.*" *Did that motherfucker give her a nickname? No. This ends now.*

Madison looks at him and then back at me. "Put. The guns. *Down.*" I can't believe my eyes as I watch the goddamn *Bone Breaker* lower his.

What the fuck is happening right now?

"You need to go, Liam. The deal was over the second you stepped foot onto this island," Diego hisses. Anger and irritation radiate off of him. "My uncle is outside in the hallway right now with a fucking gun to my sister's head." He pulls a cell phone from his pocket with camera footage of the hallway. Killian has his gun aimed at Geraldo, who has Selena pressed up against him—a pistol shoved against her temple.

"I'm not fucking leaving without Madison," I say between gritted teeth.

Madison's hands wrap around my arm as she leans down to watch the live feed.

"If my uncle thinks you are dead, he will count that as retribution for Basilio. Alan's death will be paid for through Madison. Listen, Liam. I don't have time to explain everything. This whole thing has become a fucking headache. Nothing went as planned." Diego pinches the bridge of his nose as he focuses on the feed again. Geraldo is offering Killian a new deal:

"I'm not a forgiving man, Killian. But in my old age, I find myself giving out a few rare second chances. I am changing my offer. You can take Selena with you to do as you please with her. I will be keeping Madison and whoever else my men have

captured in your little ambush. Madison will no longer be staying in the dungeon. I think she would warm my bed well or perhaps I'll gift her to my nephew—El Rompe Huesos. She will do well pumping out a bunch of his heirs. I won't be around forever."

A growl rips past my throat. Madison's hand squeezes my bicep. She leans up and kisses me quickly—*too quickly* for my liking.

"Get to the beach, Liam." Diego tosses me a boat key. "There's a door in my closet. It will lead you directly to the docks. Lay low until I contact you or Killian. I *will* protect Madison. You have my word. I'm not the monster my reputation portrays me to be—well—not towards *her*, anyway," he fucking chuckles and Madison cracks half a smile. *The fuck?* Not a second later, he's tugging Madison against him and walking to the door.

She turns her head to look back at me. "I love you, Liam. Just trust me on this." Her eyes are pleading with me.

And then she's gone.

Wake up. Wake up, you arsehole. I try convincing myself this is just a bad dream. A product of too much alcohol, cigarettes, and *severe* lack of sleep.

My throbbing jaw and the taste of Madison on my lips says otherwise.

I linger by the door, staying hidden in case some bastard decides to sneak up on me. The small opening gives me a visual of them. Diego has his gun pressed to Madison's head. I want to barrel out there and shoot him *and* his fucking uncle—but that would put everyone at risk. Madison said to trust her. As much as I fucking hate this, I know she wouldn't say those words unless she meant them. We are missing something here...

"Take the deal, Killian. Liam is already dead. Madison has nothing left to live for. She's already agreed to stay here if you take Selena and go." Diego plays with her hair as if he owns her. *"I*

happen to like this one. I think she would make a great little pet. Thank you, tío."

He needs to get his fucking hands off my woman. His hold on her is too intimate for someone who just told me they would protect her.

"Just fucking do it, Killian. Take Selena and get the fuck out of here." Madison's raspy voice carries through the hallway. Damn, I don't think I have ever seen her like this. She's a woman who knows how to get what she wants...but something has changed in her. It's how she's speaking, so cogently. I knew she always had this tenacity in her but never had the pleasure of watching it bloom.

"Okay. But I am taking the men that are left with me. My brother's body will also be coming with us." Killian says firmly, agreeing to the terms.

"I will deliver him to you myself. Can't promise he'll be in one piece," Diego sneers.

"You're just like your father," Geraldo says tauntingly. *"Deal."*

Diego turns his head to look at me, lowering the gun from Madison's temple.

"Go," he mouths.

THE TUNNEL COMES OUT EXACTLY where Diego said it would. A more excluded area of the island. The helicopters are no longer here. Boat motors rumble in the distance—that must be our pickup. I'm tempted to jog the beach to get to them, meeting up with Killian and whoever else made it, but I can't risk being exposed.

I suppose I'll remain dead—*for now.*

I pull the key out from my jeans pocket while walking over to the dock. One small speedboat—a very expensive speedboat, I might add—is docked there. Leaping over the edge, I jump in and start it. Luckily, I know how to drive this fucker. The purr of the engines is surprisingly quiet for a speedboat. *Perhaps it's electric.* With one more pained glance behind me, I take off toward the lights of Miami.

My mind is replaying everything that unfolded tonight. *Why wouldn't Madison just come with me?* I had her in my arms. And I had that bastard within brain-splattering range. *Why did she stop me from killing her tormentor?*

Grabbing my smokes, I light up, pulling the smoke deep into my lungs. I let the nicotine saturate my bloodstream and calm my fucking frayed nerves. I am leaving this island empty-handed, and that feeling is fucking God-awful. Keeping one hand on the helm, I dial Seb's number. On the first ring, he answers.

"Hello, Liam. I see things didn't go as planned." *Cryptic bastard.*

"No they fucking didn't," I growl into the phone.

"What can I do for you?" he asks calmly.

"I need the best route back to Declan's house via boat. I'll also need to know where I can leave this fucking thing that won't raise eyebrows." I take a drag of my cigarette, blowing it out slowly. I've got to calm down. I can't think straight or rationally right now. It's going to get me killed. *I need to fucking focus.*

The rapid clicking of a keyboard fills the line. Not a minute later the phone vibrates against my ear. "I sent you all the details. Follow the GPS link. It will take you to the exact spot you'll need to go. I took the liberty of contacting Kieran and Conor. They will be meeting you at the dock."

"Thank you."

More clicking fills the line as I take another drag of my cigarette.

"Killian, Selena, and Declan are also accounted for and en route to the compound." I exhale smoke and relief simultaneously.

"Thank fuck for that." I hang up and flick my cigarette into the ocean. The darkness will help this process move more smoothly.

Selena knows something. She will be the first person I look for when I get back. Killian, I'm sure, is happy to have her back.

I, on the other hand, don't trust her.

Until further notice, she's on my shit list.

"SO YOU'RE A DEAD MAN, HUH?" Colin jokes from the driver seat of the Range Rover.

"It's not funny, *arsehole*," I grumble from the back seat.

"How's Madison?" Conor turns around to ask, with genuine concern on his face.

"Different," I deadpan.

It's raining out. Typical Florida weather. I hit the storm a bit as I was pulling up to the dock. I'm fucking drenched, irritated, and needing a stiff drink. *Fuck that.* I'm going to need the whole bottle tonight.

"Can I at least tell Lexi she's okay? I haven't told her Madison was taken. She keeps questioning me about how she is. Alexis says she hasn't heard from her in weeks and that, I quote, "it's so not Madison'. I swear that woman has some weird witchy connection with her. She even had a strange dream the other night...claiming she could *feel* that Madison was in pain."

"They do have a weird connection. I've watched those two have a full conversation using only facial expressions." I run a hand over my face and wince. *That fucker got me good.* I move my jaw back and forth. 'Least it's not broken, just gonna be sore for a few days.

"Ya gonna be alright, mate?" Colin looks at me in the rearview mirror.

"Physically? I'll be fine. Emotionally? I'm about to shatter." I don't even care that the guys see me as weak right now. Madison is my world.

"Did you at least get a few good punches in on *The Bone Breaker*? Conor attempts to bring back my dignity.

"Yeah, I got him in the ribs a few times." Feeling the crunch beneath my fist was beyond satisfying.

I hope his goddamn lung collapses too.

WE PULL up to the gate after circling the block a few times and triple-checking we weren't tailed. After talking to the head of security at the gate, we are granted access. Colin pulls us into the underground garage, complete with limited edition cars and motorcycles.

Killian is waiting there, leaning against a black Porsche Cayenne. Arms crossed at his chest and a deadly scowl on his face, he's about to lace into me. His eyes narrow as I step out of the SUV.

"Relax, *sweetheart*. I'm alive." I put my hands up in mock surrender.

He pulls me into a tight embrace before punching me right into my already bruised jaw. Luckily, he didn't put all his weight into it—because if he had —it definitely would have dislocated.

"You're a fucking lunatic!" I massage my throbbing jaw. *I deserved that.* I didn't listen to Killian's command. He's always been the logical and rational one.

Me? Not so much. I'm more of the... *Savage. Brute. Arsehole* variety.

Just to name a few.

"Not only did you not listen to me, Liam, but you almost got yourself and the rest of our men killed. By some miracle, Geraldo was being merciful—if you'd even call it that. Madison is still stuck on that damn island with two sadistic fucks. If you would have just *listened*, perhaps tonight would have gone differently."

"You don't know what happened, brother. I saw Madison and Diego...*briefly*. We have a lot to catch up on. But first, I want to speak with Selena. Where is she?"

"Maeve took her upstairs to get cleaned up." I raise a brow at that. Killian throws up a hand, "Declan is with them...if you're worried about her pulling some shit while I'm not there."

"Do you trust her?" I ask as we walk to the entrance of the garage.

"I don't know. I want to. Guess we'll have to hear her out before we can decide that." Worry is sketched all over his face.

I get it. He wants to believe she wouldn't betray him. *He loves her.* Who would want to find out the woman they love betrayed not only them but their entire criminal organization? *Sure as fuck not me.* I just hope she can help us get Madison back.

"Don't let her out of your sight. Not until we know for sure."

"I don't plan on letting her out of my sight ever again."

CHAPTER 7

MADISON

DARKNESS ENCOMPASSES me in this little room behind his closet. If I were claustrophobic this would be a nightmare. My pulse is pounding in my ears with anxiety. Moisture clings to my palms as I ball them into fists. Is this an attack from another rival syndicate or gang? *Or is this...*I can't say their names. I don't want to jinx it.

There is banging against the balcony sliding door, followed by glass shattering. Tremors course through my body. I close my fist over my mouth in an attempt to stifle a scream. Diego isn't even here to stop whoever is about to find me. *What if I get taken again? How will anyone find me then?*

Whoever is in here is looking around the room. The sound of glass crunching beneath their shoes is growing significantly louder. *They must be coming this way.* I press my ear against the door, listening for any indication they may have entered the closet. Of course, the fucking latch gives and I tumble out.

Fuck. I try to scramble to my feet as the closet door swings open. A big ass gun is aimed at my head. A pair of black boots are firmly planted before me. My eyes track up a muscular pair of jean-clad thighs to a body I must have touched a thousand times by now. His handsome scruffy face peers down at me in a mixture of awe and relief.

"*Liam?*" My voice comes out so weak and raspy, I'm not sure he heard me.

The few seconds of shock wear off before he drops to his knees and pulls me against his solid chest. His secure embrace is everything I need to let the tears fall. My arms lace around his neck, nearly strangling the poor guy. I bury my face into his chest and just sob.

"Liam, it's *really* you." Warm powerful hands run along my ribcage as he begins taking quick inventory. "You're here. You're really here." If I say it enough, will it convince me this moment is real? *I know what will...*

My fingers tremble as I pull his face to mine and smash my lips against his. Instant relief sweeps over me as he opens up and deepens the kiss. Liam's fingers clasp both sides of my tear-stained face as he devours me. A throaty moan slips from my mouth when his tongue slides between my lips. He must mistake it as pain and backs off. Adjusting his grip on my face, he cradles my head like I'm the most precious thing in the world to him. The intensity in which he loves me brings on a whole flood of fresh tears.

He's here.

We are together again.

I'm safe.

Liam moves to stand, helping me up, and wrapping a protective arm around me.

"I would go to the ends of the Earth to find you. Even death itself couldn't stop me from getting to you. I would fight tooth and nail, and drag my sorry arse out of the depths of Hell, just to have you back in my arms. You are *mine*, Madison. Anyone who has touched what's mine will no longer be breathing by the end of tonight."

His declaration is everything I needed to hear and more.

Our hands intertwine as he leads us out of the closet. He stops so abruptly, I almost smack into him. There's a person in front of us. Instinctively Liam pushes me behind him. An animalistic growl rips out of him.

Diego is now chest to chest, practically nose to nose with Liam. Those ocean-blue eyes dart to mine, briefly distracting him. Liam lunges out a hand and viciously wraps it around *The Bone Breaker's* throat.

An almost apologetic expression crosses Diego's face before he swings. The sound of his fist slamming into Liam's jaw makes me gasp and recoil. Liam practically howls, tackling Diego to the ground and pinning him there. Deadly fists pound into Diego's ribcage before wrapping around his neck. Those blue eyes widen with a hint of fear before he cracks his fist against Liam's lip, sending him reeling backward.

Watching those two beautiful beasts fight with their bare hands has me in a trance. One filled with fear...and coated in a bit of lust—if I'm being honest. I snap out of it when the crimson liquid dripping off Liam's lips grabs my attention.

"Stop!" I scream at the two of them.

Neither one of them is dying tonight.

My stubborn, rage-filled man shuffles me behind him before aiming his rifle at Diego.

He is a few seconds too late–*thank God. Ocean Eyes* already has his Glock pointed at my man. My feet move on their own, and I find myself standing between the two weapons. Liam immediately lowers his at the sight of me. Horror and confusion are written all over his face.

"Madison, baby. Move."

"Dale, *Mariposita*," Diego agrees.

I look between the two of them. No one is dying for me. I won't let it happen. If I could just tell Liam what is truly going on, maybe he will understand. *Or maybe he won't.*

Rage is blinding him right now.

"Put. The guns. *Down*." Surprisingly Diego listens and Liam lowers his all the way. Liam's face is twisted into that of disgust. *Is he upset that I am protecting Diego?*

"You need to go, Liam. The deal was over the second you stepped foot onto this island," Diego says between clenched teeth. *I get it.* His whole plan just imploded. If they had just stuck to the plan, this all could have gone differently.

"My uncle is outside in the hallway right now with a fucking gun to my sister's head." A gasp leaves my lips. *Geraldo is going to kill her.* Then this whole thing would have been for nothing. Diego will do whatever is necessary to protect his sister.

He pulls out a cell phone from his pocket with a live feed of the camera in the hallway. Killian has his gun directed at Geraldo and Selena is being held against her uncle at gunpoint. His gun presses angrily into her temple.

"I'm not fucking leaving without Madison," Liam states between gritted teeth.

I rest my hand on Liam's arm, leaning over him to get a better look at what's unfolding.

"If my uncle thinks you are dead, he will count that as retribution for Basilio. Alan's death will be paid for through Madison. Listen, Liam. I don't have time to explain everything. This whole thing has become a fucking headache. Nothing went as planned." Diego pinches the bridge of his nose as he focuses on the feed again. Geraldo is offering Killian a new deal:

"I'm not a forgiving man, Killian. But in my old age, I find myself giving out a few rare second chances. I am changing my offer. You can take Selena with you to do as you please with her. I will be keeping Madison and whoever else my men have captured in your little ambush. Madison will no longer be staying in the dungeon. I think she would warm my bed well or perhaps I'll gift her to my nephew—El Rompe Huesos. She will do well pumping out a bunch of his heirs. I won't be around forever."

Take the deal, Kil. Selena will be safe and so will Liam—if he leaves right now. I can manage to stick around here a bit longer if that means they all leave *alive*. *We can get Geraldo another day.*

My decision has been made.

Diego won't let anything happen to me.

He promised me.

I plant my hand on top of Liam's and lean in, placing a brief kiss on his lips. If I linger too long, I won't follow through with this. Liam looks shocked as he processes what I am about to do.

"Get to the beach, Liam." Diego tosses him what looks like a boat key.

He's helping him.

Ocean Eyes is definitely redeemable—*even if he doesn't believe it.*

"There's a door in my closet. It will lead you directly to the docks. Lay low until I contact you or Killian. I *will* protect Madison. You have my word. I'm not the monster my reputation portrays me to be—well—not towards *her* anyway," he laughs, his eyes holding mine for a brief moment as if saying 'thank you for staying'.

You're welcome, asshole. The hint of a smug smile tugs at the corner of my lips. With not even a second to get my bearings, he tugs me flush against his sculpted body and shuffles us to the door.

I risk one more look at Liam, afraid to see betrayal, or perhaps anger there. Instead, it's just confusion and pain. He looks just as broken and angry as he was the night I was taken.

"I love you, Liam. Just trust me on this."

Diego pushes me roughly through the door and raises his gun to my temple.

Killian's eyes dart to mine the second we emerge. Horror glazes over his features as he takes in Liam's blood all over my face and lips.

"Take the deal, Killian. Liam is already dead. Madison has

nothing left to live for. She's already agreed to stay here if you take Selena and go."

Poor Killian. His eyebrows come together in pain and bewilderment. The two of them would do anything for each other. They only just found out about being blood brothers a few months ago.

This will wreck him.

I want to scream that it's all a lie just to wipe away that look on his face.

Diego breaks me out of my reverie by combing his fingers through my hair. "I happen to like this one. I think she would make a great little *pet*. Thank you, tío."

Killian looks between me and Selena. He doesn't want to have to make this choice. It's a decision no one should ever have to make. Choosing between the love of their life and their ex-lover/brother's woman. The brother he just found out he lost a few seconds ago.

"Just fucking do it, Killian. Take Selena and get the fuck out of here." I nod my head ever so slightly, trying to convey with my eyes that it's okay.

He doesn't say anything. So I try harder, mouthing, "*Trust me.*"

With a pained but understanding look, he turns to Geraldo. "Okay. But I am taking the men that are left with me. My brother's body *will* also be coming with us."

Diego's deep voice cuts through the silence before his uncle speaks. "I will deliver him to you myself. Can't promise he'll be in one piece." Killian's face pales at that, but he nods.

"You're just like your father," Geraldo scoffs at Killian. "*Deal.*"

"YOUR CAGE WAS OPEN, *Mariposita*. Yet you didn't fly away."

Diego is packing a bag for us in his room. His uncle surprisingly kept his word and let Killian, Selena, and the rest of the men leave. There were a few casualties. Mostly the men Diego was hoping would be killed. Which I guess is a win— considering his sister is safe, Liam and Killian are alive, and some truly detestable men are now dead.

I'm leaning over the sink in his bathroom scrubbing Liam's blood off my face with a washcloth. Part of me is tempted to leave it there as a reminder that he was here. That he was holding me in that closet and his lips were on mine.

He came for me.

And I forced him to leave here without me.

"Your uncle had a gun to your sister's head." My words are muffled behind the washcloth.

Diego walks into the en suite, grabs a few items, and tosses them into a small cosmetic bag. He pauses his task, leans a hip against the countertop, and crosses his arms over his chest.

"Liam hadn't even been discovered. You *both* could have fled here and left me to deal with the consequences of the mess I created."

The washcloth leaves my hand as he grabs it and cleans the rest of the blood off of me. He lifts my chin, looking down at me. Topaz-blue eyes pierce mine with an emotion so intense, so raw, it makes my stomach take a nose-dive.

"So, I'll ask you again, *Mariposita*. Why didn't you fly?"

"I didn't have much of a choice," I mumble, pulling my face out of his grasp.

"Bull*shit*." Strong hands, capable of crushing my skull, cup my cheeks so gently. He swivels my head back, forcing me to look at him. "*You did have a choice. And I would have let you leave, had you not decided to walk with me into the hallway.*"

My eyebrow raises in astonishment. "You would have let me go?"

"Yes. You knew that though. So why did you stay?" His fingers fan out so the tips of them slide into my hair. The pad of his thumb now rests against my lips.

I release an exasperated sigh. "Because *you* need me. *They*— need me." *Ocean Eyes* nods in silent understanding.

His uncle and right-hand man Mateo are still alive, along with a few corrupt stragglers. That still leaves too many innocent people exposed to his sadistic ways. Now that shit hit the fan with Diego's original plan, maybe Selena will be able to convince Killian to help—once the dust settles.

Problem is, we can't move too soon. Geraldo will be expecting another attack.

"We need to get your uncle vulnerable again," I whisper. "So if that means playing the role of your little... *pet*," I glare at him. "Then so be it."

"I like the sound of that," he winks at me. "*Mmm*...maybe I'll even get you a pretty diamond collar." His index finger traces the column of my neck.

I playfully punch him in the ribs. He instantly doubles over. "Coñoooo," he groans.

"Oh, *shit*. I forgot! I'm sorry!" I can't help the nervous giggle that escapes. *Liam did this.* I bet he was so proud of himself for getting a few good hits in on my captor and tormentor—*The Bone Breaker.*

"*Jesus*, Madison." He whooshes out a breath while clenching his side. After a few moments of him catching his breath, he grabs the bag and my hand. "Come on, let's get moving. We have a pit stop to make before we get the fuck out of here for a little while."

Ocean Eyes places the cosmetic bag inside the overflowing weekender bag. With a zip he tosses it over his shoulder, wincing and clenching his teeth. He walks to his dresser and begins rummaging through it. Finding what he was looking for, he tosses me a pair of gray drawstring sweatpants and a black zip-up hoodie.

"Put these on—or your *boyfriend* will have a heart attack when he sees you looking like *that*. I think it was too dark in here earlier for him to notice you in *just* my tank top. Surely he would have tried harder to kill me if he had."

"We are seeing Liam again?" My heart picks up speed at the possibility of it. I step into his sweatpants, push my arms into the hoodie, and slide the zipper up.

"That's the plan....but we saw how well my plan worked out earlier," he pouts. *Fucking pouts.* This grown-ass man, with a reputation that could put the devil to shame, pouted. I giggle. My mood has significantly lightened, now that I know we may see Liam for more than a brief moment.

"I'll call Killian or Liam on the way to the airport. You and I are going to take a little vacation while things cool off around here. Geraldo will think I am breaking in my new pet. Which is a good thing—it will keep us off his radar for a while. In the meantime, I have a 'body' to deliver." He air-quotes the last part and shoots me a devastatingly beautiful smile. I can't even stop the smile I give him in return.

No, he's not a monster.

Definitely redeemable.

Oh, God. Is this what Stockholm Syndrome feels like?

CHAPTER 8

DIEGO

MADISON'S HAIR is blowing in the salty breeze as we cruise toward South Beach. Her arms are wrapped tightly around herself. The blue glow of the interior lights makes her look even more angelic than ever.

I'd love to know what she's thinking right now, yet there is beauty in silence. I don't want to interrupt her brief moment of peace. She seemed satisfied with her decision, knowing that the ones she loves are safe. Although, I don't think she'll be *truly* satisfied until Geraldo is dead. It's the desire to help others that drives her.

We have that in common.

As if sensing me staring at her, she opens her eyes and turns her head my way.

"What are you staring at, *Ocean Eyes?*"

That's the first time I have heard her call me that. It's a nickname—and not one that creates panic when you hear it.

I shrug, currently tongue-tied at the moment. "I was just admiring your beauty. Liam is one lucky son of a bitch," I say truthfully.

A shiver rocks her body. I'm proud enough to know that my words affect her. *It's a rather warm night. Even out on the water.*

"You ready to call your man, *Mariposita*?" A flare of jealousy hits me as the words slip off my tongue.

"Yes," she says simply.

I pull her into my lap and fold her hands over the helm. She gawks at me. "Keep the front of the boat heading toward the coast."

Taking out my phone, I dial the number we have been using to contact them. I put it on speaker, holding the phone close to us. My other hand snakes around her flat stomach. Which reminds me—she must be *starving*. Her last meal was a sleeve of saltines. *Fuck*. I'll make sure from this day forward this woman never goes hungry again. On the third ring, Killian picks up:

"Diego?"

I give Madison's waist a gentle squeeze, encouraging her to speak.

"Kil, it's Maddy."

"Madison, *Jesus fucking Christ*, are you okay?" The sound of shuffling and crackling fills the line before Liam's voice fills the space between us.

"Baby, are you hurt? Where does he have you? Are you on a boat? What's that sound? I swear to—"

"I'm *fine*, Liam. Calm down and listen to me. Is Selena there? We need to talk to all of you."

"Hello, Liam." I cut in.

"You *motherfucker*. What are you playing at?"

"Your man is quite the hot head, *Mariposita*," I laugh, directing my words at Madison. *It's too much fun.* Getting her man all riled up, knowing it would ruffle her feathers as well.

"Cut it out, Diego or I'll punch you in the ribs again." She giggles, losing her composure.

"Good job, baby," Liam commends her.

"Diego, it's Sel. We need to fill them in."

"No shit, *Sherlock*. I told Killian I would be delivering his

66

brother's body to the house. We are en route to you with one of ours lost tonight. Do what you may with him."

There are muffled arguments going on. My sister is trying to convince Killian and Declan to let us come to the compound. After a few minutes of them bickering, they finally all agree. Whatever Selena had said was enough for them to hear me out.

"When you arrive we will be taking Madison to get cleaned up and fed in the main house. *You* will remain with Selena and the rest of us in the pool house. We can discuss everything there," Killian's calm yet assertive voice fills the line.

Interesting. My sister has managed to pacify him. They really are perfect for each other.

"Where Madison goes. I go," I state, in a *this is non-negotiable* kind of way.

Madison tenses, anticipating a fight. I know she's excited to see Liam. So I won't push it—*for now.*

"It's fine, Kil. I'll shower and eat in the pool house. I *will* be present for this. We all need to talk." Her voice holds no room for argument.

It's sexy as hell.

"We should be there within the hour." I hang up, placing the phone back into my sweatshirt pocket. My fingers wrap back around Madison's and I rest my chin on her shoulder. "Selena told me you're going to be a nurse." Her fingers clench, gripping the helm tighter.

"I was *going* to be. I'm not sure that's even an option anymore," she says dryly.

"Well, I think your *boyfriend* broke a few of my ribs. So, if you would be so kind as to take a look at them later...that would be much appreciated."

"You'll need to ice it periodically throughout the day. Maybe take some ibuprofen. I'm surprised *The Bone Breaker* doesn't know this. Bones are your *specialty* aren't they?"

She's teasing me—and I fucking love it.

I lean in closer to whisper in her ear. "Keep running that smart mouth of yours and I'll show you my other *specialty*." I raise my hips in warning and nip at her neck. Her thighs clench together. A movement she tried to conceal, but failed miserably at.

"Fuck off, *Ocean Eyes*."

That's twice now she's called me that.

WITH A *THUD*, I toss a black Christmas tree storage bag on the floor of the underground garage. Declan looks somewhat amused. Killian's face is screwed up from thinking too hard. And Liam looks murderous and ready to go round two with me. Of course, my sister is the first to run over, pulling us both into a hug.

"I'm so sorry, Madison. Will you ever forgive me?" Tears roll down her face as her hopeful eyes search her former friend's.

"I'm still pissed. But I get why you did it. So yes," she squeezes her hand, "I forgive you."

Selena pushes me aside and pulls Madison into a warm embrace. "If my brother hasn't already told you, thank you. You don't realize how much you are helping not only us but countless others."

Liam forces his way between the two of them and pulls Madison into his arms. A wave of jealousy hits me *again* and I brush it off.

She's not mine.

I point to the bag and then at Liam. "That could have been you," I say cryptically. I'm not looking for a thank you. *Just stating the obvious.*

Liam steps forward in challenge, but my *Mariposita* tightens her grip on him. "Stop. There's a lot to discuss and beating the shit out of each other isn't going to help anyone."

"Get this taken care of," Declan points to one of his men. "The rest of you follow me."

My sister falls behind to walk with me. Madison and Liam are in front of us. Mr. Hothead's arm is secure around her waist, supporting her weight as she leans into him. Killian trails behind us with a few other men who are armed to the gills.

We are led out of the garage and to the back of the property where the pool house resides. It's half as big as the main house. There is an expansive dining table in the center of the open-concept space. Declan motions for us to sit. He and Killian take the two seats at the head of the table. Selena and I take a seat next to each other, and Liam and Madison sit across from us. The rest of his men remain standing around the table. Some are stationed outside of the sliding glass doors that access the pool.

"Selena informed us of the basics while we were on the phone with you. There are still many pieces to this terribly thought-out plan that we need to put together." Killian has his arms on the table and hands clasped together. He turns towards Madison with a gentle smile on his face. "I know you are probably starving and in need of a hot shower. You wanted to be here, so would you rather us wait while you do that? Or did you want to wait 'til after we discuss everything?"

"I'll just take a plate of whatever you've got. If there's any chance you have espresso, I'd kill for a quad with some sugar. As for the shower, I took one this morning. It can wait until after we are done talking." She leans back in her chair and crosses her arms across her chest.

Liam drapes his arm around her shoulders, planting a kiss on top of her head. The bruises on his face are starting to darken. *Can't say I mind looking at him like that.* He should have fought harder to take Madison with him. Even if that meant dying for her. Even if that meant she would hate him for it. *But I'm starting to understand why he didn't.* She is a force to be reckoned with.

This woman currently has every man here looking at her in awe. Commanding the room without even trying. A Queen to everyone in her presence.

My little butterfly is a goddamn *Monarch*. Her power was unveiled during the transformations she was forced to endure. Good luck to anyone who mistakes her delicate beauty for weakness.

Because under those beautiful wings is poison.

A poison so strong, that as it makes its way through your bloodstream, your heart will pick a fight with your ribcage. Eventually, the incessant beating will slow down. And as it starts to skip a beat you will feel like you're dying. You will lay there as it consumes you, admiring the beautiful creature before you. The one you selfishly took down with you because you had to have a taste of her.

I let out a shaky breath. I'm such a fucking selfish bastard for putting her through this. I could let her go right now. Leave her here where she belongs and sort out my uncle on my own. Now that I've held her in my hands and felt the power beneath her skin, it's damn near impossible to do that.

She is sacrificing everything to help others. Her happiness, her safety...her *relationship*.

I can't let her.

"Change of plans, *Mariposita*. You're staying here."

Her head snaps up as she narrows her eyes at me. "*No.* I agreed to help you, and I will. Everyone I love is safe now. We can finish this."

"It's not up for negotiation," I stand, slapping my palms to the table and leaning over it.

She stands, mirroring me. "You'll end up getting yourself killed. And all of this would have been for nothing."

Liam slams his chair back and looms over the table. His eyes darting back and forth between the two of us. "For the love of God, does *someone* want to explain what the fuck is going on?"

With a frustrated sigh, I sit back down. Madison does the same, followed by Liam.

"As you all know, my father was a ruthless, sadistic son of a bitch. He killed my mother with his bare hands and would beat my sister and me every chance he got. I protected them as often as I could, but my father always found a way to conveniently keep me away when he was in the mood for a fix." There are a few gasps and some quiet curses released around the room. Sel's face falls with the horrific memories being dredged up.

"Killian and I made an agreement last year. He would kill my father if I got Selena and him to reunite, ultimately keeping her safe and happy. This was before Killian had met Madison. A week later Killian had called me to let me know he met someone and that he would still kill my father—but Selena was no longer part of the agreement."

Killian looks at Selena with remorse, reaching out for her hand across the table. She places her hand in his and gives it a gentle squeeze.

"It's okay, Kil."

"When my father was shot and killed last year, I knew it was Killian who had been responsible. I was ecstatic, knowing that I would now be able to take over and lead the Cuban-Miami Syndicate in a new direction. My asshole of an uncle, *Geraldo*, had other plans. Ultimately, deciding he would be the one to take over. His equally disgusting followers all agreed. I couldn't let that man continue in my father's footsteps." Everyone at the table looks relaxed at this point which is ... promising.

I look to my sister, who nods, encouraging me to continue. "After Selena had...*met up*...with Killian the night of Madison and Liam's accident, she came to see me at my hotel. I was on assignment in New York, paying a visit to a client. She told me everything about Chase and Alan. The bastard had called me to tell me about the accident. He wanted Madison's blood for the death of his son. Because of his association with Geraldo, I knew

71

I could work this to my advantage. I told him to break into your home and wait there until Selena arrived. Then and *only then*, would he be allowed to take Madison and bring her to me." Madison inhales sharply, looking royally pissed I didn't tell her this part.

"Selena was under my instructions to head back to your house with the story that she didn't feel safe in New York now that Alan was still out there. Which in her defense wasn't a fucking lie. That bastard is just as bad as my uncle when it comes to women. I knew he wouldn't hurt her in your home, because too much was at stake in retrieving Madison. Alan was under strict instructions. If he so much as touched even a hair on Madison's head, he would meet *El Rompe Huesos* and then get a one-way ticket to see his son."

"So Alan was in my fucking home because of you? After everything I did to rid this world of your father?" Killian's voice bellows around the room. *Ahh. Spoke too soon.*

"Let him continue, Kil. I want to hear the rest," Madison glares at me. Killian relaxes a fraction, sits back in his chair, and nods his head.

"As you know, Alan was successful at breaking in. He met Selena in the guest room. By that time you had arrived. He was caught off guard, using Selena as a bargaining chip to get out alive. And from what I understand, you shot him dead. Which changed my plans. I needed to get Madison some other way. I left Selena out of the rest of my plans. Lying to her and telling her that we would find another way to get you to help us kill Geraldo. I didn't tell Selena my new plan until we were on the jet home with Madison."

"And I was fucking livid, Maddy. You have to believe me. My brother wanted to kill Geraldo and his followers himself. And he would have, but he was protecting me. He knew that if anyone found out the truth, not only would he not be trustworthy as the next leader, but we would both find ourselves dead."

"So you took Madison so that we could do it for you?" Liam interjects.

"Everything became easier when Killian placed everyone on lockdown. He and Selena reconnected and she befriended Madison. None of that was fake." I glance up at everyone and they all seem to accept that Selena is mostly innocent in all this. *Good.*

"I would catch up with her like any brother would, checking in on her here and there. Everything she unknowingly told me, gave me hope that this plan would be successful. The original plan was to grab my sister and Madison and stage it as retaliation. I knew you and Liam would do everything and anything to get them back. The goal was to keep Madison and Selena together—an extended sleepover, if you will. She was never meant to see that filthy dungeon."

Liam huffs angrily, clenching his fist and slamming it against the table. *See what I'm saying about hot and cold?* Madison's plate of food leaps half an inch off the wood surface.

"Then why *the fuck* was she there?"

"Because Geraldo caught wind of it and made an appearance. He was never supposed to be involved. I just needed you to *think* Geraldo had her so you would come down and kill any motherfucker who took part in this."

"And we will. Now that you forced our fucking hand. Have no doubt about that. But why shouldn't we kill *you*?" Killian hisses.

"I have a plan for the future of my syndicate. For the future of the De La Cruz name. I am *not* my father or my uncle. There are innocent lives at stake. Innocent lives that Geraldo and his lackeys take advantage of and torment. My sister is safe now, which is one person off my list. But I can't abandon the rest. Business owners, women, and children. They need me to protect them. And I will."

"So will I," Madison chimes in over a mouthful of chicken. *A properly cooked and seasoned one at that. God, how did I let her eat that disgusting chicken back on the island?* I'm shocked she only raised her brows at the poultry dish placed in front of her before digging in.

Fucking adorable.

"No, you won't. You're staying here," Liam states. Turning to me he asks, "What was the point of even keeping her?" He's calmer now. His voice still holds a threat to protect his woman, but there is understanding.

"If you both would have just waited *one* more day and went to the meeting, this would have all been over by now. Every man that was meant to die that day would have been killed at that meeting. I have no doubt you would have slaughtered them all. That's just the consequence of war. No other syndicate or cartel would have batted an eye. Madison would have gone home with you and I would have hopefully been alive long enough for Selena or I to tell you the truth. Since that didn't happen, and you raided the island, only half the men were killed and Geraldo was left alive. Fortunately, I was able to think of a new plan under the pressure of a gun pressed to my sister's head. *Thank fuck* you took the deal, Killian. That left Sel safe, Liam able to go home and not be on my uncle's radar any longer, and Madison under my protection. I still need her to keep Geraldo convinced that nothing is astray, but I'll figure it out."

"What a fucking disaster, Diego. Why didn't you just ask me for help?" Killian asks with genuine curiosity.

"We both know you wouldn't have helped me. Your father was dying, you were about to be the new leader, and starting a war didn't seem like something on the top of your to-do list."

Killian rubs the five o'clock shadow on his chin. "No, I wouldn't have. Taking Madison and Selena was a huge fucking risk. Anything could have gone wrong. *It still can.* But you officially have my attention. Those motherfuckers need to die."

"Agreed." Liam and Declan say in unison.

CHAPTER 9

MADISON

LIAM'S ARMS wrap around my waist from behind and his chin rests on my head. We are in the bathroom of one of the guest rooms here in the pool house. Everyone agreed to reconvene after I freshened up.

Killian still doesn't fully trust or like Diego, but after privately talking to Selena, he's calmed down a bit. Declan and Killian are with him now, trying to plan the best course of action moving forward.

Me? I'm staring at the shower, but have made no attempt to move an inch. Exhaustion hits me hard—even after my quad espresso. I sway on my feet and Liam's arms tighten around me.

"Tell me what you need, baby," he says gently against my neck.

Spinning around, I press my lips to his. "I need you to let me help you guys with this," I whisper against his lips. Liam pulls away, putting space between us, and looking at me like I just punched him.

"Why are you so hell-bent on helping? Diego has your mind all sorts of twisted right now," he groans in disbelief.

"He isn't *forcing* me to do this. *Clearly*, he let me go. Diego never meant to hurt me. He was just protecting his sister and all those innocent people."

"It was a stupid fucking plan. Goes to show the kind of leader he will be. *Regardless* of whether he planned to hurt you...or not...you *did* get hurt, Madison. *In more ways than one.*" He taps my temple with his index finger before caging his arms around my body again.

I'm tired and extremely irritable, so I lash out. "What the fuck is that supposed to mean, *Liam*?" I wiggle myself out of his arms. He just pulls me back in.

We're back to this game again.

Push and pull.

"It means that he has your mind in a place that isn't healthy. You aren't thinking clearly. To the point that you were joking and laughing with him and not even realizing it. That man *kidnapped* you, let unspeakable things happen to you—*which I could kill him for*—and then made you believe *you* had to finish what *he* started. *You don't.* Let me and Killian handle this. You're safe now, baby." He massages the tension out of my shoulders, then leans over to turn the shower on.

He isn't completely wrong. If I'm being honest, I *am* seeing Diego in a different light. I still don't believe he is the monster everyone makes him out to be. He only shows that side of himself to those who truly deserve it. Underneath the monster mask is just a *man*—like Liam or Killian—who wants to do the right thing with his power. With the incredibly difficult cards he's been dealt. And I'm not sorry for believing that. Because if I looked at him as a monster, that would make Killian and Liam one as well. *Then what would that make me for loving them?*

Liam clasps my face between his palms and kisses my forehead. "I'm so fucking sorry this happened, love."

I unzip Diego's sweatshirt and peel it off me. Liam tugs me forward by the band of my sweatpants and loosens the string. They fall and bunch at my ankles. I kick off the flip-flops Diego gave me on the boat ride here before stepping out of his sweatpants. Liam's eyes linger on the tank top covering my body, his blood staining the places he touched me earlier. After a few harsh blinks, he grabs the hem of it, clutching it tightly. His bruised knuckles come up and caress my cheek.

"Did he or anyone touch–" I interrupt him before he can even go there.

"No. No one touched me like that."

"Hands up, darling." Summoning the rest of the energy I have left, I obey. He lifts the shirt over my head and drops it onto the growing pile of clothes on the floor. I took off my split-open sports bra back in Diego's bathroom. *It's not like it did much to support me anyway.* That leaves me standing in just the black lace thong.

Goosebumps spring up across my skin and my nipples harden. Watching Liam's pupils dilate stirs something in me. Something raw and carnal. *I want him.* As exhausted as I am, mentally and physically, I *need* him right now.

He on the other hand seems hesitant.

Nervous even.

His eyes don't hold the same type of hunger they normally do —they hold *pain* and *anger*. Those dark brows draw together as he notices all the weight I've lost. The electricity of his gaze is hard to ignore as he takes in every bruise and bug bite that cover my body. Tracking the marks like a constellation and guiding him up to my neck where the worst of the bruising is.

"Geraldo is as good as dead," he growls while softly tracing the fingerprints blotting the column of my neck. His fingers strum along the dip between my collarbones. *Oh no! My raven necklace is gone. Was I wearing it the night of my graduation dinner?* Hopefully, I left it at home.

I reach out and wrap my hand around his. "Do you understand now, *why* I want to help so badly? Think about Selena and all the other women who he's done this to. Who he

77

continues to do this to. I want to help, Liam. In any way I can. And if that means me going away with Diego for a little while to convince his uncle that he got what he wanted—then so be it. That's when you attack. When his guard is down again. And make sure you make him fucking suffer."

Shimmying out of my thong, I step into the shower and leave Liam standing there. He runs a shaky hand over his face and through his unruly hair, inhaling roughly.

My heart breaks for him. He looks so fucking broken. In a matter of just two weeks, I've changed dramatically. I'm not the same Maddy I was before, and I'm not sure I ever will be again. It couldn't possibly be easy for him to process all of this. To see the evidence of abuse all over my body.

Liam removes his clothing in record time and steps under the hot stream of water. Circling his arms around me from behind, he tugs me flush against the hard surface of his body.

"I can't lose you again, Madison," he whispers into my ear.

"You won't."

"Then why does it feel like I am?" He grabs the shampoo and starts massaging it into my hair. The pressure of those strong fingers against my scalp feels amazing. *Heavenly.* My eyes close with a sense of calmness washing over me.

"Because you know that I'll always help everyone I can. That's why I wanted to become a nurse, to help people."

"*Wanted?*" He spins me around and cradles my head back to rinse the suds out.

"I'm not sure what I want anymore," I sigh, pushing past him and grabbing the conditioner. We trade places as he washes his hair and then rinses it.

I close my eyes again, lathering the coconut-scented conditioner through my hair. The smell reminds me of piña-coladas...and the beach. Which makes my thoughts go to the ocean.

Ocean Eyes pierce mine behind my lids.

Fuck. Why am I so enamored with him? I'm reunited with Liam. Safe in his arms. I shouldn't be thinking about another man. *Especially the one who brought me into this mess in the first place.*

"Do you still want me?" Calloused hands slide down over my waist and grip my hips. My eyelids slam open as Liam pulls me closer to him. His handsome face is filled with worry, making my stomach fill with butterflies.

"Of course I do. I just need some sleep and time to process everything. That's all." I wrap my arms around him reassuringly and lay my head on his chest. The hot water pours over us, soothing my aching muscles. I let out a shaky breath and tighten my grip around his tense frame.

He is my home.

I love him.

And I'm going to show him exactly how much.

Determined hands glide from around his waist to his perfect set of abs. I skim them up and over his pierced nipples, giving each ring a gentle tug. A hiss slips out between his teeth. My palms fall flat over the ravens that sit on each of his pecs. His heart beats rapidly against my hand. Always so scarily in sync with my own. Leaning down, he captures my lips in a sweet kiss. Water sprinkles down over us from the rain showerhead.

It's gentle. And soft.

That isn't going to do. *That's not us.* We are always wild and crazy for each other. *Reckless even.* I don't want or *need* him to be gentle with me right now.

I slide my tongue along his bottom lip, before sucking hard and dragging it over my teeth. The metallic taste of blood from his split lip coats my mouth, followed by a hint of whiskey and smoke.

Our tongues dance wildly as we devour each other. Each of us clawing and desperate, trying to gain control. He releases a pained groan as I clasp his chin between my fingers.

Shit. I forgot about his jaw. *Diego got him good.*

"Fuck, baby. I missed you so much," Liam moans into my mouth.

Fiery kisses trail across my neck as he runs a hand down the curve of my spine. Traveling lower, he grabs a handful of my ass, drawing me even closer to his body. There is virtually no space left between us. The friction of our skin makes me come alive again. I gasp, tilting my head back to give him better access to latch on.

The hard length of him sits between us, pressing against my heated skin, just begging to be stroked. Dropping my hand, I grip him, sliding slowly from base to tip. My thumb rubs a circle over the sensitive head of his cock. Liam nips my neck and bucks his hips into me.

Rapacious fingers thread through my hair and grip it firmly. He tugs my head back even more and latches on to my neck, alternating between biting and sucking. I close my eyes and revel in the feeling of him becoming unhinged. He's replacing the bruises that caused pain and fear, with those of love and devotion.

Healing me with each touch.

Each kiss.

Each breath.

One of his hands drops between us, slipping between my folds. His smile broadens against my neck as he's met with my desire for him.

"Always so wet for me," he says approvingly in my ear, licking the shell of it.

The slow circles he is making around my clit are driving me insane.

More. I need more.

He teases me some more before sliding two fingers through my slick entrance, adding pressure where I need it most.

"*Mmm*, Liam. I thought about this every day I was away from you."

His lips claim mine again—almost bruisingly. I pump him harder, making him thrust against my hand. Those talented tattooed fingers continue to work their magic on me. High-pitched, staccato sounds are coming from my mouth. I am right on the cusp of an amazing orgasm.

We both are panting heavily when he pulls away.

"I need to be inside you, love." He's holding back, gritting his teeth, and ready to come right alongside me.

"What are you waiting for?" I raise a brow at him. *That always sets him over.* Here comes the savage beast I adore...

He removes his fingers with a sense of urgency and grips my thighs, hoisting me up. My back slams against the tile wall as his body presses against mine. I wrap my legs around him, resting my ankles on his sculpted ass.

Seriously though–this man does squats religiously. A smile tugs at the corner of my lips, reminiscing about our first gym interaction. *Man, my legs and ass were so sore that night. Even the hot tub didn't help much. What did Liam say that night? Oh, that's right...*

'*What is it about hot water and you, that gets me so fucking hard?*'

Hot water *does* make Liam ravenous—and I freakin love it. Linking my arms around his neck, I pepper kisses up and down his bruised jaw.

He lines the head of his cock up with my entrance and in one swift move thrusts inside.

"Ahh," I cry out. "Jesus, Liam. Every time...you take my breath away." I tighten my arms around him, burying my face in his neck. His impressive size is always a shock at first. The instant sting of my walls stretching; the overwhelming fullness and pleasure. It's that delicious balance of craving more and needing a reprieve.

His fingers dig into my hips as he pounds in and out of me.

More. I still need more of him.

The combination of our breathing, the sound of my ass slapping the tile wall, and the look on his face is about to be my undoing.

"*Harder*, Liam. Give me all of you. *Everything* that you're holding back—*don't*. I can take it."

A guttural growl rips from his throat. Deeper and deeper he sinks into me. He reaches between us circling my clit with his middle finger, pushing me into oblivion. The edges of my vision are starting to go. Sparkles twinkle across my eyes. Liam is panting and gritting his teeth, holding back for me.

Hearing him frantic for release gets me *every time*.

"Liam," I cry out, as an earth-shattering orgasm rocks through me. My legs tremble and spasm as wave after wave of aftershocks hit.

"Fuck, Madison. You're *everything* to me. I love you so fucking much baby," his voice is strained as he picks up his pace. His grip tightens on my thighs, supporting my now unresponsive lower half. I'm surprised I don't split in two as he roars out his release and empties himself inside of me.

We stay wrapped up in each other as we catch our breath. Tears stream down my face while I sob into his neck. "I love you," my voice breaks. "I love you so much."

He backs away from the wall and wraps his tattooed arms around my back, crushing me to his broad chest.

"I've got you, princess. You're safe now.

CHAPTER 10

MADISON

I'M nice and snuggly in Liam's oversized clothes. They smell like him—*cedarwood and lavender.* I inhale deeply, my eyes practically rolling to the back of my head at how intoxicating that smell is. He notices and chuckles.

"I did the same thing our first night without you. After destroying half the house in a rage, chain-smoking, and splitting a bottle of whiskey with Killian...I went to our room and grabbed your university sweatshirt you left on the desk chair. Like a goddamn safety blanket, I slept with it that night and every night thereafter—*not that I got much sleep.*" His eyes are softer now, less guilt and vexation plague them.

Liam tugs me closer by the sweatshirt, planting a gentle kiss on my lips. It's innocent enough to prove he's sated—for now—but the undertones of it hold a promise of making up for lost time. The corners of my mouth raise and my cheeks flush with thoughts of just exactly *how* we will be making up for that lost time.

"That smile looks so fucking lovely on you, Madison. I'll do anything just to keep it there." A delectable smile of his own creeps onto his face. He wraps his burly arms around me and holds me tight against his chest. *This is home.*

"You have two options, baby. Sleep or grab some dessert and see what everyone else is up to. *Hmm.* Perhaps we can add a third option...dessert in bed..." he trails off, his greedy fingertips sliding down my waist.

I pinch his nose between my fingers. "As much as I'd *love* to be persuaded into option three...I think we need to see what everyone else is up to first. There are still a lot of plans to be made. Plans that I can help with."

A moment of trepidation carves his features before he grabs my hand and leads me down the hall to the kitchen.

Aaand there goes our postcoital bliss.

Everyone is talking in hushed tones as we enter the space. All eyes are directed at us as Liam and I make our approach. One particular set of eyes narrow as they graze over me from head to toe, lingering on my hand wrapped around Liam's. His teeth clench and the muscle in his jaw pulses before Liam speaks.

"I offered her sleep," he shrugs. "You know Maddy. She wanted to be here."

"Seems you offered her a lot more than that," *Ocean Eyes* spits. "The entire house could hear you two." His eyes lock with mine, making me feel a moment of guilt.

Wait. Guilt for what? Fucking my boyfriend?

And why should I care? It's not like *Ocean Eyes* means anything to me. We share a trauma bond.

That's all.

Killian purses his lips, evidently *bothered* by our loud reunion as well. Selena covers her mouth with her hand, suppressing a giggle. And Declan just stares down into his teacup like it's telling his goddamn fortune.

Liam's hand squeezes mine possessively, a low growl rumbles in his chest. "We're just getting started," he clucks his tongue. "Perhaps it's time for you to fuck off to your yacht if silence is what you require."

"I could use a coffee and maybe a little snack," I cut in,

slowing the buildup of testosterone that's threatening to decimate the entire room.

"And I could use a fucking cigarette," Liam grumbles. "Want one, love?" He pulls the pack of menthols out of his pocket and wiggles them in my face.

"As tempting as that sounds, I'll pass. I *seriously* need some more caffeine." The smile I shoot him is meant to be reassuring. "Go, babe. I'm perfectly capable of putting a K-cup into that Keurig over there." I plant a kiss on his cheek before making my way to the machine.

His eyes dart over to where Diego is sitting and then back to me again. Without another word, he opens the sliding door and slams it shut. All you can see is the silhouette of his large frame and the glow of his cigarette in the night. Declan has kept the lights surrounding the property to a minimum, preventing Liam from being seen.

Killian breezes by me, heading in the same direction as his brother. I'm sure they would like to discuss a few things away from Selena and Diego. My back is turned to them as I load a coffee pod into the machine.

"I need to take a leak," Declan announces, his chair scraping against the tile. "Selena, I trust that you will keep your brother in check while I'm gone."

She huffs, "Haven't you all decided he is no longer a threat?"

"He may not be a *physical* threat to anyone here...but I see the way he looks at Madison."

"I'm right here, *asshole*," Diego retorts.

Dude, same.

"And that's where I'll find you when I get back. *Entiendes?*" he sneers.

There's a heated moment of silence. I'm tempted to turn around to diffuse it when I hear Declan's retreating footsteps followed by Selena whisper-shouting.

"*Es suficiente, Diego! You* are the reason everyone is in this situation in the first place. Even if they understand, it doesn't mean they forgive you for what happened to Madison. And seriously, *hermano*, if you know what's good for you...stop looking at her like that."

Once again. Right here, Sel.

The sound of the machine brewing fills the room. I open the refrigerator and look around for the half-and-half. Coming up empty, I close the door. *Fuck it.* I'll drink it black at this point. I let out a little yelp when I spot Diego leaning against the island with the carton in his hand.

"Looking for this, *Mariposita*?" He shakes it for emphasis.

I grab the carton from his hands more aggressively than intended. "Thank you," I say in a clipped tone.

Turning my back to him, I snatch my mug of freshly brewed dark roast and bring it to my nose, summoning feelings of instant relief and comfort. It enriches and awakens my soul. My eyes close as I lean against the granite countertop.

"Ahhh, I missed you so much," I whisper.

"You weren't gone *that* long, baby. But, I missed you, too." Diego's gravelly voice breaks into a chuckle.

Slamming my mug down, I open my eyes to scowl at him. Scalding hot liquid sloshes over the rim, burning my finger. I pop the knuckle into my mouth and suck on it to relieve the pain. Diego's eyes blaze as he takes in my lips. Heat scorches across my body, much hotter than the coffee spilled. I pull my finger away and continue my task...temporarily ignoring the intensity of those blue orbs while sprinkling in two spoonfuls of sugar and a healthy splash of half-and-half.

Knowing I can't ignore him forever, I lean my hip against the counter and turn toward him a fraction, clutching the steaming mug between my hands. "And for your *information*—I was talking to my coffee."

He barks out a laugh again, his arms crossed over his solid chest. Every tendon and vein is on display. "What did I tell you about talking to inanimate objects, *Mariposita*?" He arches a brow at me.

A light-hearted laugh tries slipping past my lips. I bite them instead and shake my head. Diego's throat bobs. He swallows a few times before regaining control of his features. If I am going to ignore this thing between us I'll need to do the same. I grab a banana off the hook of the fruit basket and make my way to the table.

Selena is sitting there sipping on coffee and watching us interact. I completely forgot she was there. Her eyes volley between us over the rim of the mug looking more amused than anything. It's when Diego pulls out the chair adjacent to his, that her eyebrows raise then come together in vacillation.

Diego takes a seat and Selena shoots him a stern look. Some unspoken words are exchanged between the two siblings. Diego just smirks and flips her off. She sticks her tongue out before responding. "Flip me off one more time tonight, and *I will* break that finger off your hand," she hisses.

"*Oooh.* Trying to steal my M.O., Sel? You'll have to break a hell of a lot more bones than that to get my title. *Thousands.*" He smirks at her playfully before taking a sip of his coffee and leaning back in his chair. He winces briefly before masking the discomfort of his ribs.

A shiver runs up my spine hearing just how lethal this man truly is. My eyes linger on his hands resting on his stomach with ease. I could catch flies with the way my mouth is hanging open.

Thousands of bones.

Those hands have the power to obliterate anyone or anything in his path.

Just when I thought his hands were the most lethal thing about him, my eyes meet his.

Nope. *Those eyes are.*

Like a siren, they lure you in with their beauty and hold you captive—slowly dragging you under the surface until you can't tell which way is up. I didn't even realize how long I was drowning in them until the chair next to me scraped against the floor. A tattooed arm laces around my shoulders, pulling me close. Smoke and lavender permeate the air.

Killian comes striding in from the sliding doors. He leans down to kiss the top of Selena's head before plopping next to her with a sigh. Declan returns from the bathroom a few moments later, eyeing Diego the whole time. His green eyes swirl with wariness.

Silently, I take it all in, sipping my coffee, and humming my approval. Liam chuckles beside me. "Feeling better, love?"

"Much. How about you?" I raise an inquisitive eyebrow.

"Better—*for now.*" He gives the back of my neck a gentle squeeze. His index finger lazily traces circles on a spot I didn't even know was erogenous until now. The feather-light touch is ticklish and sensitive at the same time. All of my nerve endings are firing off. I squirm in my chair already wishing to head back to our room for the night.

Liam takes advantage of my moment of weakness, gliding his hand over my shoulder and down my arm until his fingers graze my thigh under the table. He continues his expedition, finding the seam of my sweatpants and sliding his middle finger up and down it. My hand shoots out as he makes contact, digging my nails into him in warning and trying to swat his hand away. *He needs to knock it off.* We need to focus on ways to take down Geraldo.

I clear my throat when he ignores me, increasing his pressure and circling my clit. The soft lace of my new panties dampens as liquid heat begins to pool.

My cheeks grow hotter.

"So...what we were discussing while you were showering, *Madison,*" Killian begins, curiosity and amusement shadowing his face as he redirects his focus to me. He inhales deeply through his nose, "Was that...it will be—" reprimanding eyes dart to Liam's before continuing, "—*important* to keep things just as we had agreed upon with Geraldo."

"Mhmmmm," I moan and respond simultaneously.

My hands begin to shake from the impending climax building inside me. I grab the banana and start peeling it, giving myself some form of distraction. Liam just continues with his tactical ministrations, discreetly snorting with laughter and satisfaction. I don't think he is even paying attention to what's being said. He's too busy admiring the flush crawl across my skin.

"Liam won't like this." Killian eyes his brother again. "It will be best to keep up the guise that we are recovering from his loss. We will appear distracted and not a current threat, encouraging Geraldo to slightly drop his guard. With that being said, Liam will be heading to Ireland to spend some quality time with our family there. He needs to stay off the radar for this plan to work. If Geraldo even catches a whisper of Liam being alive, this whole plan will go to shit. He won't trust Diego, and we won't have the ability to strike together." Diego nods his head in my peripheral, agreeing with Killian.

I raise the banana to my lips, taking a vicious bite out of it while glaring at Liam.

Stop it. I can't. Fucking. Focus... Ahhh.

I know why he is doing this. He's pissing on his territory. *Men.* I roll my eyes.

And then they roll back for an entirely *different* reason.

"*Fuuuck*," I cover my face with my hands, feigning interest in the conversation.

I'm going to come right here at this table in front of everyone. I lower my hands to focus on Liam. My whimpers become garbled behind the mashed banana. Liam's eyes drop to my mouth, a wicked grin carved onto his face. Deft fingers continue to unravel me as I barely register what everyone is saying around me. *My mind is as mashed as the damn banana!*

Diego swivels his head and leans his elbows on the table to glance over at us. His eyes widen and smolder before looking away. What he sees has his hands balling into fists and his nostrils flaring. Killian is even turning red as he continues to speak. Selena's eyes gleam with laughter and a bit of envy, while Declan's have zeroed in on Diego, his brows furrowing.

"As for you, *Madison*...with your permission of course...it would be best if you spent some time on Diego's yacht. We know it's not ideal for you, but it could help immensely. I know that was an important factor for you earlier. We can make sure proof is sent to Geraldo, which will make him feel confident that his plan worked. If we keep quiet on our end, Geraldo will think he's won. That's when Diego will invite him to his yacht for dinner. The rest of his crew will be in attendance as well. Our men will be ready and waiting below deck. The rest will be on my private yacht, close by and ready to attack if anything goes astray."

I grip the table until my knuckles turn white and gasp. Diego's attention snaps back to mine. He inhales sharply, realizing my reaction was not due to our discussion. Fire races up my chest and my breathing grows heavier. I am two seconds away from seeing stars.

Diego clears his throat and adds, "We will end this once and for all. I will become the head of the De La Cruz Syndicate, and we will initiate a new alliance with the Tri-State Syndicate. Liam can come back from the dead—" Diego's hand slaps the table.

Liam's hand jerks away from between my legs. *Are you fucking kidding me?!* I let out a *woosh* of frustration.

"What the fuck did you just say?" Liam curls his lip to reveal his perfect teeth. All the blood must have been directed back to his brain, for he's just now catching on to what's been said.

Killian speaks before Diego can. "*Liam.* It's Madison's choice whether she will go with Diego or not. He has changed his opinion about having her there. *So have I.* She can help us significantly—"

"Abso-fucking-lutely-*NOT*!" he roars, standing and knocking his chair over.

"You, on the other hand, have orders to go to Ireland. I will not have a war looming over our heads and threatening everyone we love because of your stubbornness. We saw how *well* that played out earlier. Madison *will* be safe. You both will come home to each other when all of this is over. You can't be seen, Liam. Plain and simple. Your presence near her or even in this country is a fucking risk right now."

"*No*. You may be the leader of this organization, but I am still your brother. This is MADISON we are talking about." He points to me. She isn't going *anywhere*. And neither am I. We will go away somewhere *together* while this is taken care of, but she isn't leaving my side," he says with finality.

"Liam," I whisper, curling my hand around his bicep. "Look at me, babe." His head tilts down a fraction. Unshed tears are gathering in his eyes. My hand reaches up to caress his cheek and my thumb glides over his lips. "I have to do this. I told you I want to help. It will make everything transition more smoothly. It will keep you safe, too. If Geraldo finds out you're alive, who do you think he's coming after first?"

Liam shakes his head like he wants to disagree, but he knows I'm right.

Geraldo would come for *me*.

And then he would try to kill his nephew and his niece for conspiring against him, followed by Liam. He would leave Killian alive to live in misery, while the threat of having them as rivals continued for years to come.

Liam must have seen the same image unfold in his mind. His warm calloused hand overlaps mine on his face. A single tear drips down and rolls over his cheek.

"I can't," he whispers. "Baby, this *can't* be the only way." Resignation makes his words come out shakier than intended.

"Even if I don't go with Diego, I can't come with you. I have a target painted on my back. If either of us were found, the same fate would still unfold. Until Geraldo and his evil disciples are taken care of, we can't risk it." Tears well and spill over my eyes as my arms circle his waist. I lay my head against his chest. An erratic heart drums against my ear. Strong arms circle around me, cocooning and shielding me from the stares I feel on my back.

"My soul is yours, Liam. No matter how far away you go. No matter what lifetime we are living in–together or apart—it has and always will be *yours*. I will always find my way back to you. That's a promise." My voice wavers as I speak.

"I'm holding you to that, Madison. Because if something happens to you and I wasn't there to protect you, I will tear apart every city, every town, every crevice of this Earth until I find you again. Even then, I will spend the rest of eternity making it up to you. Doing everything I can to prove to you that I am worthy of your love. Of your forgiveness. And hope I didn't make the biggest fucking mistake of my life by letting you do this and not fighting harder to protect you. For not preserving your beautiful wings when I had the chance, and selfishly choosing to tarnish them with my darkness."

Big fat tears cascade down my cheeks, dampening his shirt. My fists cling to the fabric as my lips meet his. I'm not sure how long we stay like that, devouring each other in front of everyone after our elaborate confessions of love.

That sinking feeling kicks in. One I've become familiar with. *This feels like goodbye.*

The worst kind of goodbye.

I don't have to do this. Even if I decide not to, it still won't change the fact that we won't be together for a while.

The room starts to spin.

Exhaustion and grief hit me like a sack of bricks to the face. My legs buckle and Liam catches me, twining his arms around me before I hit the ground. He swings my legs up and cradles me against his chest.

We start moving toward the bedrooms. He glances behind him before reaching the threshold of our room.

"She needs rest. You can leave tomorrow after she gets some sleep," his words are directed towards Diego. Then he turns to brush past Killian who is standing by the door. "Killian, I can't even look at you right now, mate. Get the fuck out of my face before I completely lose my shit. How could you do this? How could you use your rank to force me into something that *you* would never be okay with yourself?" Liam walks us into the bedroom and kicks the door shut forcefully with his boot.

My body shifts in his arms as he pulls the comforter down and places me on the mattress. The softness of the down feather comforter engulfs me as Liam tucks me in. The bed dips as he sits on the edge of the bed. His head is slung forward in defeat, hands covering his face. I want to get up and comfort him, but I'm so fucking weak. My eyelids are beyond heavy. I can barely keep my eyes open. The last thing I see before the darkness takes me is Liam leaning over me and placing a tender kiss on my forehead.

The sliding glass door leading to the pool glides along its track.

And then there's silence.

No buzzing. Or whooshing.

CHAPTER 11

LIAM

FUCK HIM. I am two seconds away from abandoning my plan to blow off steam, and go in there and give my brother a piece of my mind—*or my fists.* He's done this once before during lockdown. When we were forced to stay under the same goddamn roof.

And that was for *his* benefit.

My house would have accommodated Madison and I *just fine.* Killian used that situation for his gain, trying to win Madison back. *So now what?* Sel is safe and happy, back in his arms, and he suddenly forgets how important Madison is to us?

As I said—*Fuck. Him.*

It took everything in me not to scoop Madison up in my arms and get us the fuck away from here. I don't even give a damn where we would go. *Anywhere but here.* They all lost their fucking minds. The only thing tethering me to this plan is the oath I took for Killian and the Tri-State Syndicate.

Killian's word is final.

However, I am starting to consider plans to take over my brother's role. He never wanted it in the first place. We are brothers after all—only born a few months apart. Perhaps it's time I use that card.

I am a goddamn Kennedy.

No one takes what is mine.

Stripping down to my boxer briefs, I pull my black t-shirt over my head and toss it onto a nearby lounge chair. Inhaling deeply through my nose, I take a running start before diving into the blue-lit pool. I hold my breath until my lungs burn and scream out, and push myself across the length of the pool and back. When I breach the surface, I inhale on a snarl, breathing in and out through my clenched teeth like a feral animal.

A plethora of questions are racing through my mind, one after the other pouring in. With a sigh, I fold my arms over the pavers and lay my head against them.

Fuck my life.

How am I supposed to let the fucking devil himself take my woman with him on his private yacht? How can I just sit here and let her go? Not only that but I am being sent across the pond. I can't protect her from there. Even if Diego means every word he says about keeping her safe, I don't trust his intentions. You would be a damn fool to think he didn't develop feelings for her. You can feel it sizzle in the air between them. Like butter on a skillet, my woman can't help but melt for him.

I don't blame her. Diego De La Cruz has the looks. I'll give him that. Perhaps Madison is drawn to his surfer vibe. Although, she is rather fond of my beard, piercings, and tattoos...

That's what I am worried about most. No matter how many times Madison has confessed her love for me, my heart just can't fully grasp that she wants me.

That she chose me.

Blackened soul and all.

She is the only person who sees past my darkness. Madison is all that is good in this world. Every person she comes in contact with opens up to her and confides in her. Even complete strangers. She's a magnet for helping others and aiding in their healing.

When we finally got our chance, she made herself right at home, ripping open the curtains drawn on the dusty windows of my soul. One by one she yanked, until only bright healing light beamed through. Fear by fear, memory by memory, every bad deed I've ever committed washed away. I see the world in such a different way now that she is in it. I'm a better person because of her.

I have purpose.

More than just being a criminal. More than playing a role in the underworld.

I'll be damned if I let her slip away from me, again.

I will always protect her. For she is a goddess walking amongst us mere mortals. Madison truly is too good for this fucking cruel world. And one of these days, she's going to give too much of herself. So much so, that she won't be able to come back from it.

I just pray this desire of hers to help Diego—isn't going to be that day.

AFTER A FEW DOZEN laps in the pool, I push myself up over the pavers and sit. Footsteps approach me as I'm reaching over to grab my smokes from my pants pocket. A shadow makes its way over to me. Her beautiful features become illuminated by the blue light of the pool. Steam swirls around her, making her look even more ethereal. *My Goddess.*

Black—now chipped—painted toenails catch my attention as she pads towards me.

"Aren't you supposed to be sleeping, baby?" I ask, my brow cocked as I drink her in.

She slips her fingers into the band of her sweatpants, pushing them down her sexy legs, and steps out of them. Maeve had provided her with a fresh set of panties—which are now hugging my favorite part of her. Suddenly, I am extremely envious of a lace pair of panties. My cock springs to life under my boxers, ready to pick up where we left off.

She takes a seat next to me, dipping her long sexy legs into the water, and rests her head on my shoulder. "I did—for a little while. I don't want to waste time sleeping when I can be spending it with you."

That makes my heart soar. As much as I'd love for my cock to take a deep dive into that sweet wet pussy, I just want to hold her.

"Ya want a cigarette?" I rasp. She chews on her lip and her eyelashes flutter as her head swivels to look up at me. Those gorgeous eyes meet mine, stunning me into silence, *as always*. My hand comes up to cup her cheek, my thumb stroking the soft skin beneath it. I lean in and claim her lips, the sweetest sin a man can covet. They are lush and full and speak the filthiest things when I'm inside her.

"I'd love one, but right now—your lips are going to pacify my need." Her arms come up and circle my neck, bringing me closer to her.

"We are going to be okay, baby," I concede. "No matter what happens now, no matter how far away I am. I will always be yours. You need me, sweetheart—I'm on a plane. A boat. I'll fucking swim there. I don't care about the repercussions. Part of me is ready to just say *fuck it all* and come with you. Except, after calming down, I realized they're right." I lower my head until our foreheads touch.

"If we stick to the plan, we can save countless lives *and* change the future of the two syndicates moving forward," she says. The cutest smile forms on her face. One full of pride in herself.

I would give anything to go back to a few weeks ago. When life wasn't like this. So fucking complicated and painful. I mean —it was still complicated—this is *just completely fucked*.

Pressing a kiss to the tip of her nose, I reach behind me and grab my lighter and smokes. I pull two from the pack and light them both, handing her one. Her head falls back onto my shoulder as we look out and watch the hint of the sun rising along the horizon. Vibrant purples, oranges, and pinks start to creep into the sky.

I take a deep pull of my cigarette. From my peripheral, I watch her do the same. We sit in silence for a while, enjoying this moment of stillness and temporary reprieve from the chaos.

Smoke billows out from the side of her mouth with a sigh. "I need to take a pregnancy test before we leave."

Believe it or not, I've never been tased before. But I could imagine this is what it feels like to be slammed with 50,000 volts.

"Why? I thought you said no one—"

"No one did. In the bathroom at the steakhouse three weeks ago was the last time we had sex. I haven't had access to my birth control pills since then, so who knows." She shrugs, taking another deep drag of her cigarette.

Christ. My child—*our child*—could be growing inside her right now. That elated feeling is quickly replaced with dread. The realization we are about to part ways rears its ugly head.

No. *Hell no.*

If that stick shows two pink lines, we are changing course on everything. I am hiding Madison on the other end of the continent.

Warm, firm hands grip my bicep, pulling me out of my rampant thoughts. "I doubt we are, but I have to be sure. I also need to get my birth control or some other long-term form of it. I am going to be away for a while."

My brows pull together as I turn to her, pulling smoke into my lungs and exhaling above our heads. "Why would you need birth control if you and I are apart?"

"My periods are really bad, babe. I have PCOS. I'd rather not deal with painful cramps and erratic periods while being out at sea and in the company of Diego and his staff." The muscle in my jaw pulses at the mention of that fuckers name. I also feel like a dick now for assuming the worst.

Told you I'm a savage.

I slide the ashtray over to us and snub my cigarette out. Madison takes one final drag before doing the same. "Listen—" I reach out and stroke her face, "—I apologize. I never really got into detail with my mum about periods and all that. I'm sorry for assuming it was strictly for prevention. And for assuming that you...perhaps...would need it at some point. This whole situation has me on edge. I see the way Diego looks at you and how you respond to him. It scares the hell out of me, Madison."

Leaning in, she places a brief kiss on my lips. "You don't have to worry about him. He may enjoy his women submissive, but he would *never* touch me. He promised not to touch me like that unless I asked. And since I never will, you will never have to worry."

That doesn't comfort me in the least. I told myself the same thing when Madison was dating Killian—and I was too weak. I gave into temptation with her.

She made me crazy.

She still does.

MADISON SITS cross-legged on the bed. Light from the morning sun is streaming through the sheer white curtains. The pregnancy test is face-down on top of the end table like a ticking time bomb.

Three minutes.

Three grueling minutes is how long it takes to find out if your world is about to change.

I pace the room like a madman, brooding and biting my lip until I taste copper.

"Calm down, Liam." Madison giggles as my phone timer chimes.

She makes no move to take a look at the test. On a deep breath, I pick the damn thing up and flip it over, holding it out in my palm between us.

Both our heads are bent over it, nearly touching. I hear her sigh before I take in the one pink line.

Part of me feels deflated at the thought of my baby not growing inside her. Or that I could have had a reason to go guns blazing into the other room and tell them all to fuck off with their plans. I would take my woman and run the hell away from here.

The other part of me is relieved.

I want this all behind us.

I want my ring on her finger.

And I want as big or little of a wedding as she wants before we build our family.

The selfish bastard I am wants to spend more time with her —*as much as I can get*—before baby Kennedy claims their mommy's perfect tits.

If they are anything like their father, they won't want to share either.

My knuckle drifts under her chin, lifting it. Tears coat my gorgeous woman's eyelashes. Before I can speak she's in my arms. Her head rests on my chest and her hands, still gripping the test, wrap around me. A sob slips past her lips.

"Oh, Liam." *I can't tell if she's upset...or...?*

Lifting my left hand, I rub soothing circles over her back. The other tangles into her hair, massaging her scalp. "What is it, princess?"

Madison hiccups and sniffles. "I always wanted a baby. And I want a baby more than anything with you. I guess I wasn't expecting to be so upset over a negative test." She releases a small shaky giggle. "Now would definitely not be the best time to find out I'm pregnant. Still sucks seeing one line. I'm worried that my PCOS has caused me to become infertile. The longer we wait, the harder it can be to get pregnant."

A chuckle of my own follows her admission. "If you want a baby, we will find the best doctors around to get you pregnant. I'll fuck you from sunrise to sundown. And if we exhaust that option—not that I will ever tire of having my cock buried inside of you—we can find a surrogate or even adopt. Our family will be just as blessed, no matter how that baby was brought into this world—because they will have you as their mum." I kiss away her tears and bring my lips to hers.

She slaps at my chest. "Why are you so perfect?" Her glossy, red-rimmed eyes find mine.

"I'm far from perfect, baby. You just make me want to be a better man. A man worthy of not just your love, but of our future children, too." I angle my head to whisper in her ear. "Ditch the birth control. We could have conceived in the shower earlier." I am pulling at strings here, trying to find a reason for her not to go.

"My period should be coming any day now. I'm not sure that we would have had much luck."

A knock interrupts our moment, snapping me back into reality.

With an annoyed groan, I drag my feet to the door. Killian's stupid face greets me. It's tight with unease as he shoves a small cooler bag into my chest. "Madison's birth control," he mumbles.

I open the bag, pulling out the three boxes inside. It's some sort of monthly ring that you insert. How Killian knew she needed it is beyond me. Fucking detail oriented, organized, lunatic probably tracked her cycles.

"It needs to be kept on ice until they reach the yacht, so leave them in there." Killian's voice is void of any emotions and it's pissing me the fuck off.

Robot boy strides right past me and walks toward Madison. His eyes dart over to the pregnancy test in her hand.

"Fuck. Am—Are you guys...?" The stumbling eejit apparently found his emotions again. They flash across his face like he's playing a speed round of charades.

"We aren't. I was just making sure." Madison shrugs, tossing the test into the garbage bin in the corner of the room.

Killian lets out a sigh of relief. Which I don't fucking like. *Why is he relieved?* That could have been his niece or nephew.

As the time inches closer to her leaving, my nerves short-circuit. I clench my fingers into fists. I want to punch Killian in the mouth the more he stands there not saying anything. His lips are slightly parted as if weighing what to say next.

He pulls an iPhone from his pocket and places it in her palm. His hand lingers on top of the cell and curls around hers. "Our hacker Sebastian set this phone up. It cannot be traced by anyone other than our men. It has Liam's number, mine, Selena, Lexi and your sister Mikayla's programmed in there. As of right now, your mother thinks you and I took a nice vacation to Greece. Which isn't *technically* a lie. You'll be heading to Mykonos with Diego. He plans to stay off the coast, anchoring in the Aegean Sea."

Madison looks down at her new phone and then over Killian's shoulder at me. For the first time since she came here, I see real fear in her eyes. The idea of what she just committed to is settling in. She won't even be in the States anymore.

"Thank you," she says simply.

Kil turns around and pushes a phone to my chest. "This is yours. Your flight leaves in an hour. The members of our Northern Ireland Syndicate will meet you at the airport. You will be staying with them until further notice," he shoves past me. "Declan is keeping an eye on things down here until we are ready to move and has generously provided Selena and I transportation home," he sneers while crossing the threshold of the door.

I spin around angrily, gripping his arm with force. "Did I do something to piss you off, Kil? Cause the way you've been acting, it's as if we are back to fighting over the same woman. Yet—you have Selena now... so why the need to push me and Madison apart?"

His eyes narrow as he looks down to where my hand grips him then back up to meet my eyes. There is a flash of sympathy before they harden again. "You couldn't just listen to me. You *had* to do things your way. *So here we are.* Dealing with the cards we've been dealt because of *your actions*. And please, correct me if I'm wrong, but Madison wants to help. She always has a choice, Liam. I think you forget that sometimes."

"You're a fucking hypocrite, Kil. You never wanted this power. Yet here you are using it to make me bow down to what you need. And for the record—*you* are the reason we are in this mess. *You* had me kill Basilio. How dare you use Madison as a pawn in this war. This would *never* have been the case if it happened back in December. You would have done *anything* to protect her from all this, to shield her." I grip his t-shirt and get in his face. We are practically nose to nose.

"*Madison will be protected,*" he says between gritted teeth. "Diego swore on his life she would leave that yacht unharmed. She is strong, she is smart and she will help our syndicate. She knew what she was getting into when she came into our lives. *Let. Her. Choose.*"

"Um, hello...I'm right here." Madison's sweet angelic voice chimes in.

I turn my head to look at her in apology. Her arms are crossed over her chest as anger simmers across her features.

"Baby, tell me what you want me to do. You know I will *always* protect you. And if that makes me a total arse for bypassing your decision to walk right towards danger, then so be it. You are *everything* to me, Madison. To your friends and your family. I'll be damned if anyone hurts you because *Killian—*," I growl, spinning my head in his direction, "—thought this was *best.*"

An internal war is brewing behind her eyes. She isn't as confident as she was last night. *Please just change your mind.* Her hand goes up to where her necklace—*my* raven necklace—once sat. Red stains her cheeks as she realizes it's missing.

"You're not an ass. I love that you protect me so fiercely, Liam. I never want you to stop doing that...but I have changed in such a short period of time. I'm not afraid. *I can do this.* I want to do this. And when you finish the job, I will come home to you. Let me help."

Time feels like it stops. I take this small window of opportunity to stare at her beauty and process her words.

After a beat, I'm striding over to her and pulling her into my arms. "Okay," I acquiesce. Her arms come back around me and we just stand there as Killian clucks his tongue and leaves.

"I love you, baby. Please never change. You wouldn't be *my* Liam if you weren't so brash, so willing to end anyone who could hurt me. I love that about you. I know I can help. If that means bringing peace to our foreseeable future—then I am willing to do this for us."

"And I love you. I love that you are so full of passion for the people and things that inspire you. I love that you are *selfless* and giving and kind. Baby, know this...When you exhaust yourself and there is no energy left to give others, let alone to put yourself back together... I will be there to catch you. To nurture you and bring you back. Don't let this world—*our world*—turn you cold. Don't let the darkness win. Keep those wings pure. I know my fingerprints may have stained them, but it's because I was holding you too tight. I promise to loosen my grip and trust that you've got this. If I let you fly without me hovering above and casting my shadow on you, will you still come back for me? My dark soul, foul mouth, mood swings, and all?"

The most beautiful sound pierces through the tension. Her laugh is so fucking perfect. "I will always come back for you. And I happen to like your foul mouth." Her fingers trace my lips while shooting me a wink. "As for your dark soul—you don't see yourself very clearly. Your soul isn't damned, Liam. You are the most loving, protective, altruistic person I know. You took a bullet for me. Remember that."

"I would do anything for you." I get down on my knee and hold Madison's hand in mine. Her eyes go wide seeing me there. "Marry me, Madison. It doesn't have to be today, tomorrow, or even next year. I will do this the proper way. With the proposal you deserve and a ring you will adore. Right now, I just need to hear you say it. That it's always you and me. Forever."

Tears spring to her eyes as another fucking knock on the door interrupts us.

A slow, derisive clap begins.

"For fucks sake! Maybe the Universe really is trying to keep us apart," I roll my eyes.

Diego leans into the room with his hands grasping the molding above the door.

Impeccable timing, arsehole.

"That was beautiful. Truly brought tears to my eyes," he sniffles sardonically. The knuckle of his index finger swipes under his eye to wipe away the faux moisture. *"Mariposita,* it's time you say goodbye to your *fiancé."* He clears his throat. "We've got a plane to catch to Mykonos, and I have a few places to stop along the way. My chefs are preparing a late dinner for us when we board my yacht." He winks at her.

Madison ignores him and presses her lips firmly to mine. "Yes," she whispers against them. My smile grows beneath hers. I know this isn't official, yet hearing her say that one word, damn well eased my fears.

In a daze, my feet carry me to the chaise lounge where my duffle bag is. Madison's eyes light up and she gasps as I retrieve the black diamond raven necklace from it. Dangling it off my fingers, I motion for her to move her hair. Which she does, collecting it and parting it to the side. I return the necklace to where it belongs, reveling in the knowledge that this goddess of a woman just said *yes* to me.

To being my wife, my forever.

She leans up on tiptoe and kisses me one last time.

Diego leans against the door frame, arms crossed over his chest. Impatience and annoyance mar his features.

"Take care of her." I jab my index finger at his smug face as Madison takes her place by his side.

"*I certainly will,*" he goads, curling a hand around her waist.

CHAPTER 12

SELENA

I'M LOOKING out the window of the private jet Declan was kind enough to lend us. Killian and I are heading to New York. *To my new home.* The place I should have called home years ago. Diego did everything in his power to give me another opportunity to live in peace. It's not his fault it took this long for Killian and I to get the chance for a redo.

I am so incredibly thankful for my brother.

Since we were children, he's always been there for me. Protecting me. Teaching me. Guiding me.

If a guy from school, or even one of my father's men looked at me the wrong way, they would find themselves at the other end of my brother's hands. Sometimes they ended up with a broken rib. Sometimes a broken jaw. Or his personal favorite—a fractured skull.

The nickname *The Bone Breaker* was birthed way before he rose up the ranks in the underworld.

Waves of guilt slam into my gut as I sit here. A mimosa in one hand and Killian's in the other. *Technically, it's* just orange juice—Killian doesn't know that. I asked the flight attendant to put it in a champagne glass with a splash of seltzer.

This morning was eventful in more ways than one. While

emotions were running high and everyone was saying their goodbyes, I was puking my brains out in the guest bathroom of the pool house. I knew Killian and I had been going at it like crazy before my brother took Madison and I, but I never expected to see two pink lines show up on a pregnancy test. Once the shock wore off, I cleaned myself up, hid the test in my suitcase, and grabbed myself a bagel.

Now is certainly not the time to tell Kil. When the time is right I will. I feel uneasy about this, I am finally getting back to a good place with him. What if he doesn't want children right now? What if God forbid something horrible happens with their plan? Will he look at my brother and me differently?

I made out better than anyone in this crazy plan my brother created. Although I agree it could have been orchestrated better, he meant well. He really did. Experiencing what we did as children was devastating enough. But hearing bits and pieces of what Diego witnessed firsthand alongside my papá, breaks my heart.

He has and will always want better for us. His vision for the future of the De La Cruz family is inspiring. I just hope Killian and Liam can see what I see.

He would never have wanted anyone who wasn't deserving to get hurt.

Madison was never supposed to get hurt in all of this.

She has to be halfway to Mykonos by now. Probably mentally preparing herself for her stay on my brother's luxury yacht for the next several months.

It's not fair. She doesn't deserve this.

Even if she is willing to sacrifice so much of herself for those she loves. For me and Diego. And the lives of so many innocent people. She doesn't deserve to be in this position.

Listen, Diego may be my brother, but he's still a man. His interest, or should I say infatuation with Madison is going to be a problem. I'm calling it now. Liam and Madison will find themselves in a strained relationship after this is all said and done.

I can't help but feel extremely guilty about that. About my part in all of this.

We became good friends over the last few months. She trusted me. Regardless if she forgave me for my involvement in this, I know she'll never fully trust me again. And that fucking sucks.

I never had best friends growing up. As I said, boys were out of the question. Even though there were plenty of guys who were amazing towards me, I was always too frightened to drag them into my fucked up life. The girls at school kept away from me altogether. Their parents made sure of that. No one wanted their daughters to befriend the child of Basilio De La Cruz.

Becoming friends with Madison was refreshing and exciting. She didn't have to give me the opportunity, either. *Yet she did.* It was the first time in my life I had made a true friend. Someone to gossip with. Someone to get drunk with and shake our asses to 90's pop with.

Her history with Killian could have made our relationship extremely awkward. I suppose it was for a bit—especially Valentine's Day.

Damn. What a night that was. Talk about Killian not being over her.

Yet, that never really bothered me. The moment she chose to put aside our history and actually attempt to be my friend proved why he still cared.

We became gym buddies, working out together as often as we could. HGTV was always on while we did our cardio. The two of us would talk about our future with our men, the houses we saw ourselves in, our dream vacation homes, and even talk of the desire to have children.

Children. I can't believe I have Killian's baby growing inside of me right now.

It was so simple then.

Time is such a funny thing, isn't it?

A few months ago, we were just two *regular* women discussing our dreams of a family and domestic life. I wasn't the daughter of a sadistic Mafia leader and she wasn't the girlfriend of the new leader of the Tri-State Syndicate (well— that's what the rest of the underworld thought Madison was at the time).

Poor, Liam. Since the beginning, besides Maddy's love, he really got the shit end of the stick. Dealing with Killian in the beginning, almost losing her during the accident, losing her to my family, and now the two of them being forced to separate.

My mind begins to race with visions of their future—*and it's not pretty.* Liam has always been so protective of the ones he loves. Last night he was the worst I have ever seen him. Real worry etched his features. The thought of losing Madison plagued him. And it wasn't fear of her losing her life. He knows she'll be kept safe.

It was fear of losing her to another man.

Madison is going to change through all of this. *She already has.* I'm afraid that when she comes home to him she will have changed so much, she won't even know what or *who* she wants.

Hopefully, my brother is not the catalyst for that.

"You okay, Lena?" Killian's thumb skates across mine. His eyebrows come together with concern as his other hand tucks a strand of my hair behind my ear.

"Yeah." I sip my mimosa, buying myself some time to find the courage to tell him what's been bothering me. I adjust in my seat to look at him and sigh with frustration. "No, I'm not okay."

"What's wrong, baby?" He squeezes my hand, giving me some reassurance to continue.

"Why did you send Liam to Ireland? You and I both know we could have kept him under the radar in New York. Hell, he could have stayed in his home in Connecticut until this all blew over."

Killian's features turn stone cold. A mask slides into place before he speaks. "He deliberately disobeyed me when we tried to extract you both from the island." Dark amber liquid swirls in his glass as he takes a healthy sip.

"You would have done the same thing. I'm actually surprised you didn't. And not for me...for *Madison*. You knew it was a possibility—*a big possibility*—that I had turned on you. The love you have for her will always be there, Killian. I have accepted this, come to terms with it, and honestly—I'm fine with it. I know the love you have for her has dulled down. What once stemmed from passion and desire, has now evolved into wonderment of the woman who helped you rediscover the meaning of those four letters."

I glance up at him when he remains silent. He empties the remainder of his drink and signals the flight attendant for another.

"I would have done the same thing, you're right." A crystal tumbler with two fingers of whiskey is placed on his coaster.

"Then why punish him?" I push for more information. I'm really trying to make sense of how he could be so cruel to his brother. In all the years I have known him, he's never been this callous.

Liam is bleeding out over Madison and Killian is standing over him with a knife instead of sutures. *This needs to be fixed.* If I can try and put a tourniquet on to stop the bleeding, maybe just maybe, I can salvage their relationship.

Maddy and Liam belong together. He's dark and brooding. A hot head. Doesn't believe he deserves happiness. She is kind-hearted and patient. A healer and a true believer in love—in its power. I see the way she has captured his heart.

Never. And I mean *never*. Have I seen Liam act so romantic and emotional. He's always been cold and distant. Non-committal. IDGAF mentality.

"Love makes you reckless. I can't have him being a liability to this entire operation. The stakes are too high. Too many lives are at risk. Where I can be somewhat level-headed, Liam is not." His fingers rake through his hair, messing it up and making me squirm in my seat. He's so freaking hot with his hair disheveled like that.

"When it comes to Madison, he doesn't see clearly. Diego taunting him isn't helping, either. I see the way he looks at her. I think *everyone* can tell what's going on in his mind. And my brother is extremely territorial. Could you imagine trying to keep him in New York or Connecticut with her on a yacht with your brother? I *had* to use my rank to force him to Ireland."

"What if there is another way? What if we talk to my brother and see if Liam can join them in Greece? Even if he isn't on the same yacht. Can we at least arrange for him to be in the same *vicinity* as Madison?"

Killian stares at me for a beat before caressing my face and twining his fingers into my hair. "I love that you are their biggest fans, but for the time being, Liam is staying in Ireland. Let's see how this plan begins to pan out before I make any changes. I'm not saying no, I'm just saying not right now."

Nausea swirls in my stomach. I stand abruptly, letting Kil's hand drop from my face as I slide past him.

"Are you alright, love? Ya look a little pale." His voice carries behind me as he follows me to the bathroom.

"I'm fine, I'm not great with flying," I white lie, cupping my mouth with my hand as another vicious wave of nausea assaults me.

Bolting to the toilet, I drop to my knees and dry heave into it. Killian is behind me in seconds, patting my back and holding my hair back for me.

"Jesus, Sel. Is there anything I can get you?"

"It'll pass. I just need a moment," I groan, laying my forehead against the cool porcelain.

Kil rubs gentle circles around my back until the nausea subsides. "I think I'll lie down in the bedroom for a bit. I know you've got some work to take care of. I'll be alright, sweetheart." I kiss his cheek and stand up.

I bypass our seats, snatching my phone and bottle of water. Kil's warm hands wrap around my back and under my legs. He swings me up into his arms and carries me to the small bedroom at the back of the jet. Gently, he lays me down and covers me with the softest cashmere blanket.

Pressing a kiss to my lips he says, "If you need anything, call out for me." He pulls the door behind him, keeping it slightly ajar.

Anxiously peeking through the crack in the door, and seeing Killian back in his seat, I slide my phone out from beneath the covers. Scrolling to Madison's new number, I type out a text:

SELENA

> Girl. I could really use my bestie right now. Hope we are still able to talk like that. I miss you. 😿

Hitting send, I crack open the water bottle and take a few small sips. I feel better now that I am lying down. My phone chimes and my stomach drops again for a whole other reason. *Does she truly forgive me?* Glancing down, I see the first few letters, and a smile spreads across my face.

MADDY

> I miss you, too. 🤍 I told you I forgave you, Sel. And I meant that. After hearing how your brother kept you in the dark about the night we were taken, I can't really blame you. With that being said, what's up? Is everything okay with Killian?

SELENA

> Promise me what I am about to tell you, you won't tell Kil... or Diego.

115

The bubbles pop up on my phone and then disappear. Then pop up again.

> **MADDY**
>
> Okay... I'm nervous now. I don't think I can take any more bad news...

I bite on the tip of my acrylic nail. *Just spit it out, Sel.* I speed-type and hit send before chickening out.

> **SELENA**
>
> I'm pregnant. I just found out this morning.

> **MADDY**
>
> What?! Selena!! That is amazing. Congratulations. Are you happy about this? What's wrong with telling Killian? Your brother, I can understand... but Killian is going to be ecstatic.

> **SELENA**
>
> Thanks, girl. I am excited...and nervous, too. Are we biting off more than we can chew? Especially right now? We just got back together. I selfishly wanted more time with him before we started building a family. And I'm not telling him because he's super fucking stressed right now.

> **MADDY**
>
> I think the Universe sends us blessings exactly when we need them. Sometimes we don't even know we need them until they present themselves. This baby is a gift from your mother, no doubt. Everyone has been at each other's throats and chaos has been unfolding on every corner. It's your time to finally look forward to your future.

You're safe now and by the end of all of this, you and Killian will get to enjoy the life you always wanted. Without fear of your Uncle Geraldo or anyone else threatening that dream. Everything just needs to go according to plan this time. Now I have even more of a reason to help end his reign.

Salty tears drip down my face and onto the pillowcase. Stupid hormones! *See what I mean about Madison?* How can you not love her? She is on a flight across the Atlantic with my brother. Her man is miles away, and yet, *she* is comforting *me* right now.

The sudden urge to tell Killian strikes me. Madison gave me the perspective I needed. We live our lives so worried about the future, that we end up missing the important moments of the here and now. *What if tomorrow never comes?* Killian deserves to know he is going to be a father. I think I'll tell him when we get back to New York. *But how?*

SELENA

You are an angel, Mad. I hope you know that. Everything you say is always so comforting and inspirational. Even when your life is upside down, you still find it in you to make others feel better. I'm going to tell Killian when we get back to New York. Thank you for making me see that. Life is short. We all know this. Too well.

MADDY

Ahh! I am going to be an aunt! Killian is going to freak! My lips are sealed. Your brother won't find out from me.

SELENA

Speaking of lips... I know it's not my place, and it's probably really awkward that Diego is my brother... He's being respectful to you, yes?

117

What the hell? Liam proposed, and Madison still went? I wonder if Killian knows?...Or if Diego knows. He may be playing the respectful role of having Madison decide if she wants his attention but that won't last long. My brother's tastes in the bedroom have always been about it being consensual. The thing is, they were always contractual. Nothing remotely involving emotional feelings.

I suspect what my brother feels for Madison is more than the need to have another notch on his bedpost. Or a way to live out his wild fantasies. Which means his usual set of rules may not be ironclad enough.

Jesus.

He's going to slip up.

And by slip up—I mean slip and fall onto Maddy's lips. *Feelings are such a bitch.*

Killian is right...love makes you reckless.

Of course, the one woman my brother falls for is perfect for him—and *spoken for.*

Watching them interact over the last few weeks has me questioning who's going to end up hurt at the end of all this. As much as I am rooting for Maddy and Liam, I can't help but feel something brewing here. Something that could spell disaster for them...and that person is my brother.

118

MADDY

We were saying our goodbyes this morning. He told me that it wasn't official...he just wanted to hear me say that I was his forever. He even got down on one knee. There is no ring. He plans on doing it the proper way one day. Obviously, I said yes! He's my world, Sel. We will get through this. We can get through anything.

SELENA

You will. In a few more months you'll have your happily ever after, too.

At least, I hope so.

CHAPTER 13

DIEGO

"WHO IS PUTTING that smile on your face?"

Madison looks up to glare at me before continuing to type like she drank two Red Bulls in a row. Which she pretty much had. The flight didn't even take off and she was already finished with her iced quad espresso.

She clucks her tongue. "That is none of your concern."

"I told your *fiancé* I would protect you. So, yes, you are my concern. Everything you do is my concern."

Her chestnut eyes laser focus on mine. A pink blush warms the apples of her cheeks. Those straight white teeth of hers bite down on her full bottom lip. It's a nervous habit, she isn't trying to be feisty. Regardless, it's sexy as hell. I want to pry them open with my tongue and taste all her dirty little secrets. Her eyes hold mine captive, refusing to drop until mine do.

Such a power play, baby.

I fucking love it, this fight for dominance. With a smirk, I raise my coffee to my lips and look out the window. Ultimately, letting her win this round. Or at least that is a better explanation of why I submitted.

Madison looking at me like that has me hard as stone. Just a few seconds longer of our staring contest, and I would have been pulling her down onto my cock and letting her feel *exactly* what she does to me.

"If you must know, I am talking to your sister." Her nose scrunches as she shoots me a snarky expression. The one that says *are you satisfied?*

Well, I certainly am not *satisfied*. Although, I am happy to hear it's Selena instead of Liam.

"I take it you two have reconciled?"

She shrugs. "We have. It's not like *she* kidnapped me." She shoots me another glare over her phone while multitasking talking to me and Sel.

I chuckle and drain the rest of my coffee. "Best decision— ever," I whisper over the rim.

"What was that?" Madison lowers her phone to her lap, raising a delicate eyebrow.

"Nothing to *concern* yourself with, *Mariposita*." I throw her words back at her.

She places her phone back into the Chanel bag I purchased for her and stabs a piece of pineapple with her fork.

I had the black calfskin purse waiting on her seat along with a pair of Louis Vuitton sunglasses resting next to it. When she sat down and ran her hands along the bag, I knew her mood had significantly taken a turn for the better. She was in such a shit mood on the way here. I'm sure that had a lot to do with the fact that Madison would be away from her man for a few months.

And damn...putting all that aside, this woman is cranky without her coffee. She finally fell asleep in the car on the way to the airport after mindlessly staring out the window. Exhaustion and emotions from the last few weeks finally caught up with her. It was actually quite adorable when she woke up on my shoulder.

Madison is nowhere near as annoying as most women are when they wake up. She is needy in the way a toddler wants cuddles before bed. With the sleeves of her sweatshirt, she rubbed at her sleepy eyes and groaned about how she needed coffee.

"Pleaaaase tell me there is a fancy espresso machine on your multi-million dollar jet."

I just laughed and shook my head in disbelief that this sassy woman would be spending the next few months with me. Grabbing her hand, I led her up the stairs and straight to the machine. With wide eyes, she took in the stainless steel machine and the different options it offered.

Caffeine addiction is something I can admit to having as well. That machine cost a pretty penny, too. I crave coffee almost as much as I've been craving to get a taste of the gorgeous female sitting in front of me.

The red-headed flight attendant walks by and places a hand on my shoulder. "Mr. De La Cruz, would you like for me to set up the bedroom for your guest?"

I glance down at my watch, we have another five hours until our arrival.

Madison glances up, holding the pineapple-speared fork inches from her succulent lips. She's waiting for me to respond.

"That would be great. Please leave the bags I picked up on the bed as well." The redhead leaves us, dragging her glossy red nails across my shoulder, and licking her candy apple lips as she retreats to the bedroom. I drain the rest of my coffee and snatch the fork out of Madison's hand, popping the fruit into my mouth.

"Mmm. Love me some pineapple. You know, they say—"

"I know what they say," she snaps.

I stand and reach out my hand to help her up.

She crosses her arms over her chest in defiance. "I'm fine right here. Enjoy your nap, old man."

"You need to sleep, *Mariposita*." I mirror her, crossing my arms over my chest.

"I'm not tired."

I lean over her chair, caging her in with my arms. "*Liar.* If it's

123

one thing I am good at, it's detecting bullshit. You *are* tired. Don't lie to me, Madison. I said I wouldn't touch you but that doesn't mean I can't punish you."

She turns her head to look out the window, a blush creeping onto her cheeks. I grab her face and turn her head so she's looking at me again. Her hands slide up my waist and over my ribs. Just when I think my wildest fantasy is about to play out, she squeezes my ribcage. The air leaves my chest and silver stars sprinkle my vision.

"How are those ribs doing?" Her eyebrow raises as she places a firm hand against my chest and shoves me back in my seat. Then this maddening woman dares to fake a yawn. "You know, maybe I will take that nap."

She stands and shuffles by me, heading to the back of the cabin toward the bedroom. The flight attendant and her chat for a few minutes before she leaves Madison, clicking the door shut behind her. I grab her hand and tug her close to me as she passes me.

"Can I help you with something, Mr. De La Cruz?" she asks while running a hand down my chest.

"You can, actually. Interested in joining the Mile High Club?" I run my hand over the swell of her ass in the tight pencil skirt she has on.

Lacing her fingers in mine, she follows me to the bathroom adjacent to the bedroom. Once behind closed doors, I slam her against the adjoining door to the bedroom. She drops down to her knees, begins unbuttoning my jeans, and slides the zipper down.

I push her hands away and lower my jeans to the floor. "Take off your shirt."

She does as she's told, slipping off the scarf around her neck and unbuttoning the white blouse in a strip tease. Slowly, her fingers release each button until she shimmies out of it. A cherry red lace bra supports her generous set of fake tits. Eager hands reach for my boxers but I push them back.

"No touching, *Red*." I run my thumb along her lips then bend over to grab the red scarf off the floor.

I lean over and tie her hands behind her back. "Are you okay with this?" I whisper, nodding my head to her hands. Her eyes light up in a way that tells me this isn't her first rodeo.

"Yes, sir."

"Good." I lower my boxers and twine my fingers into her hair, pulling her closer to my cock. Red opens wide and wraps her silicone lips around my shaft. I lean back against the adjoining door to the bedroom with a loud thud. She licks and sucks, swirling her tongue around the head.

I've got about ten more seconds of letting her get adjusted to my size before I take over.

"Mmm," Red moans with a mouthful of my cock.

Usually, watching a woman give me head is the biggest fucking turn-on. Watching my cock disappear between two pillowed lips and seeing saliva pool down her chin turns me into an animal. *But right now? I* don't want to see Red's face. And don't get me wrong—she's gorgeous.

Moving my hand to the back of her head I slam my eyes shut and see a brown-eyed, smart-mouthed goddess.

"Fuuuuck." I pump myself harder into the back of her throat, making her gag and slurp. I take a quick peek, making sure Red's alright. She grins up at me and seductively flutters her wet lashes, so I shut my eyes.

Madison's gorgeous face fills my vision, once again. Her on her knees as I deliver her punishment for her sass and her lying. She's taking my cock like such a good girl. Invisible hands run up my thighs and grip my ass, encouraging me to go deeper. I fist the back of Red's hair and fuck her mouth faster with even more desperate thrusts. I am about to come when the door behind me jolts forward.

"For fuck's sake, I'm trying to sleep. Could you keep it down?" Madison's irritated voice fills the room.

I laugh. *Fucking laugh* while getting a blow job from the flight attendant. Never in all my years of kinky sex have I *ever* laughed. "Care to join us, *Mariposita*?" I ask while pulling my cock out of Red's mouth. "I guarantee you'll sleep great after."

"I'm engaged, *asshole*. If you still want my help then please refrain from having oral sex in my vicinity. Or any kind of sex for that matter."

My cock is aching for release, yet I no longer feel like using Red's mouth for it. I'd rather deal with a set of blue balls and spar with my little butterfly than empty my load at 36,000 feet above the ground.

"Can't promise that. We will be living in close quarters for a few months," I say over my shoulder while tugging my boxers back up.

Madison shrieks out her frustration, slamming the door shut in her retreat.

Reaching over, I untie the scarf from around Red's wrists and hand her her top. "Sorry about that, Red. She's got quite the temper." With haste, I pull my jeans up and fasten them, before extending a hand and helping Red up.

She buttons her shirt before rubbing shaky fingers under her eyes to wipe away the smudged mascara. "I'm sure you can find my number if you are ever interested in finishing what we started." Shooting me a wink, she adjusts her skirt, leaving me alone in the bathroom.

I glance at my reflection in the mirror and let out a frustrated sigh. *Fuck.* Madison has me all wound up. Guess now would be the perfect time to ask her to wrap my ribs...right?

CHAPTER 14

MADISON

THIS MAN IS INFURIATING! *I mean really?* I'm starting to question why I even agreed to this plan. I should have just stayed out of it and found a way to go with Liam. I sit on the edge of the bed and lay back, covering my eyes. *This is bad.* Bad. Bad. What's worse, was hearing what they were doing in there.

It turned me on.

God, I can't even trust my own mind anymore. That should have disgusted me. Instead, it intrigued me. It's not like I planned on interrupting them. One minute I was trying to sleep and the next, the erotic sounds filled the room. I was on my feet, heading to the door before it even registered to me that I could have seen him naked.

Opening that door, I realized that part of me *wanted* to. *Which is awful.* Part of me needed to know what it would have felt like to be that flight attendant. *Ughh, Madison. You're engaged!* I mean not officially, but Liam is your man. He always will be. You said YES! You promised him forever!

I can't be thinking like this. It's reminding me of the Killian and Liam situation all over again. Yet, it's different. I'm starting to believe that Killian was my rebound in a way. Someone I did genuinely find a connection with. But the truth is, Selena and him are perfect for each other. They were always meant to come back together.

Liam was always the one for me. Since the day I met him, I knew he was going to be an important part of my life. Isn't it just peachy, that I'm here questioning my sanity over none other than Selena's brother? I don't even *know* him. So why is my body reacting this way when I am so ready for a future with Liam? *Is it too soon for cold feet?*

All I can say is that I need to get my shit together. *And* set some major boundaries. *And* call Lexi. *Stat.*

The bathroom door opens, revealing Diego shirtless and in navy blue jeans.

Yep. Definitely need to set some major boundaries.

Dark blue bruises cover his ribs on both sides. *Liam got him good.* What's even more interesting is the black ink curving its way from his hip bone, around his ribcage, and disappearing behind his back. It looks like tentacles. They wrap around his ribs and one curls around his shoulder.

Diego must notice me staring, for he offers me a wide smile and touches the ink on his left shoulder. "Interested in seeing the rest?"

Yes.

NO.

I shift my weight, pushing my left hip out and crossing my arms over my now hardened nipples. *Traitors!* "We need to set some major boundaries, Diego."

He pads closer to me until we are an inch or two apart. "Consider *that* your punishment."

"Cocky much?" I raise my eyebrow at him. "I don't care one bit that you were fucking the flight attendant's face. I *care* that you chose this bathroom over the one at the front of the cabin."

"Already eager for another punishment? There was a truth there *and* a lie."

"I am not yours to punish. And I didn't lie. I don't care who you fuck, Diego. Just do it away from me." His blue eyes pierce mine, hungry and glittering with mischief. They dip lower down my body and back up again, holding mine captive.

"You're not a bad person for admitting that turned you on. I promise I won't tell Liam." He winks and walks past me, taking a seat at the edge of the bed. In my peripheral, I catch a glimpse of the enormous octopus inked on his back. The beast is crushing a skull in one of its tentacles.

The Kraken.

I turn to face him. "As I said, we need to set boundaries. I understand you are a very...*sexual* man. You have needs. If you could be more... respectful while I am around, that would be great. Remember why I'm here and the reason I am doing this." I stare him down until he laughs.

"As I said, I can't make any promises. I will try though. And make sure you *remember* our conversation. All you have to do is ask, and I can ease that ache you have between your legs right now. I won't lie to you, *Mariposita.* I want you. *Badly.* But until you are ready to accept my offer, I'll try harder to be aware of your boundaries."

"I guess that's better than nothing." I roll my eyes at him which causes him to narrow his.

"Sheesh. You really do like your woman submissive."

"I do–you're the exception."

Before I can ask him to elaborate, and realize this isn't just about the sex for him, he continues talking. "Now that we've discussed our *needs*, would you mind wrapping my ribs? They hurt like a motherfucker."

"Uh, yeah. Sure. No problem."

He points to the bag I moved to the nightstand. "There's a pair of satin pajamas in there—if you choose to sleep the rest of the flight, a sundress and sandals for our trip to *Pontus,* and some Ace bandages to wrap my ribs."

I walk over to the bag and dig around, catching a glimpse of the gorgeous pajama set before removing the bandages. Turning back around to face him, I hold them in my hand, "They don't recommend wrapping your ribs anymore as treatment. It can cause pneumonia or even a collapsed lung."

"I'm well aware, *nurse Maddy.* Sometimes in life, you have to outweigh the good versus the bad. I prefer them wrapped, they heal faster. So I'll take the risk. This isn't the first, and this certainly won't be my last time with broken ribs. But hey, at least I'll have a nurse onboard in case my health deteriorates." He shrugs while shooting me a dazzling smile.

Uneasiness eats away at me as I walk over to him. *Hmm... how to go about this?* I could easily wrap his ribs by standing in front of him. Except, that would mean I would need to look into those intense ocean eyes...and be at risk of standing between his legs.

The desire to take a closer look at his tattoo has me crawling onto the bed and kneeling behind him. His body vibrates with a silent chuckle.

"I don't bite, *Mariposita.*"

"Who's lying now?" I counter.

He barks out a laugh again, "I'll take the punishment, I'd love to see you take control. *Preferably naked.*"

With a sigh, I unravel the two Ace bandages, trying my best to ignore him. My eyes roam his muscular back, each muscle sculpted and visible with the way he is sitting.

He's tense.

It's incredible how much detail went into this tattoo. The octopus on his shoulder blade is insanely realistic and definitely intimidating, covering the entire left side of his upper back. At the curve of his spine, a tentacle wraps around a skull, crushing it.

"It's a Kraken," he says, his voice like gravel.

"I can see that. Makes sense, *El Rompe Huesos.* Hands up, please."

I place the bandage at one end of his ribs and start to wrap where a tentacle snakes around his abdomen and another curls around his hip. The one on his back dips low beneath the waistband of his jeans—I'm sure that one rests on the top of his ass cheek.

On my final loop of bandaging the front of him, he grabs my arms and gently folds them around him. The movement forces my cheek to press against his shoulder blade and my breasts against his back. *Too much contact. Too intimate to be clinical.*

"Thank you," he whispers in that raspy deep voice.

"You're welcome. Now, go. Let me get some beauty rest." I try to pull away but he tugs my arms a little harder, shackling me in place.

"Not just for this," he guides my hands along the fabric of the bandage. "Thank you for all of it. For choosing to help me and Selena, even after what you endured because of me. Thank you for trusting my plan and leaving behind the man you love. I know that couldn't have been easy."

I sigh against his shoulder blade. "You're welcome. Now *please* let me get some sleep before the next leg of this trip."

He releases me and presses a kiss to my palm before sliding off the bed. "I'll be right outside if you change your mind and decide you need that ache relieved."

Shaking my head, I threaten, "You're on your own the next time you need your ribs wrapped."

With a deep chuckle, he leaves, closing the door behind him.

KNUCKLES LIGHTLY CARESS MY CHEEK, stirring me from sleep. "We are landing shortly, *Mariposita*. Time to get changed and seated back out front."

The blankets are tangled at my feet, I must have kicked them off of me. I've always been a furnace when I sleep. Diego is sitting on the edge of the bed next to me. His eyes blaze hungrily down the lavender satin tank top and shorts I'm wearing.

"I knew you would look beautiful in these."

"Out." I point to the door.

He raises his hands in surrender. "We are going to have to get used to seeing minimal clothing on each other. The climate is very warm and unless you plan on getting heat stroke, I'd recommend lighter clothing—or none at all."

"Let's see..." I start counting off on my fingers. "Kidnapper, prison guard, tormentor, and now my stylist...any other titles you would like to add?"

"Just one," he says cryptically as he leaves.

What the fuck does that mean?

I throw the pillow over my face and scream into it. This is just the very beginning of being around this man. We're off to a great start.

God, help me.

THE SUNDRESS he chose for me is gorgeous. *Not that I'll be telling him that.* His ego is inflated enough as it is.

A beautiful light blue chiffon maxi dress dips into a V in the front and back. The slip underneath cuts off at the thighs, leaving my legs visible and silhouetted through the sheer fabric. Simple beige leather sandals wrap around my feet along with a blue butterfly ankle bracelet to complete the look.

I quickly use the bathroom and freshen up before twisting my hair into a low bun. Gazing into the mirror, I find myself pleasantly surprised. Sleep has helped immensely. No longer do my eyes have sunken dark circles beneath them. If anything, I look well-rested. The bruises around my neck are still visible but are now a bit of a yellow color. Even some of my bug bites have gone away.

With one last glance in the mirror, I start making my way back to my seat. Diego is on the phone, talking in hushed tones.

"I said I understand, Sel. *Calm down.*" He looks up and smiles as I take my seat across from him and buckle myself in.

"I can't promise that." He rolls his eyes in the most childish way and holds the phone away from his ear for a second. "Coffee?" he mouths to me while holding a hand over the phone. I nod my head in approval. He motions to the flight attendant to come over and places the phone back to his ear.

"Sel, seriously. *Calm down.* Are you PMSing or something? You're crankier than a vegan at a steakhouse...I'm fucking 33, I can handle myself. If it comes to that, I will let you know."

Huh. 33. For some reason it doesn't feel like we have eleven years between us.

The flight attendant hands me a coffee—iced and light. *Perfect.*

Diego raises his eyes to the ceiling and taps his thumb and fingers together, mimicking his sister talking.

"Alright, *hermana*, I have to go. Glad you're settling in okay. Let Killian know I'll be in touch." He hits the end button, leans back, and tosses his phone onto the table between us.

"Damn, you women can talk."

I take a sip of my coffee. "*Mmm.* This coffee is delicious. Please tell me you have the same machine on *Pontus*?"

"I do. And a helipad. Have you ever flown in a helicopter, *Mariposita*? His lips twitch and he laughs like he's enjoying his own private joke.

Holy crap. This has to be a mega yacht.

"No, I can't say I have." My leg bounces under the table.

Diego reaches across and takes my hand. "You have, but you don't remember. You weren't exactly...*coherent*. Don't be nervous. I'll be right next to you. Once you realize how beautiful the view is, you won't pay attention to the size, or see it as any different than a regular flight.

I scowl at him. The empty spots in my memory are from being drugged by this asshole. "I sure hope so," I mumble.

"Do you get seasick?"

"Now you ask me?" I ask incredulously. "When I'll be on a damn yacht with you for the next few months."

"When would you have liked for me to ask? When I told you that you weren't coming with me or when you threw a tantrum and demanded to come along?"

I sip my coffee to hide my smile. "I did not throw a tantrum."

"Oh really? So standing up and slamming your hands on the table isn't a tantrum? You've got quite the temper, *Mariposita*."

"Says the pot calling the kettle black. And to answer your question, I haven't been on a *yacht* before. I wouldn't know."

"Well, I guess we will find out."

"I guess we will." I'm *soo* tempted to stick my tongue out at him, but that would only help prove him right.

"You look beautiful, by the way," he says more gently. His topaz blue eyes shimmer as they make contact with mine.

"Thank you," I whisper. Butterflies start to swarm my stomach as the plane begins its descent. It's totally the reason for their coincidental arrival and nothing to do with him calling me beautiful.

"Lying again?" I can almost hear Diego's voice questioning me. *Get out of my head, Ocean Eyes.*

The flight attendant comes back toward us and rests her hand on Diego's shoulder. "Mr. De La Cruz, we will be landing now, please make sure you and your guest remain seated."

"Will do, Red," he replies, maintaining eye contact with me.

I'm the first to break, looking down at his phone which glows with a text message from Selena.

> I mean it Diego, don't fuck with her head! She's not like your other women. Your little playthings. She deserves someone who wants to stick around—not someone who wants to stick their dick in her for a few weeks before moving on to the next woman. Leave Madison and Liam's relationship alone. Don't fucking meddle. Killian said Liam

The screen goes dark before I can read the rest of what she wrote. Killian said Liam what?!

Diego grabs his phone, reads the message, then places it in his jeans pocket. His brow furrows and his mood sours almost instantly.

The jet touches down on the runway, jolting me forward and banging my knees into his under the table. He doesn't respond or joke, just silently looks out the window as the jet slows to a stop.

"Welcome to Mykonos, *Mariposita*," he says dryly.

CHAPTER 15

KILLIAN

SINCE BEING BACK HOME in New York, everything feels off. This house feels emptier than I care to admit—considering the love of my life is here with me. And not just for a reunion with an unknown expiration date. I mean Selena is here for good.

This is our second chance.

Despite that, without Madison and Liam around, it feels... eerily...*quiet*. Of course, my men and staff are around, but it's just not the same. The emptiness I'm describing is due to a lack of sarcasm, lightness, and banter. *That* is what I miss most.

Selena believes I was taking a risk sending Madison to Greece with Diego. At the very least she feels Liam should be there with her, that perhaps I was acting too harshly by sending him to Ireland.

And I was.

Liam doesn't know that though. He probably damn well hates me right now for being so hypocritical. It just about killed me sending Madison with Diego. That being said, it's the only way for *my* plan to work out.

Keeping them all out of this is required.

You see, the way I was raised, the way my Da and many other leaders run things is that we leave the women *out* of our wars. They are to be respected as the wives and daughters of our organization and *never to* be used as pawns for bartering or retaliation.

Diego did no such thing.

I understand he was out of options and is doing this for the good of so many other innocent people...but bringing Madison and my woman–*his sister*–into this, cannot be forgiven. This situation couldn't get more fucking complicated. Selena will hate me for the rest of her life if I kill her brother.

Which is why *I* can't kill him.

She won't be hearing about any of this, nor will anyone else. That is exactly why I left Liam out of the equation.

Madison is going to be Diego's weakness. I can already see it —I know Sel does. It's not just a character flaw or a way of getting attention. Maddy does this without even trying. She just lives and breathes and men become completely infatuated with her. She is a bright white light in a pitch-black room. You can't help but draw nearer to the source, even if it blinds you.

I'm starting to understand why Liam left before involving Madison in all this shit. He's right—she's too good for this world. Just eight months with us and she's already experienced so much death and trauma. More than *anyone* should, let alone someone who was never raised in this life.

I grip the marble counter and lean over the bathroom sink, bowing my head. *Deep breaths, Kil.* On an exhale, Selena's warm hands rub gentle circles around my back.

"What's going on in that head of yours, my love?" I look up and gaze at her reflection in the mirror.

My God, she's a vision, wearing that sexy black satin nightgown and matching robe. I turn around to face her, pulling her in close, needing to feel her warmth. Her robe shifts, revealing the swell of her gorgeous breasts, which somehow look fuller in this set. *Not that I'm complaining...*

My thumb skims her jaw as I lean down and kiss her neck. She moans and leans her head back, granting me better access to trail my lips across her collarbone and down over her breasts. They rise and fall at a quicker pace. Her fingers lace into my hair, massaging my scalp. I hook a finger into the cups of her nightgown and pull it down, exposing her to me. Circling my thumb around her nipple has her squirming against my erection. Through gritted teeth, she releases a hiss, when I close my index finger over the tight bud and tweak it.

Her hand comes down and slaps mine away. "Sorry, they are just really sensitive tonight."

Lowering my lips to hers and pressing our bodies together, I show her *exactly* what I desire. Where she normally would begin to tease me and actively participate, she seems withdrawn and lost in thought. It has been an exhausting few days. I'm sure she's just—

"I'm pregnant," she blurts out, gripping both my shoulders. Her eyes burn into mine, looking for any sign of life. I guess that would be because I immediately went rigid, straightening my spine.

After opening my mouth a few times like a fish out of water, gasping for air, I cup her face between both my hands and capture her lips in mine.

"I just found out at Declan and Maeve's," she says between sweet kisses. I continue to kiss her, unsure of what to say just yet.

Her hands slide up my forearms and over my hands, wrapping them around mine. "You don't seem excited..." She pulls away to look at me with watery eyes. A single tear escapes, sliding down her cheek. I swipe at it with my thumb before rubbing the color back into her cheeks.

"I am, sweetheart..." *It's just that I plan on having your brother executed* "...with everything going on right now, and these last few weeks...This is wonderful news! *Damn.* I am going to be a father. I AM GOING TO BE A FATHER!" I shout while picking her up and spinning her in a circle in our bathroom. *Jesus.* I can only hope to be as good of a father as Jack Kennedy was.

Giggles and sniffles fill the space between us as tears drip onto my bare chest. Hers and mine. "I love you, Killian Kennedy. You are going to be an amazing father. I really am so incredibly thankful for Diego and Madison, for giving us the second chance we deserve. It feels so right to be back here in your arms, to call this my home—*finally*—and not temporarily."

I pull her into me, circling protective arms around her. In return, she nuzzles her face into my chest, sighing in relief. The mention of Diego and Madison makes my heart throb. Guilt gnaws at me. *How can I continue with my plan?* Selena is carrying my child. The grief of losing her brother will only hurt the both of them.

I shouldn't.

Fuck the plan. Fuck my need for revenge.

I need to call Liam and sort out getting him as close to that yacht as possible.

Although Madison is no longer what I crave...*romantically* (even though from time to time a shred of jealousy hits me)...she is still someone I genuinely love and care about.

It's just *different.*

Madison awakened a part of me that I don't think I knew was there. The part I had assumed was dead and gone a long time ago. She made me see the importance of not giving up on love. Even when it doesn't make sense. Even when it seems impossible that it will work out.

She found me as a raw, uncut diamond and returned me to

Selena, a brilliant new version of myself. And for that, I am eternally grateful. She is an incredible woman. Liam certainly is a lucky bastard—as am I for having had the chance to encounter such a beautiful soul.

However, Madison was wrong about one thing. My heart does belong to Selena, so she was right there. But she was wrong when she said I loved her like a rebound or that we were two people who found comfort in each other.

A piece of my damn soul belongs to her. And that piece will never belong to anyone else.

It's the part that Selena never got to witness. The dark part of my soul that was afraid and anxious about becoming the next leader of the Tri-State Syndicate. The part of my soul that was cracked over the loss of my Da. The part that got the chance to experience being a regular, simple man and not a '*mobster*' as Madison once called me. The version of me who enjoyed cooking Thanksgiving dinner in a blizzard. The same one who snuck their girlfriend out of her family home before Christmas ended, just to get the chance to kiss her.

Let's make one thing clear. I will always, *always* protect Madison as fiercely as if she were still mine. The only reason I agreed to Diego bringing Madison along with him to Greece was because I know he feels that way too. I can see it in the way he looks at her and can feel it in the air around us. It's how I felt when I met her.

"About what you were saying on the plane earlier..." I collect Selena in my arms and carry her to our bed. She maneuvers her body once under the sheets as I slide in next to her. My arm wraps around her as she lays her head on my chest, resting a gentle hand on my stomach. "I think you're right. I've been too harsh with Liam. Perhaps I could arrange something with your brother. Figure out a way to have Liam remain close by on my private yacht. He can keep an eye out for any potential threats, have occasional meetings with Madison, and be there as backup in the event things go south prematurely."

Sel lazily trails her hand up my stomach and then over my sternum. She leans in and presses a kiss to my chest. "That's a much better plan. Plus, I'd rather have Liam close by. I don't trust Geraldo." She yawns, covering her mouth. "He could be planning something."

"He's not the only one I don't trust."

"Diego made a mistake, Killian. It was a dumb plan, but there was no malintent. Please try to get along with him. He's going to be your brother-in-law one day and our child's uncle. I owe him so much. He's saved me more times than you can count. I wouldn't be here right now if it wasn't for him."

It kills me to say, but she's right. His good does outweigh his bad. Fuck, what was I thinking? *Like an eejit, that's what.* Da always said 'Never make decisions out of anger. Sleep on it. If in the morning it still holds the same intensity, the same passion as it felt in the heat of the moment, then it is a sound choice.'

I woke this morning feeling indifferent, wavering between wanting to plot Diego's death and wanting to tell him to fuck right off.

Taking his death off the table, he can find a way out of this mess without us, and I'll bring my family home as one. The problem is, Madison is just as stubborn as Liam. She wants to help and I won't be the one to take that choice away from her. Neither should Liam. No matter how much having her away with another man bothers us, it is still her choice. The best we can do is sit close by and monitor. If we need to step in, we will.

Sel's eyes start to flutter closed. "Sorry, I wanted to spend some *quality* time with you tonight, but I can't even keep my eyes open. Damn hormones."

I place a kiss on the top of her head and rub her arm reassuringly. "Don't worry about it, baby. I do have one last question. How far along are you?"

"I'm not sure exactly, but if I was to guess, maybe about eight weeks or so. I need to find an OBGYN around here."

"I'll schedule an appointment first thing tomorrow morning. The doctors we have on payroll will provide me with the name of their best associate." Placing one more kiss on the top of her head, I say, "Get some sleep, love."

"I love you, Kil."

"I love you, sweetheart. Welcome home."

MY EYES SLAM open in a panic. Selena wriggles her way out of my sleepy embrace and runs toward the en suite, slamming the bathroom door behind her. The sound of muffled retching filters through the door.

Hormones.

The toilet flushes and the sound of running water fills the space between us. I make my way out of bed, rapping my knuckles against the wooden door. Opening it a crack, I stick my head in.

"You alright, love?"

"I'm okay...just give me a minute."

Giving her some privacy, I close the door and sit at the edge of the bed, reaching for my phone off the end table. The sound of her brushing her teeth has me silently laughing.

She hasn't noticed yet. I glance at the clock—4:30 a.m. Lena is probably still half asleep.

While she refreshes herself, and I wait patiently, I shoot out a text to Liam.

I made a mistake sending you to Ireland. Keep this between us. Head to Mykonos. I'll have the staff prepare The Triquetra for an extended stay. It should arrive there in a few days. Leave tonight. Lay low in town until the yacht is ready. I'll call you with more details. Until then, stay safe, sweetheart.

LIAM

I'm already in Mykonos. I was hoping you would come to your senses, dickhead.

My finger hovers over the call button. I'm about ready to ream him out for not listening to my original orders when the bathroom door flies open. Selena leans against the door frame in nothing but my black t-shirt, and holds her left hand up.

"Killian, what is this?" Her voice cracks as she points to the 3-carat pear-shaped diamond on her ring finger. Tapered baguette diamonds sit on each side of the center stone, collectively resting on a gold band.

I saunter over to her, and grip her fingers, placing a kiss to the top of her hand. "*This—* is back where it belongs."

Her delicate hand comes up to cup my face. Tears pool at the rims of her warm chocolate eyes. "You kept it."

I kiss each of her flushed cheeks, followed by her cute little nose, then press my lips against those luscious lips. "I always hoped one day we could rewrite our story," I whisper against her lips before deepening the kiss.

Her fingers clench my hips, pulling me closer to her body. Little moans and mewls mix with the mint on her breath, making my lips tingle. I walk us backward until my legs hit the mattress and gently tug her down with me. Wasting no time, she straddles me and leans down to plant kisses all over my chest and across my stomach. Her fingers trace every inch of ink on my arms by memory. Greedily, they glide lower through the trail of hair below my navel and slip into the waistband of my boxer briefs.

I help her shove them down my thighs, wanting to be inside my woman *right the fuck now*. Sel situates herself, hovering over my rock hard cock, teasing the head of it at her slick entrance. My *fiancée* strips the black t-shirt off herself and teasingly throws it in my face.

It's amazing how her body has changed already. She's always been fucking gorgeous. Now? She's *glowing*. I suppose now I understand just how accurate that description is.

Those incredible breasts are plumper. *Fuller.* Small blue veins spider web across her sun-kissed skin. I cup both my hands around her tits, giving them a delicate squeeze as I lift my hips and enter her. She lowers herself all the way to the hilt and moans, arching her back, and pushing her tits further into my hands. My thumbs lightly rub her darkened nipples until they peak, making her chest rise and fall as her curled hair cascades down her back.

My hands graze down her waist and grip her hips. We start to move together, an erotic dance of two people who never forgot the rhythm.

"Shit, Kil. I'm so fucking sensitive *everywhere*." She moves her hips with more haste until her breathing becomes labored and sweat begins to bead on her forehead. Not breaking the connection between us or leaving the warmth of her tight swollen pussy, I lean up and roll us over.

"More, Kil. I need more. You aren't gonna hurt the baby. Fuck me the way I like," she purrs in my ear while her teeth graze the shell of it.

Goosebumps spring up over my arms as my thrusts quicken. She's fucking dripping for me and the sounds of my cock sliding in and out of her is turning me into an animal. I rest my elbows against each side of her face and claim her lips. She rings out my name as her pussy clamps around me like a vice.

"Sel. Marry me, baby," I groan out, holding back another second just to hear her say it.

"*Yes!*" she says in garbled words as she climaxes. "Yes, Killian Kennedy! *Yesssss*. I'll. Be. Your...Wife...*Ahhh*." Her eyes roll back like she's possessed as the most intense climax of my life hits me.

Sel wraps her arms around my back and clutches me to her chest. We are both panting and drenched in sweat. Her fingers lace into my hair as she massages my scalp.

"I love you both." I lean up to steal another kiss while rubbing her stomach.

CHAPTER 16

LIAM

I BOOKED a hotel right near Tourlos Bay. The rectangular infinity pool overlooks the port, giving me the perfect view of Diego's private yacht—*Pontus*. I offered Seb a hundred grand to get me the name and coordinates of Diego's yacht. And fuck, he works quickly. I had the name within fifteen minutes *and* he threw in a nice bonus. I need to remind myself when this is all said and done to find a way to send him a thank-you gift. Without him, we may not have found Madison as quickly as we did.

Speaking of Madison, the two of them should be arriving shortly. Diego's staff have been busy loading supplies on board since I checked in. I drain the rest of my beer and glance at my phone, fixated on the *bonus* flight route Seb sent me. The blinking yellow helicopter indicates they are only a few minutes away from the helipad of *Pontus*.

My heart accelerates and I feel like I'm about to have a heat stroke, which would be pretty bad, considering I'm in a pool. *I need to calm the fuck down.* Just the thought of seeing her with *him* makes my skin crawl. I've contemplated marching down to the dock and getting on that damn yacht with them.

Except, Madison can't know I'm here yet.

The Triquetra needs to get into port. *And fast.* I plan on having the staff anchor a few nautical miles away from them. I don't trust Geraldo. *Period.* I can guarantee you he is already plotting and scheming some more shady shit. The way he described Madison as Diego's 'pet' makes me sick to my stomach.

If that *Tales From The Crypt* motherfucker shows up unannounced, I'm going in guns blazing.

Killian's orders to lay low be damned.

After arriving in Ireland, I wasted no time hopping on the first commercial flight here. I had time to think on the flight and I've come to the conclusion it's not possible for me to be away from her. *Haven't we already learned that lesson just a few short months ago?* I'd *never* forgive myself if something happened and I wasn't there to help. Trust me, I want to respect Madison's wishes—*and I will*—for now at least—by remaining on Killian's yacht.

That doesn't mean I won't interfere if that bastard Diego tries to move in on my fiancée.

Just as I crack open another beer from the ice bucket and take a swig, a helicopter flies overhead. Cupping a hand to my forehead, I shield my eyes as it hovers and lands on Diego's helipad. I waste no time bringing the binoculars I purchased from a tourist to my eyes. I adjust the focus just in time to spot my woman being helped down onto the platform by none other than Diego De La Cruz.

Madison is laughing at something he said. Her eyes are masked by oversized designer sunglasses. It's hard to say without looking at her eyes, but she looks refreshed. A delicate blue sundress graces her beautiful curves. The *Bone Breaker* places one hand at the small of her back and the other gestures to the guard rail. My fingers clamp down on the binoculars as I turn the dial that brings it into focus. For a moment it becomes blurry.

"Shit."

When I finally get my girl back in focus, I find her lips parted in awe at the beauty of the island before her. Her head swivels as she scans the coast. For the briefest of moments, her gaze lingers on the balcony where I am. Most likely she can't see me from here. Yet, I wonder, if in some spiritual way, she can sense that I'm here. *Hi, princess.*

Diego laces his fingers through hers, breaking her out of her serene moment, and leads her down the steps obscured by black glass.

"Fuck." That's going to be a problem. I wasn't planning on them leaving so soon.

The dock master and staff begin to untie the ropes and a horn blazes, signaling their departure. I know they won't go far, yet I feel uneasy not having my eye on her. *Especially* with the way he so casually touched my woman and had her laughing.

They say jealousy is an ugly bitch—but I can't help it.

I can't shake this awful feeling that I am going to lose her.

PUSHING MY EMPTY PLATE FORWARD, I wipe my mouth with a napkin and take a sip of white wine. I'm not much of a wine drinker; nowhere near a wine snob like my girl, but I do enjoy the occasional glass with dinner every now and then. I have Maddy to thank for that. She taught me quite a bit about different wines and their pairings on her birthday trip to Vermont.

Such simpler times then.

For all of us.

I check my phone for the billionth time tonight. Madison has my number, so why is it taking her so long to contact me? I'm trying my best not to smother her, to give her some time to process this all. But my patience is wearing thin. I've got about another hour left in me before I turn caveman, lose all control, and call her.

"Will that be all for tonight, Mr. Kennedy?" I barely register what the waitress says. Her warm hand comes down on my shoulder shaking me out of my musings. I'm so wrapped up in thoughts of what Madison could be up to right now that I haven't been paying much attention to my surroundings.

The waitress is quite young and smiling down at me. She's beautiful, but nowhere near as stunning as my future wife. Returning the gesture, I smile and shake my head. "Yes. Just the check, please."

Her face falls with a tinge of disappointment as her hand falls from my shoulder. She pulls a black leather bill folder from her apron and leaves it on the table.

"I may be presumptuous in saying this, but I hope that whoever stood you up tonight realizes what they've lost." She nods her head to the empty chair across from me before shifting her eyes to my phone. "If you find yourself looking for a good time tonight, or maybe just to get your mind off things, give me a call."

I'm about to correct her and tell her that I'm not interested when my phone rings.

I grab the damn thing like I've been drowning and it's my last lifeline. A chance to breathe again. *Finally.*

Then I realize it's Killian.

"What's the craic?" I growl into the phone.

"Hello to you too, *sweetheart.*"

I throw a bunch of bills down into the folder and slam it shut, leaving the waitress' number in there. "Have you or Sel heard from Madison?" I question as I start walking back to my hotel.

"No. Diego only sent a text confirming they arrived safely and have anchored a few nautical miles off the coast of Mykonos."

"I'm starting to worry that he's getting in her head, Kil."

"I know," he lowers his voice to a whisper. The sound of a door clicking shut echoes through the receiver. That's why I have you there. Listen, I'm sorry, brother. I made a mistake sending you to Ireland. Although there is still a substantial risk of Geraldo discovering you *alive*, it's worth it. *She's* worth it. You and Diego will keep her safe if that were to happen. The rest of us will protect Selena over here. No one will touch our women. *Ever again.*"

"What made you suddenly change your mind?" I walk through the crowded lobby and press the button for the elevator.

There is a moment of silence before he speaks. "I thought about what it would feel like had roles been reversed. Orders or not I would have done the same thing for her, for Sel." He releases an exhausted sigh. "We will always be a team, Liam. We are brothers. Not just by oath, but by blood. Truth is, I'm no good at this leadership thing without you. I'm sorry for playing the rank card on you," he sighs.

"I forgive you, *asshole*. Now, tell me, when is *The Triquetra* going to be here? It's been almost four fucking hours since Madison left port and I'm going stir crazy. I need eyes on her."

The elevator doors open directly to my suite. It's dark. A silhouette of someone on the balcony catches my attention. In an instant, my hand goes to my waistband where I have my Glock.

Killian chuckles. "So do I. *The Triquetra* is ready and currently waiting for you to board tonight. It's already anchored within visual distance of *Pontus*. Oh, and for the love of God, please don't shoot Conor—Lexi and Maddy will kill us both. He should be in your suite by now."

"A warning would have been nice." I place my gun back into my waistband while walking to the sliding doors to greet him.

"I would have preferred to be there myself, but Selena isn't too comfortable flying long distances at the moment...and I haven't exactly told her of my plan just yet."

"Okay, *Mr. Cryptic.* Is she alright?" I ask, my curiosity now officially peaked.

"She's pregnant, Liam. I'm going to be a father." You can feel his smile and joy radiating through the phone.

"Christ. Congrats, man. That is wonderful news." I run a hand through my hair as I approach Conor. A twinge of jealousy hits me. Kil finally got his girl back and is now expecting a child. *What would that have felt like had Madison's test been positive and we weren't in this fucked up situation?*

"Thank you. She was seen by our doctors just a little while ago. Both of them are healthy. They set her due date to New Year's Eve."

Amazing how this past New Year's Eve he was proudly sporting Madison on his arm at the gala. This New Year's Eve, he'll be welcoming a baby with his ex fianceé. The way things work out is fucking bizarre. Another round of anxiety slithers its way through my veins. *What does my life with Madison look like a year from now? Will I still have a place in her life? Or will Diego worm his way into her heart and replace me?*

"Looks like you'll need to reconsider hosting the Masquerade Gala this year."

"Perhaps I'll pass the baton over to you. You've always been cut out to lead." His tone is light but I can tell he is seriously contemplating stepping down and letting me take over.

This is something we need to discuss after Geraldo becomes shark chum. Not just with each other, but the council too. It's not a normal occurrence for one to step down in our line of work. Considering we are both Jack Kennedy's sons, the council may agree to the switch in leadership.

"I'll be in touch when we get settled in." I disconnect the call and shake Conor's hand, pulling him into a back-slapping embrace.

"Ya know Lexi and Maddy would have your balls if you shot

me just now." A half smile forms on his face as he squeezes my shoulder firmly. "You holding up okay, mate?"

"I've been fucking grand, Con." I roll my eyes at him and reach into my shorts pocket for my pack of smokes. I offer him one as I always do. Normally, he would indulge. He shakes his head to decline and places both hands into his jeans pockets.

"Lexi and I are trying to quit." He shrugs his shoulders in a nonchalant way. The kind of way that tells me Conor has it *bad* for Maddy's best friend.

I raise an eyebrow, pop the cigarette between my lips and light up. Conor takes a seat at the wicker table and I follow suit.

"So, when's the wedding?" I smirk while taking a drag.

"Fuck off," he quips while flipping me the bird.

Smoke swirls toward the star-filled sky on a laughing exhale. All jokes aside, I'm happy for him. He's been smitten with her since the moment he met her at the gala. The both of them share a similar set of values. Collectively having a sense of humor and a bit of a spontaneous side. If you were to ask me, I think Lexi could drink Conor under the table—but I won't ever tell him that.

Though, as adventurous and wild as the two of them can be, they still remain focused on their responsibilities and loyalty to their friends and family. She'll fit right in.

Madison couldn't have found a better best friend. I feel the same way about Conor. How poetic the two of them are getting serious.

"Has Lexi spoken to Madison?" I ask after taking another drag of my cigarette.

The smoke curls around each letter of her name. *Please say she hasn't. Please give me some hope that my woman hasn't been avoiding me or putting distance between us.*

"I'm not supposed to say anything...you know how women are. They tell you to keep their girl gossip a secret. I know you are concerned for your woman, as am I, so I'll tell you the truth. Yes, they were on the phone for over an hour earlier this evening. From what I gathered, there were a lot of tears..." He hesitates a moment before continuing. "Something to do with your proposal."

I stand abruptly, tossing the cigarette into the ashtray, and start to pace the balcony.

"Grab your things, Conor. We are leaving for the yacht. *Right. This. Fucking. Second.*"

On a frustrated growl, I slam open the sliding door to the bedroom, nearly knocking it off the track. My nerves are fucking shot. I've barely slept in weeks. And right now, I *need* to hear Madison's voice. *Does she not want to marry me?*

I never really unpacked, which makes my life a hell of a lot easier. Conor is fresh on my heels as I make a quick circle of the suite, stopping every few paces to grab a few remaining belongings. I shove all of my toiletries into the front pouch of my luggage and rip the phone charger plug out of the wall in the kitchenette.

Conor follows me into the elevator with his suitcase and mine in tow. I jab my finger against the lobby button repetitively while retrieving my cell phone from my back pocket. Searching the contact list for Madison's name, I scroll until I find her new number.

My thumb hovers over the call button.

Fuck it. She doesn't need to know that I'm here yet. I just want to check on her.

The elevator doors open to a lively lobby, littered with people as I place the call. Conor and I enter like a dark cloud over Disney World. We receive a few concerned looks, some downright terrified. *You know what they say, if looks can kill and all that...* On the third ring, it goes to voicemail. *Did she hit the F-U button or was it that snake Diego?*

For the third time tonight, I feel like something is off. And I don't mean Madison's phone.

My phone chimes with a text notification:

MADISON

Stop worrying. Little complication, that's why I
haven't called sooner.

My heart feels like it's about to explode in my chest. From
worry or relief, I can't tell.

LIAM

I'll never stop worrying about your safety,
Madison. What complication?

The bubbles pop up and then disappear.
I wait and then wait some more.
But no response comes.

LIAM

Madison. So help me God...I will come get you
and burn that fucking yacht to the sea floor if
you don't clue me in.

CHAPTER 17

MADISON

DIEGO'S YACHT IS STUNNING. Its black matte exterior makes it appear sleek and dangerous, yet the interior is all warm fixtures and golds. *A paradox like him.* Like Liam and Killian. I haven't even seen the entirety of it, but could only imagine the intricate details.

The view alone from the helipad is jaw-dropping. Diego places a hand on my lower back and gestures for me to get a closer look.

I lean over the railing, enjoying the warm salty breeze, and run my eyes along the beauty of the coast. My eyes take in the white buildings and the people lightly scattered along the beach. All those magnificent boats and yachts docked in port. It's incredible the amount of wealth in just one small area. The yachts range in size—*Pontus* being one of the largest superyachts here. It is beautiful and overwhelming at the same time. I pull a deep breath into my lungs to try and relax my nerves.

Okay. This may come off as crazy, but my life has been exactly that for months now. *So...crazy thoughts it is.* I can almost *feel* Liam here with me. Like a warm embrace or the tingle of the sun on your skin, the wind wraps around me like one of Liam's hugs. I barely register Diego's hand on my back.

Instantly, my eyes are drawn to a building in the distance. There is a man there on what seems like a private hotel balcony. He's in a small infinity pool holding a set of binoculars directed at our yacht. I shield the sun from my eyes, trying to focus more clearly on him. He's got Liam's build and I can faintly make out some tattoos. A beard.

There is no way Liam is here.

Killian made it very clear with his actions and use of authority that Liam was to be sent to Ireland. I even told him it was for the best. As much as I love Liam, his temper and need to protect me would put our plan at risk. The sooner this is over, the sooner I can be with him. I just need to keep remembering that. It's part of the reason I haven't reached out to him yet. He needs to settle into how this is going to be for the next few months. So do I...

Diego's fingers lace with mine, breaking me free of my uneasy thoughts.

"Ready to take a tour of the place you'll be thriving in for the next few months, *Mariposita*?"

He leads me down the steps to the entrance of the main level. "Why did you say it like that?" I raise an eyebrow at his verbiage and cross my arms over my chest.

Diego lifts my sunglasses so that they rest on top of my head. His thumb caresses my heated cheek. "Because you *will* be thriving. Life is different living out on the water. My staff is extremely accommodating, anything you need they are here to assist you with. Plus, there are no distractions out here—other than myself," he winks. "Take this time to figure out what you want from life. What you truly want. Read, relax, swim. You are safe here. Until Gerlado comes with his men, you can move freely around the ship without my shadow."

My lip raises in a defiant smile. "Good. Cause you're kinda like a gnat. Every time I shoo you away you keep coming back."

He shakes his head and laughs, walking a few steps ahead of me. "Maybe it's your sweetness that I can't resist."

His arms open wide to show me a beautiful kitchen area that has indoor and outdoor dining. There is a large kitchen island with black leather bar stools beneath it. An array of fresh fruit, pastries, and refreshing cocktails line one end to the other. Diego walks over to the island and snags a grape, popping it into his mouth. "Help yourself, dinner will be ready shortly."

I reach for a pretty purple cocktail, garnished with a dried lemon and lavender sprig. There is a small honey dipper used as a stirrer. Diego brushes his shoulder against mine to grab his own as I take a sip of my drink. *Holy crap this is delicious.* So many different flavors are having a party on my tongue. Honey, lemon, lavender, and a hint of blueberry—*maybe blueberry-infused vodka?* My eyelids close as I take another sip. Wow, this is delicious and refreshing. The perfect remedy to calm my nerves.

"The one you have is my favorite." He raises his glass to my lips, encouraging me to take a sip. "But the blood orange, agave, and rosemary margarita is easily my second choice."

I wrap my hand around his to control how much he pours and tilt my head back slightly to take a sip. Those ocean eyes of his drop to my lips as the cool liquid and all its glorious flavors interact on my tongue.

"Mmm," I practically moan out my agreement.

He pulls the glass back with a satisfied smirk and takes his own healthy sip. For such cool eyes, they sure seem to melt me to my core. He licks the salt from his lips and uses his thumb to rub a few flakes off of mine. Fire erupts within me, and warning bells go off in my head, but all I can do is stare at him and the depths of his eyes.

The need to learn all the secrets hidden beneath them is becoming a problem. Getting Diego to open up means opening myself up the same way. Which means I could be making a *very* big mistake and quite possibly putting my relationship at risk.

With a sigh, Diego steps out of my space and walks outside. I follow him after snatching a small lemon tart. *Fuck this is amazing, too.* If the drinks and food are going to be this delicious, I am going to go back to New York a few pounds heavier. That's not such a big deal, considering I must have lost quite a bit these last few weeks. After playing chicken roulette—this is heaven.

What I really need is the gym to gain back some muscle and strengthen my body again.

"Do you have a gym?" I ask over a mouthful of lemon tart.

He turns to me and leans against the deck railing that overlooks a gorgeous seashell mosaic tiled infinity pool. "I do. Feel free to use it. In fact, feel free to let me train you."

We stand in silence, finishing our drinks and admiring the views before I speak.

"I may take you up on that, *Bone Breaker*," I laugh lightheartedly. "I don't ever want to be weak again. I should have been able to defend myself the day your men scooped me up and at least fought back against your uncle. Speaking of that lovely, not so memorable night—" I scowl at him, "—who did you trust enough to kidnap me and Selena?"

Diego pushes off the railing and cages me against his body, dredging up memories of that night. He cups a hand over my mouth and his lips hover close to my neck before his teeth graze over the skin and he nips me.

"After learning all about you, courtesy of my sister, I didn't trust anyone else to retrieve you. If anyone was going to be stupid enough to cage a butterfly, it was going to be me."

I buck my hips and try to squirm out of his hold but his grip on me only tightens. "My cousin Antonio is the only other person I trusted enough to disclose parts of my plan and handle my sister. His mother, my mamá's sister, died when we were kids. His dad was a deadbeat. My mamá practically raised him as her own. I view him as a brother. We can trust him."

160

"You fucking drugged me, Diego," I grit through my teeth and try to kick my foot into his balls. He just laughs at my attempts and then releases me.

"I wasn't sure how trained you were or how much of a scene you would cause in public." He rolls his eyes. "Selena had mentioned you were gym buddies—but, *fuck*. Liam and Killian *really* dropped the ball on training you for situations like that. Rule number one of being part of this life...the kind of 'life' I don't think you should be involved in...regardless, is learning self-defense. Your man and I can swear up and down we'll protect you, but surprises always happen. The worst thing would be for you to be vulnerable. I want to teach you, *Mariposita*. Let me teach you."

Diego extends his arm out for me, his eyes more gentle and less intense than they were before. I back away from him, needing some air that isn't saturated with his signature scent.

"Show me the rest of your superyacht, *Ocean Eyes*." Not caring if he follows, I walk back toward the kitchen area and get another drink, this time the blood orange one, because that shit is delicious and citrusy and full of *tequila*. I need to cleanse myself of Diego and bring back some comforting memories of Liam.

Tequila will always remind me of him.

Without stopping for another drink, Diego passes me, heading upstairs.

WE ENDED up touring the ship rather quickly. Diego's mood instantly soured after our earlier interaction. The uppermost level hosts the Captain's quarters, which was where I met the majority of the staff. Diego quietly let me know anything we discuss in front of them is fine. All of them understand the risks involved in working for the De La Cruz family and are paid handsomely for it.

Other areas of the upper levels accommodate a gym, sauna, small spa and the helipad. One of the decks has a jacuzzi with a perfect birdseye view of the pool below. It seems like an ideal place to relax at night, read a book, or even do some stargazing.

We took the elevator down to the lower level in silence. This is where all the staterooms and suites are. The staff sleep in some private cabins and community rooms on the main floor off of the kitchen. There are four staterooms down here along with *Mr. Bone Breaker's* master suite.

It's incredible the amount of detail that went into designing these rooms. Each one has a similar vibe, with small differences in aesthetics.

I'm walking around Diego's suite admiring all the accents of gold, black, and teakwood. His bed frame has me at a loss for words. It's nearly impossible to describe its beauty. A custom-made, cast iron Kraken sits in the center of the room. The damn mythical creature even has blue Swarovski crystal eyes like *his*. Black satin sheets embroidered in gold add to the dramatic effect. Topaz blue, blown glass pendant lights give the room a feeling as if it's underwater.

The HGTV lover in me is squealing.

Don't even get me started on the en suite. The space is almost as big as his bedroom, equipped with a shower spacious enough to accommodate at least four people. *Maybe that's its purpose.* How many women he has had in there at one time?

"Honestly, none." The deep timbre of his voice startles me. Diego leans against the door frame right behind me. And apparently I just said that out loud.

"I find that hard to believe," I scoff, leaning my hip against the vanity.

"And why is that?" His eyes narrow as he steps across the threshold of the door, towering over me. The veins and tendons in his arms pop out as he grips the marble counter, always caging me in. We are practically nose to nose now, those ocean eyes swirling like a crystal ball. They have me captivated and peering into his fucking soul in search of my future. *Or where my brain went, for starters.*

"Judging by your little *performance* with the flight attendant, I wouldn't put it past you to host an orgy in your ridiculous shower."

Twirling a piece of my hair around his index finger he says, "I did that for you, to make you jealous, and to serve as a punishment for that sassy mouth."

I glare up at him before smacking his hand away. "I am *engaged.* Remember? And I was not jealous, I was disgusted."

A chuckle leaves his lips as they inch closer to my ear. "Keep telling yourself that, *princess.*"

The nickname causes me to retreat, simmering down whatever was just crackling between us.

Noticing my shift, he backs away and calmly walks to the door before looking back over his shoulder. "For the record, you are not *engaged.* Your idiot boyfriend did that out of desperation and fear of losing you. He took what should have been a special moment and tarnished it for you. You know it's true, *Mariposita.*"

"You're wrong. What Liam and I share is *none* of your concern. We've already been through so much. Everything that man does for me is out of love. *And for the record*—I was more than happy to say yes."

"I'm not saying he doesn't love you. He does. The problem is you've changed and he's terrified of what that means for the both of you. Hell, *you're* terrified of what that means."

I shake my head in disbelief. *How dare he.* "No I'm n—"

He interrupts me again. Frustration spelled out clearly on his face as he charges his way back towards me. Strong hands squeeze my cheeks and tilt my head up so that I'm forced to look at him. "*And* instead of explaining that to you, he thought proposing to you would keep you from outgrowing him—or from falling into the arms of someone else. Someone who understands you more than he does." His voice is nothing more than an angry whisper.

Brooding blue eyes stare down at me, searching for...what? *I don't know.* What he eventually finds there must be enough. Sighing loudly, he drops his hands to his sides and balls them into fists, as he trudges into his bedroom.

"Pick whatever room you'd like. I have to call Antonio back, he's called me half a dozen times. Dinner will be at seven thirty on the deck off of the kitchen. I thought you'd like to watch the sunset."

The door to his bedroom clicks closed, and I exhale the breath I've been holding. I swear this man should be on a fucking Sour Patch Kids commercial.

One minute he's sour.

One minute he's sweet.

And the next he's *gone.*

Snatching my phone off of Diego's bed, I leave in search of a bedroom.

CHAPTER 18

D I E G O

"THIS IS NOT GOOD, SEL."

I pace the deck for the hundredth time waiting for my cousin and Madison to arrive for dinner. *Speak of the devil.* Antonio swaggers his way across the deck, escorted by the First Officer.

"No. I don't want you here with him. If you insist on being a brat and coming along, promise me you'll stay on Killian's yacht. Promise me, Sel."

I mouth, "thank you" to Andrew and pull Antonio into a hug just as Madison steps into the kitchen. My eyes refuse to leave her perfect body. Her face lights up and she appears calmer than I've seen her since meeting her as she laughs and socializes with Magaret, the Chief Stewardess. She looks stunning in a white flare-sleeve crop top and high waisted pants to match. What's better, she must have met Cindy, the woman who runs our salon. Madison's hair is blown-out and full of volume. Silky onyx waves tumble down her shoulders and over her perfect set of tits. More than a handful...the things I'd do just to bury my face in them.

Greedily, my gaze drops even lower, to the curve of her waist and the smooth skin teasing me there. I memorize every beauty mark, every scar, all the way down to the fresh white pedicure gracing her bare feet. I guess she got the rundown of ship etiquette. *No shoes.*

The staff have their own, designed for preserving the teakwood and prevent scuffing. I try my best to remain barefoot as well, occasionally wearing boat shoes or sandals.

A delicious fantasy stirs in my mind. *Madison on her back, gripping my satin sheets, and hooking those sexy feet over my shoulders as I—*

"Diego? Did you hear me?" Selena's voice snaps my focus off of Madison and back to my conversation with my sister. Even thousands of miles away, she can be the biggest fucking cockblock. With a frustrated sigh, I turn around and gesture for Antonio to take a seat at the dinner table.

"No, I didn't. Listen, we'll talk more later. Madison just came up and I don't want her to find out like this—"

"*Diego.* It's about Liam," my sister nags. Probably another one of her warnings I don't want or *need* to hear.

Madison's delicate hand grips my bicep. "Tell me what?"

I turn back around to face her and hang up on Selena. Wide chocolate eyes dart over to Antonio, just now recognizing we are not alone. She starts to blush, tucking her hair behind her ears. Sapphire-blue crescent moon earrings hang from them, adding to her regality, and shimmering as they catch the last bit of sunlight.

"I didn't realize you had company," she admits shyly.

I place my hand at the small of her back and guide her toward the table. Antonio stands and wipes his hands over his shorts before extending his own.

"Antonio Reyes."

"Madison," she replies curtly while shaking his hand.

He guides her hand up to his mouth and places a kiss onto her knuckles. A low growl emanates from my chest, prompting Antonio to bite his lip and stifle a laugh. His eyebrows raise and he lets out a low whistle.

166

"You don't seem like the same young woman we picked up in New York," he declares before taking a swig of his beer.

Madison and I speak at the same time.

"She's not."

"I'm not." Her cheeks heat realizing we are in agreement—well—*at least in this moment. No, shes not the same girl we took from that graduation party.* She's stronger, wittier and even more gorgeous now that she is discovering her sense of self.

I pull out her chair and wait for her to sit, before sliding it back in and taking a seat across from her. Eloise and Robert bring out the first course salads, placing them down on each of our gold charger plates.

"Would you like some wine, Ms. Marrone?" Eloise holds up a bottle of red and white in each hand.

"I would love a glass of red. And please, call me Madison." Eloise smiles in return, busying herself with opening the wine and transferring it to the decanter. She pours Madison a glass of cabernet sauvignon then fills my glass as well. This wine is my favorite. I get it directly from a small family owned vineyard in Bordeaux, France.

"Can I get anyone anything else before the next course is served?" Robert inquires.

"We seem to have everything. Thank you, Robert," I say before taking a sip of my wine.

Madison watches me with peaked interest over the rim of her glass. Taking a sip she smiles then takes another one.

"Are you a big wine drinker?" she asks, nodding her head to my glass.

"My cousin is a bit of a wine fanatic, if you will," Antonio lifts his beer bottle, pointing the neck at me. He's never been one to drink out of a chilled glass, and I don't blame him. Beer just tastes better in a bottle.

"Is he?" Madison smiles wide before taking another sip of her own.

"I don't swish and swirl or gargle—*God, that's fucking awful.* However, I do enjoy good wines from a number of different regions."

Madison bites her lip and covers a hand over her mouth at the mention of gargling. "I'd like to see that one day," she laughs, borderline snorts. Her eyes twinkle with a challenge.

I shrug, "I will if you will. Maybe our next trip should be to Italy or maybe France. I didn't know you enjoyed wine as well."

Those perfectly arched brows come together at the suggestion. "How would you? I was held prisoner for three weeks," she sneers. Checking her tone, she takes another sip from her glass. "I love wine just as much as I do coffee." Her fork shakes as she stabs at the halved cherry tomatoes.

When she finally manages to skewer one, she moves on to add a bunch of arugula and a bit of burrata. She ceremoniously shoves the salad into her mouth, wipes at the corners of it with the cloth napkin, then abruptly stands.

"Excuse me, I left my phone in the room and need to grab it in case my *boyfriend* calls."

I lean back in my chair, silently sipping my wine as I wait for her to return.

"*Dude*, she's pissed," my cousin laughs, stating the fucking obvious.

"No shit, *Sherlock.*"

At least she said boyfriend and not *fiancé.* Maybe my speech earlier gave her something to think about. After a few minutes have passed, I drain my wine and follow my little butterfly. The door is open when I reach her room, and I find her sitting on the edge of her bed. *Which is one room over from mine, I might add.* She's staring at the phone in her hand while gnawing on her lip.

I take a seat next to her and pat her leg. "What you heard earlier was part of a conversation I was having with my sister. I had no idea Antonio was going to show up here. He's been trying to call me since we left Miami. Something must have been wrong with my service because the missed calls only registered when we arrived on the ship. He even reached out to Selena this morning."

"What's the urgency?" She looks up and her eyes are wide, searching mine.

I let out a sigh. "Uncle Geraldo decided he wanted to have a little... fun with you..." I trail off, disgusted by the words coming out of my mouth. "My cousin caught wind of that, the night of the ambush, and told Geraldo that I requested his assistance. Antonio took the first flight here and has been staying at a hotel near the port. Apparently, Geraldo and all his men agreed a little vacation was in order while the island gets restored. They should be arriving in a few days." Collecting her shaking hands in mine, I give them a firm squeeze.

"No," she says in disbelief. "We had a plan."

"He won't fucking touch you. No one will. You go *nowhere* without me or Antonio. Do you understand me? This just means we get to end them sooner than we had thought. Then you'll be on your merry way back to your man." An ache in my chest forms at the thought of not seeing her every day. I shake that feeling off so as to not worry her by my change in demeanor. "The good news is my uncle gets seasick easily, so they will be staying at a hotel on the island. I'm sure he will be here for the occasional dinner or business meeting. Selena and Killian are coming as well with some backup and will be staying on his yacht. It's actually already here. I'll show you how close it's docked when we go back upstairs."

I wrap an arm around her shoulder and pull her into me, tucking her head under my chin. Her body tenses from the contact before relaxing into me.

"It's going to be okay, *Mariposita*. He is just doing this to see if I'm bluffing. I have to show him my *El Rompe Huesos* side and ease his suspicions. When he drops his guard, I'll alert Killian to make our move. In the meantime, try to enjoy yourself. We'll start your training tomorrow—if you're still interested."

MADISON BARELY TOUCHED HER DINNER. She kept fidgeting with her phone, indecision and unease haunting her perfect features. I know she wants to tell Liam, but doing so will only make matters worse. There's nothing he can do from Ireland, so I understand why she hasn't reached out to him yet.

Antonio excuses himself to his room after dinner, leaving Madison and I sitting at the candlelit table. This moment could have been romantic if there weren't so many issues plaguing it. Leaning back in her chair, she drains the remainder of her wine, then stands. "I think I'll try and get some rest before more death and chaos unfold."

CHAPTER 19

MADISON

THE SECOND I reach my room, I lock the door, leaning my shoulder against it for support. I tilt my head and press it against the smooth wood, releasing a frustrated sigh.

I don't want Diego here to witness my meltdown.

That's when I let the tears fall. I tend to hold a lot in, always putting on a smile or acting strong when inside I'm trembling with fear and anxiety. *How is this my life?* I went from being a good girl, a nursing student, ready for her first big career in the medical field. To being caught up in not one but two criminal organizations.

Ugly tears drip down my cheeks and run off my chin onto my phone screen. I've been staring at it for the past fifteen minutes like it's a live bomb.

I need to talk to Liam.

And that scares the hell out of me.

But what scares me most, is that Diego is stirring something inside me that should not exist. You see, the thing is, Liam is it for me. I know that down into the depths of my soul. Yet, I'm hurting him just as bad as I'm hurting myself by committing to this assignment. I'm putting my life at risk because it's what feels right, instead of just letting Diego, Killian, and Liam settle this.

I should call Lexi. She probably doesn't have a clue what's going on with me. Using the sleeve of my shirt, I swipe at the liquid pooled on my phone screen and dial my best friend.

"Hello?"

"Lex, it's me." My voice cracks from lack of sleep and the thick emotions churning in my gut.

"*Jesus.* Fucking. Christ, Maddy. I've been worried sick about you!"

"I know," I sigh. "It's been an eventful last few weeks. Has Conor filled you in?"

"A bit. Like the fact that you were taken by Selena's brother Diego—and not just off with Killian on an extended vacation to Greece. Your family wasn't easily convinced but somehow managed to let it go. Mikayla has her own suspicions about what happened that night. Where the hell are you?"

I stay silent, knowing I should tell her but not wanting to worry her more. The need to tell someone overrides my need to keep things on the down low. "I am in Greece...in Mykonos. On a superyacht."

"Conor said that you chose to go with Diego? That Liam and Killian had gotten you back from some private island off the coast of Miami. Is that true?" Her voice is full of frustration and a sternness I rarely receive from her.

"I did. Diego, Selena's brother, is not as bad as everyone makes him out to be." I pace my room before sitting in the little cushioned nook by the window. "He wants to help so many people, Lex. After encountering his uncle...I knew agreeing to go with him could make a difference."

"It's not safe or smart—*and you know it.* What about Liam? How is he holding up?" she whispers his name.

"Why are you whispering? Is Conor there?"

"Um...no. He left straight from Miami for an assignment."

"What are you not telling me?" My eyebrows come together, confused at her hesitancy.

"Conor's with Liam."

"Well, I guess Killian is showing some sort of mercy towards him. You know he sent him to Ireland?"

"Conor told me. Poor guy just got you back only to be separated from you."

"It seemed like Killian wanted to punish him. He blames Liam's inability to listen to his command for why we are in this situation right now. Basically, those two aren't on great terms at the moment. Besides that, Liam needs to stay off the radar for a while until this plan is...executed. Liam is supposed to be quote unquote—dead."

"*Ha.* You're bat shit crazy if you think Liam will obey that order. I wouldn't be surprised if that man is hiding under your bed right now."

Fresh tears coat my eyes and fall more freely knowing how right she is. I love that about him. How he would do *anything* for me. How his love for me knows no bounds.

Sniffling and clearing the huge knot in my throat, I say, "He proposed to me before I left for Mykonos."

"What?! Holy fuckballs, Mad. Of course you said yes?" She says it in more of a confirmation than a question.

I sniffle again then laugh. "Of course I did. I love him. I want our future. I want children one day. And for all of this to be behind us like some awful distant memory. I just know that may never really be possible. Look what happened to me in a matter of months. " A sob escapes me as I rub away the wet mascara clinging to my eyelashes.

"Mad...Conor couldn't tell me much about the time you spent on that island...did anyone... you know you can tell me anything." Her soothing voice is all I need to confess what I've been afraid to even admit to myself outloud.

"No. No one hurt me in that way. Diego's uncle is a fucking monster, he left bruises and scars all over my body— some visible and some... not—but he never got the chance to take it any further. Diego made sure of that."

Lexi gasps at my admission. Her voice wobbles as she sobs, " Oh, Madison. I'm so fucking sorry you got wrapped up into all of this. Why are you doing this? Just come home. Tell Diego to bring you back to New York. If he let you go, why are you really there with him?"

"Because I don't want any other innocent person to experience what I did, or worse, at the hands of that monster. Helping Diego will ensure that he *never* touches anyone ever again. Ughhh...my mind is really fucked up, Lex. I...I feel oddly calm and safe with Diego. And maybe that is because he was there at a time that I needed a life vest. I held onto anything that could keep me from giving up, from letting the darkness wash over me. He kept me alive. All I know is that something happened to me on that island, and it shifted how I feel about Liam."

"That's normal," Lexi says softly after a brief pause. "It doesn't mean you love Liam any less than the way you used to. You just formed a bond with Diego based on trauma. He was someone who protected you. Let's not forget he's also the reason you were on that island in the first place."

"It wasn't supposed to happen that way. I was never meant to meet his uncle or be left in a cage, bruised and starved."

"Don't make excuses for him. Madison, come home. I'm sure Killian will go get you himself if you say the word. Hell, I'll take a leave of absence from school. We can get through this together. Just come home, girl."

"I'm safe. Diego won't let anything happen to me. Plus, I think we are going to end this whole thing much sooner than we expected. After that, I'll be home. I love you for wanting to be there for me. I'll be okay, Lex. I can't explain it, not in a way that is rational. Diego is good for me right now. He's been teaching me how to be strong on my own and he's going to train me to defend myself. I need to learn that if I plan on being with Liam. If I plan on staying in this life. Events like this can happen at any time."

"I question myself and my morals dating Conor, too. Are you sure this is what you want? It's okay if you say 'fuck it' and leave everyone behind. Liam out of everyone understands that. No wonder he left after your first night together. He didn't want this to happen to you...or the car accident. I know you love him—"

"I can't let him go. Not now. We've been through too much together to let a love like ours flicker out." Longing for Liam coils its way around my lungs, making it hard to breathe. I am yearning for him in a way I haven't ever felt before. Suddenly, it feels like the day he left me crying in my bathroom all over again.

"Is Diego treating you well...all things considered?" Lexi chuckles, breaking the intensity of the moment I was having.

"Yeah. He's known in the underworld as *The Bone Breaker*. I've never even come close to seeing that side of him. Even when I got a glimpse, he still found a way to show me I can trust him."

Lexi sighs, "Just be careful, Maddy."

"I will. I miss you. I'll call you soon."

"Love ya, girl."

"Love you, too."

This little nook by the window will be the perfect place to read. Not sure how much time I'll have for that—with Geraldo's impending arrival and all. My thumb hovers over Liam's contact. I want to call him.

I should call him.

I just don't want to make it any harder on him than it already is. Deep down, I know calling him will break me, too. In order for this plan to be successful, I can't get all emotional and clingy about the man I love.

The phone rings on my end table, making me jump. Hesitantly, I walk over and answer.

"Hello?"

"Good evening, Ms—Madison. I was wondering if you'd like anything before bed. Perhaps a nightcap or tea? We have an arrangement of teas, pastries and fruit for dessert."

"Oh, that's so kind of you. Tea sounds great, I plan on reading the rest of the night."

"That sounds lovely. Would you prefer chamomile to wind down from the long day?"

"Perfect, thank you."

"It'll be down shortly. I'll add in a few of our chocolate chip cookies. We baked them fresh for tonight. Mr. De La Cruz specifically requested them for you, he thought you'd enjoy them. They are still warm—the best way to eat a cookie if you ask me."

I giggle. "Mmm. You are *so* right. Thanks, Eloise."

Placing the phone back down, I amble over to my closet. The amount of outfits Diego purchased for me is outrageous. I mean my entire closet and drawers are full of satin and silk teddies, negligees, exquisite lingerie, fancy attire, casual jeans and t-shirts, sundresses... He even went as far as to select some skimpy swimsuits and workout outfits. Any sort of clothing I could need is here.

I end up opting for a black satin negligee with a matching robe.

Grabbing the throw blanket off of the couch I dim the lights and get comfortable in my little reading nook. As if it were just another night, I open my Kindle app and choose a steamy romance book I've been dying to read off my TBR. It's about a sexy, moody billionaire who is threatened by the new female employee his father hired at the family firm. The two of them have to work closely together on a major project that will be presented to their biggest client. After one drunk steamy night, the two of them begin to blur the lines of hating each other to throwing their entire career away for love.

Gotta love a good enemies to lovers romance.

My phone buzzes with a phone call from Liam. As badly as I want to answer, I need to calm down. My mind and heart are battling each other and am in no place to talk to him right now. I'm confused. I'm nervous about what the next few days will bring and I know he'll do something reckless if he senses I'm upset. After the third ring, and my heart about ready to explode out of my chest with anxiety, I silence it and send it to voicemail.

My eyes skim over the words of my book, but I can't focus. I've been reading the same damn sentence for the last two minutes. The least I can do is text him, he deserves to know there is a bit of a change in the plan—in case Killian hasn't told him.

MADISON

> Stop worrying. Little complication, that's why I haven't called sooner.

LIAM

> I'll never stop worrying about your safety, Madison. What complication?

So he doesn't know. Killian hasn't told him about Geraldo, or about the fact that they are coming here for back up. Damn, Killian really is pissed at Liam. Those two need to make up. Whatever this spat is about, they need to reconcile. I type out a response about Killian and Selena coming here, leaving out Geraldo and his men arriving sooner than anticipated, when I realize Conor is with him. I don't want Liam finding out from his best friend what's going on. He should hear it from me. Deciding I need a minute to think of how to tell him without him freaking out, I head to the bathroom.

One look in the mirror has me washing my face and the mess of makeup smudged all over it. The drawers are filled with La Prairie skincare. All sorts of blue bottles with lip masks, serums and moisturizers. I slap on some under eye cream and nighttime regenerating moisturizer, and head back to the nook.

Worry plagues me as I take a peek at my phone and don't see another message from Liam.

Fuck it, I'll call him. Bringing the phone to my ear, I wait... but it never rings. It doesn't even go to voicemail. Diego mentioned earlier his phone wasn't receiving calls, maybe we have bad service here. I'll try calling again before bed.

I'm about five chapters in, and just about to get to the highly anticipated sex scene, when a knock on the door jolts me out of fantasyland. Checking the time on my phone, I notice it's been an hour since I spoke to Eloise about my tea.

Hmm. Maybe they forgot.

I practically skip to the door, excited for those cookies and my tea, and more than ready to get back to the scene I was just reading.

What—rather—*who* is standing on the other side of my door is not at all what I was expecting. Two sets of gorgeous eyes take in my face before dipping lower to my hardened nipples beneath this satin robe.

One set of brown.

One set of blue.

CHAPTER 20

MADISON

"LIAM," I gasp, utterly shocked. I stand there like an idiot, looking between him and Diego, the latter holding a tray with my tea and cookies.

He breezes past me and places the tray on my bed, snatches a cookie and takes a seat at the edge. "Well aren't you going to say hi to your *boyfriend?*" Diego says over a mouthful of *my* chocolate chip cookies.

I spin around and rip the half eaten cookie out of his hands, wanting to smack him for his arrogance. Pointing to him and then the door, I scream, "You. *Out.*" Then like a tornado, I whip back around and find Liam still standing at the threshold of my door. "*You.* Get in here. You have *a lot* of explaining to do."

Diego chuckles and brushes the crumbs from his shirt. He saunters over to me and snatches the cookie back out of my hand, popping the rest of it in his mouth like a chipmunk. "I knew you'd like these. Especially since you've started your period. I'll be in my room if you need me. You know the one —*right next door,*" he says, shooting Liam a look. A look that has Liam gawking at me with so many questions.

"Get out!" I scream pointing to the door.

Liam steps in and closes the door behind him. His large

frame leans against it looking delicious and livid as he crosses his legs at the ankles. Those muscular inked arms come up to do the same, resting against his chest. Heavy silence sits between us as his eyes roam every inch of my body, making me shiver with need and a little bit of fear. I've seen this look on him. It's the same one he had in his office at The Triskelion. He's going to lose control in about three, two—

Liam rushes over, grips my face and kisses me hard, stealing the breath right out of my lungs. "You make me fucking crazy, Madison," he growls, pulling my face back an inch to stare at me. He sighs and strokes his thumbs over my cheeks.

Instead of that making me swoon like it normally does, it makes me angry. *Irrationally angry.* I press my hands flat against his chest and push him back. Immediately, his posture shifts and his eyes narrow.

"What's going on, love?" His eyebrow raises in question. "Not excited to see me?"

I sit down on the bed and pat the space next to me. He takes a seat and brings my hands to his lips. Pain and rejection lace his features.

"You promised me you wouldn't do this. You told me you understood, that you would let me fly without you." The words come out rushed and shaky. I am still processing the fact that he's here right now. *What the hell is Killian going to do when he finds out?* He's going to be here tomorrow.

"I know that. I never even got to my family in Ireland. I took the first flight to Mykonos after I landed. Killian knows. I told him—only after he admitted to being a total gobshite about everything." He looks to the door and then back at me. "We don't trust Diego."

I pull my hands out of his hold. "He knows you're here? You don't even realize how much more complicated you just made this for you, Liam. Not only just for you, but everyone else. Geraldo is coming here any moment now. He's decided to take a vacation with his men after the ambush. I also think he's calling Diego's bluff, waiting to see if he'll slip up while around me."

Liam's hands nervously rake through his hair. "Fuck."

"Yeah. Fuck is right...*Liam*," I say, reaching for him and cupping my hand to his cheek. "You can't be here. I know you thought you were doing the right thing trying to keep me safe, but this is a *huge* risk. If Geraldo sees you..."

"Let him. I'll kill every single one of those motherfuckers the second they step foot on this yacht. I'm not leaving you to play house with Diego just to put Geraldo's mind at ease."

I scoff at him. "We aren't playing house."

"Sure looks that way. From the moment you stepped onto the helipad you were laughing and smiling with him. Then he brings you fucking cookies and tea as you curl up with a book and a blanket...dressed in—", his eyes travel to my exposed skin, the lace-lined satin nightgown, then back up to meet my eyes. "—*That*."

"Conor is here?" I drop my hand and cross my arms over my chest.

"Don't change the subject, Madison."

"I'm asking a question," I snap. "Lexi said he was with you. She obviously wasn't told you were here."

He nods and stands, starting to pace the floor in front of me. "It was supposed to be kept quiet. When Killian and I talked, he agreed he was wrong and wanted to send me over to keep an eye on you from a distance. It was never my intention to barge in here—unless I thought something was wrong. Killian has our yacht anchored a few miles away. I saw you land, I kept my distance, but then you never called me. *And then,* I hear from Conor that Lexi spoke to you and ya both had been crying on the phone. To top it all off, you didn't respond when I said if you didn't elaborate on what was complicated, I would come here and burn this yacht to the ocean floor—preferably with Diego in it."

"What? I didn't get that message. I tried calling you and it didn't even ring or go to voicemail. Regardless, you're acting impulsively. You and Killian *both* are. Killian is on his way with Selena and more backup. *We* will do this. Liam, you need to go. You can't be here. I can't lose you. *Please*. Please just go. And if I can't convince you to go back to Ireland, then stay on that yacht and don't you dare think of snooping around here. What if Geraldo is already here? How fucking stupid." I shake my head, and rub my eyes until I see stars. With each breath, my anger builds more and more.

"So you're mad at me now? Madison, I took a fucking bullet for you—and I would do it again in a heartbeat. I'm not going anywhere. You don't need to worry about me. Let *me* worry about me. Tell Diego I'm staying."

"No."

Liam stops pacing and turns to me with shock written all over his face. "You have feelings for him. That's what this is, isn't it?"

"No. It's not. It's about you sticking to the plan to keep everyone, including me, safe."

He takes a few strides towards me, before capturing my face in his hands and tilting my chin up. His eyes search mine, desperate for them to reveal what I said as the truth. What he sees there must not have been good enough. Liam steps back, dropping his hands like he's been burned, and lowers his head; shaking it.

"I can't do this again, Madison. I've done it once and it nearly broke me. If you don't want me anymore, I need you to tell me. Perhaps I rushed into asking you to marry me. Quite frankly, I think it scares you," he sighs. "Know that I'll always protect you. I will always watch over you. But I can't always wonder if your mind is on another man. It's me and you, baby. *Just* me and you. There's no place for my brother. *Or Diego.*"

He doesn't give me the chance to explain or respond. The door pops open and he walks out.

"Liam, wait," I shout, running after him.

A shirtless Diego steps out of the door behind me in a pair of black sweatpants that hang low on his hips. *Ass. Put a shirt on.* I rush up the stairs, taking them two at a time. When I reach the top, Liam is walking across the deck and over to the hydraulic platform at the back of the ship. That's where I spot Conor waiting in the dinghy.

Diego catches up to me and wraps a hand around my waist, but I shake him off angrily.

"Liam!" My voice cracks with the pressure building in my chest.

Liam turns around and throws his hands in the air. Tears line his red-rimmed eyes. "I think we both need some time to figure this out. Actually, *you* need time to figure out what you want. I'll stay away, like you asked. I'll respect it. I just needed to make sure you were okay. You'll always be my priority, Madison. I just hope I'm still yours."

He hops onto the boat and salutes the staff member who is operating the platform with his middle finger. The platform lowers into the sea the same way my heart sinks into my stomach watching him leave.

As I approach the back of the yacht, they start the engine and take off. Liam doesn't bother to turn around. The two of them head off into the night towards the other yachts lighting up the distance. The dinghy slowly becomes engulfed by the night, hardly visible, yet I stand there and stare at the faint white stern light until my eyes can no longer track them.

Diego's hand comes down on my shoulder, giving it a gentle squeeze. "You alright, *Mariposita?*"

"No," I squeak as the tears start to collect, threatening to spill over.

He pulls me to him until I'm tucked under his chin and he's

rocking me in his arms. I wrap mine around his waist and bury my face into his bare chest.

"I wasn't very nice to him. He didn't deserve for me to react the way I did," I sob.

Diego's hand soothingly pets my hair and he shushes me. "He knew what he was doing when he came here. You specifically asked him not to, and he did it anyway. He let his fear of losing you override his decision to stay away."

I sniffle and shake my head against his warm chest. The steady rhythm of his heart beats against my cheek.

"I think we just broke up. *Fuck*, I think we just broke up." Salty tears drip onto Diego's chest as mine heaves with anxiety.

Diego backs us up to a lounge chair and sits, pulling me down with him until my ass is on the chair between his legs and my head rests on his shoulder. My bare legs drape over his thigh, his hands resting respectfully on my hip. This isn't romantic or sexual in any sense. He isn't his normal gloating and dickish self.

At least...not right now.

He's comforting me.

There isn't any indication he's getting satisfaction over this, especially knowing there's no one standing in the way of him and I.

"It'll be alright. I don't blame the guy for wanting to protect you. I'd do the same damn thing. The problem is you specifically asked him not to, knowing the risk."

"That's not why he did it. He let his jealousy get to him," I shrug. "He thinks I have feelings for you."

Diego goes still beneath me, his fingertips grip my hip more firmly. "Do you?" His voice is full of gravel and vulnerability.

Those enchanting eyes of his zero in on me, but I'm too much of a coward to look up at him. "I don't know what this is, Diego," I shrug. "I shouldn't feel a damn thing about you. You kidnapped me. You fucking *drugged* me."

Eventually finding the courage to look up at him, my eyes

find his, and for a moment it steals my breath away. They are the most royal shade of blue I have ever seen. Diego's beautiful eyes search mine. His body vibrates beneath mine, radiating so much intensity and hope.

Suddenly, I'm way too hot in this thin fabric. Heat scorches across my cheeks and chest, traitorously dipping lower between my legs. Memories are playing like a reel in my mind.

"You chained me up to the ceiling," I continue, "and stripped me of my clothes..." I trail off, realizing I'm verbalizing said visuals and not heading in the direction I wanted this to go.

Proof of his arousal presses hard against my side.

"Go on..." His minty breath fans my face, prompting goosebumps to spring up along my arms.

"I don't hate you."

He lowers his face so that his nose is inches from mine. "No, you don't."

"But I don't like you, either. I love Liam."

"So you keep saying," his voice is smooth, no more than a sultry whisper. "What did I say about lying to me, *Mariposita?*" Our noses touch as his hand curls around my hip, adjusting me so that I'm lying back on the lounge chair.

Diego grips my legs, spreading them and pulling me closer so that they wrap around his sides. I gasp at the sudden change in his mood. My nightgown rides up over my thighs, exposing my black satin underwear to him. He leans over me, grazing his length against the flimsy fabric.

His closeness stirs something in me.

Okay his impressive cock pressing up against my most sensitive spots is what really stirs something in me—if we are being candid here.

Something I wish I didn't feel. A reaction that Liam knew I'd have. The reason why he was so upset.

This is fucking wrong. So wrong.

185

Liam just left. God knows where we even stand. I was just bawling my eyes out. What the hell is this shit with Diego?

He leans over to whisper in my ear, resting on his elbows so that our bodies barely touch, yet the heat radiating off him feels like a sensual caress. "I do believe you love Liam. But I don't think you were ever expecting me. And that scares you. Because I make you feel free. I make you crave a man who doesn't treat you like you're glass, but a diamond...precious and rare...created by intense heat—" he runs his lips along the shell of my ear, "and pressure," his hand slinks down my neck, gripping it lightly on the sides. It's overwhelming my senses, making this energy between us feel heightened and exhilarating. Instinctively, I grip his hand, not out of fear, the way Geraldo instilled in me. *No.* Out of lust and desire to hand over my need for control.

I want to scream at myself for feeling this way. Especially given the fact that Liam just broke up with me. *I think.*

Who the hell am I anymore ? I don't even know—and that's what scares me the most. What if the woman I've become isn't the woman Liam fell in love with? Butterflies and uncertainty assault my stomach at the thought.

My mind spins and my pulse hammers against his fingers as his smooth lips approach mine.

Fuck. Fuuuuck. Push him away, Madison!

"Remember, all you have to do is ask," he reminds me as his words brush over my lips. Once again, he changes direction, leaning back and extending a hand to help me up. I accept it shakily, letting out a silent breath.

Maybe even slight relief.

A prayer.

"Come on, I'll walk you back to your room."

He takes off towards the kitchen when I do something impulsive.

Something I'm not proud of.

"*Wait.* Will you..."

Diego whips his whole body back around, one deviant eyebrow arched.

Those sapphire globes of his shine with mischief, and a bit of pleasant surprise. His tongue darts out to wet his bottom lip as he stalks toward me.

It's predatory.

Unfaltering.

The real, thrillingly terrifying form of the man the underworld calls *The Bone Breaker.*

My chest rises and falls with each resolute step he takes my way. *Shit is it too late to chicken out?* I've officially lost it. I keep letting him get in my head. That guilt courses through my heightened senses, in steady competition with the need to know what it would feel like when his lips touch mine.

Lifting my chin and running his thumb over my trembling lips, he pulls my face closer. I brace for what could be the biggest mistake of my life—*at least the most reckless*—I'm still so unsure.

Diego chuckles and presses a kiss to the tip of my nose. "Consider this your punishment for not only lying to me, but to yourself. I want to do a hell of a lot more than kiss you, you beautiful girl. Tonight you broke up with your boyfriend. A man you are in love with, no matter how much I wish you weren't. You need time to process and decide if this is what you really want."

"Ugh," I push at his chest, making him take a step back. "Forget it. This was a mistake. I don't even know what I was thinking or who the hell I am anymore."

I side-step him and attempt to walk back to my room with my pride—*and sanity*—still somewhat intact. I barely make it to the entry of the kitchen when he tugs at my wrist slamming me into his firm chest. His hand cups my face as his fingers snake through my hair, gripping it at the nape of my neck.

"I think you know *exactly* who you are. *Fuck,* Madison—I want you. I have been *craving* you in ways I've never felt before.

There is no question about that. I just don't want you to regret me." His thumb runs over my bottom lip. "So ask me again. And the next time you do, no longer will you see this gentle side. I will not hesitate, *Mariposita*, in showing you just how much pleasure you've been missing."

Unraveling his fingers from my hair, he releases me and stalks off in the direction of his room, leaving me standing there flabbergasted. I clasp my hands together and bring them to my lips in disbelief.

Shit.

CHAPTER 21

L I A M

GOD FUCKING DAMNIT! I claw a hand through my hair, gripping it to the point of pain. Unshed tears collect in the corner of my eyes, blurring the lights of *The Triquetra* ahead. Conor shoots me a look I know all too well among my men.

Worry.

"This is just a lovers quarrel, Liam. The lass will be blowing up ya phone in the morning." His sentiment was meant to be reassuring. But it feels anything but. I should be turning this dinghy around, throwing Madison over my shoulder, and getting her the fuck away from Diego and the looming threat over all of our heads.

Except, this isn't some fairytale romance novel my woman reads.

This is real life.

I can't change the man I am nor the life I live. *Fuck*–it's a miracle that Madison even wanted anything to do with the likes of me. *How did we get here?* I'd give anything to be back at that college bar right now. Where the threats were minimal, that of any normal college kid trying to make it through the semester. A time not so long ago that I could keep an eye on her.

Only a few short months and here we are with imminent

threats all around us and in an all out war. She's been run off the road, held at gun and knifepoint, beaten and held captive in a filthy dungeon, and so many more atrocious moments in between. My heart continues to crack wide open with each passing thought.

The way her eyes met mine with fear and relief when I first saw her in that closet on the island.

The bruises covering her body as she undressed for a shower at Declan's.

The defiance in her eyes as she stood her ground, demanding to help Diego.

Each memory brings new waves of grief and longing. The tears spill over my lashes and down my cheeks as my heart stutters in my chest.

I wish more than anything that I could be a different man for her.

That my life wasn't this way.

The ugly truth has been hovering over us since the first day I got a taste of her lips. *She shouldn't be part of this life.* I've been stupid and reckless with her love for purely selfish reasons. I let her convince me that this is what she wants, when in reality it's not this life that she wants.

It's me.

Well, I thought it was.

If letting her go means sending her back to a life she can live without danger or darkness, then I'll break my own heart and my promise to her, and let her go.

Conor's hand comes down hard on my shoulder, giving it a firm squeeze. "Come on, mate. Let's get you some rest. I'll take the night shift. Killian should be arriving with Selena and Kieran in the morning. The rest of our men will be here no later than tomorrow evening."

I slap Con's back and squeeze the back of his neck. "Thanks, Con."

STEPPING OUT OF THE SHOWER, I dry off and don a pair of gray sweats. As relaxing as the hot shower was for my muscles, I still feel tense inside. This void in my chest is growing bigger with every passing second that Madison is not next to me. Guilt gnaws on my insides with the way I left her. When she was calling out for me. Twice now I've done that. *God, I'm such a dick.*

Taking a seat at the edge of the bed, I rest my elbows on my thighs and lean over into my hands, releasing a massive sigh. *Fuck, baby. I miss the hell out of you. What have I done?*

My phone vibrates on the end table where it's charging. I unplug it and squint down at the message. The glow of the screen, too bright in this darkened room.

MADISON

> Liam, please. Please can we talk? You didn't give me a chance to explain to you how I feel. My head is all over the place after what I went through. I'm an emotional disaster. And to top it all off... I got my period today and it's fucking awful as usual. This can't be the end for us. You and I both know that.

Her words ring true. It will never be the end for us—I'll love her til my final breath on this Earth. And even then, I'll love her for many lifetimes after. I'm realizing now that love is about being selfless. For far too long I've been a selfish bastard with her love.

My fingers hover over the keys as I take a second to really process what I am about to do next.

I love you more than life itself, Madison. It's because you went through hell and back that I have realized the biggest mistake I made in loving you. I've been so fucking selfish with you. I said it in the beginning—I'm not good for you, Madison. You don't deserve to have your life at risk by loving me in return. You deserve to have a life where you won't need to look over your shoulder every two seconds. You deserve to have the family you want one day. And a man who comes home from work and brings you flowers. Not enemies lurking in shadows. I can never be that man for you, baby. You are an incredible woman. Please listen to me this time. It's because I love you that I need to let you go. Killian will be the one to come and get you when this is all over. Until then, I'll stick to the shadows where I belong. Always watching and protecting you from a distance, just like I used to when we first met at the bar. Know that you are and always will be protected, baby. I won't let anything happen to you. Trust that. Please take my words into consideration. Move on from all of this, Maddy. Go back to New York, to your future job and your family, and never look back at any of this. I love you, princess. Always have and always will. My soul is yours. That won't ever change.

As my thumb lingers over the send button, my chest tightens and my air supply cuts off. This hurts far worse than any stab wound, being shot, or God bless my mum, *even her death*.

Fuck. Do it, Liam. She deserves so much more than this life with you.

I hit send and gasp for air, trying to convince myself I'm too young to be having a heart attack. The pounding of my heart against my ribcage won't let up as the bubbles pop up in our chat. Part of me is tempted to text Conor just in case I do go down. I need to be alive to make sure Madison gets away from all this shit. Then fuck it all after that. I'll be out of her life for good. She'll be better off without me.

MADISON

You promised me. You promised me you
wouldn't leave me again 🙁

LIAM

I know. Use that reason to hate me. It'll make it
easier for you. Goodnight, love.

Any remaining pieces of my heart left tethered together have officially snapped, leaving behind a sickening hollowness.

I drag my feet across the wood floors in search of the door. By some miracle, my legs carry me to the pool, but not before I snatched a full bottle of whiskey off the bar. Twisting the cap off and tossing it into the pool, I bring the bottle to my lips and chug a quarter of it in one go. *Damn, that fucking burns.* 'Suppose it's better to feel fire in my chest than the emptiness that's there.

My arse finds a lounge chair. I lean back on the cushion and look up at the stars, questioning their motives and role in my star-crossed love life. Reminds me of the days Madison would stare up at them. It has me wondering if she ever felt the same way about her life.

WARMTH CARESSES MY FACE. I awaken to a familiar brunette leaning over me. Rubbing the blur from my eyes, I wet my dry lips. My tongue is stuck to the top of my mouth and my head pounds like a son of a bitch as I try to sit up. I wrap my fingers around the woman's face and rub my thumb over her pink-tinted cheek.

"Madison," I whisper, pain altering my voice.

The woman clasps my hand and gently places a glass of ice water into it. "It's Lainey, Liam."

Swiping my free hand down my face, I try to shake off the confusion. The world spins and my head pounds with a fucking hangover from hell. *Perhaps I'm still drunk.*

Lainey's face comes into focus. She's sitting on the edge of the lounge chair. "What're you doing here, love?" I slur.

Dainty fingers grip my hand. She tilts the glass to my lips, forcing me to drink. I oblige, sipping slowly before chugging the damn thing. My tongue finally loosens from my palate. Lainey takes the glass and places it on the floor next to the empty bottle of my favorite whiskey and an ashtray full of cigarette butts.

Oops. I drank the whole bottle.

Forcing myself to sit up straight, I take a strand of my childhood friend's hair. "First of all, when did you change your hair? Second of all, what the hell are ya doing here?"

Lainey reaches behind her and hands me some manky looking green smoothie. "You drink, I'll talk."

"Yer absolutely *delusional* if you think I'm drinking that," I scoff, pushing the smoothie away like a defiant toddler.

She slaps my arm and plugs my nose with her fingers, once again forcing the unsightly liquid to my lips. "Drink this if ya want to be semi-functioning by the time Killian arrives. Stop being such a big baby."

I move her fingers away, toss the straw, and chug the damn thing. Not going to lie, it actually tastes quite good.

"Killian requested that I be here as head chef. The original chef, Isabella, came down with the flu. You know how he can be with his meals and all," she clucks her tongue, the corner of her lips lifting into a smile. "As for your other question—I dyed my hair back to chocolate brown because it's easier to maintain than the blonde. It reminds me of when we were younger and everyone would say I looked like my mum." She looks down at her hands in her lap. Grief paints her usually cheerful features.

I reach out and place my hand over hers. "Well, you certainly

194

look like her now. She would be so proud of the woman you've become, Lainey. We all miss her."

"What happened to you last night?" Lainey asks while nodding to the empty handle of whiskey.

"I ended things with Madison," I practically choke on the words as they leave my lips. It feels foreign and wrong. My smoothie threatens to come back up at the thought of what I did last night.

Without warning, I stand, brush past a startled Lainey, and race to the back of the boat. I puke my brains out for what feels like forever before sliding my back down the wall. Lainey approaches with a washcloth that she places on the back of my neck. She has refilled my water glass and hands that to me as well.

Dropping to her knees in front of me she says, "I'm sorry, Liam. I'm sure you had your reasons. It couldn't have been easy to do that. Just know, I'm here if you need someone to confide in." She takes my hand and rubs soothing circles over my palm with her thumb. "Looks like the smoothie did its job."

"What the fuck was in that?"

"Just a bit of activated charcoal—masked behind matcha, kiwi, kale, and green apples." She smirks in satisfaction. "Killian should be here soon, I recommend you go grab yourself a nice, hot shower. Breakfast will be ready for all of you by the time you come back up." With those parting words, she ruffles my hair and stands, leaving me a fucking mess on the floor.

I COLLAPSE into the chair across from Conor at the table prepared for our small group. Black Aviators shield my bloodshot, puffy eyes. Luckily the ibuprofen is kicking in, so I won't have to use this butter knife to pry my eyeballs out of my pounding skull. I wouldn't have time anyway—Killian, Selena and Kieran should be here any minute now.

Fluffy eggs, greasy bacon, warm biscuits, assorted fruit, freshly pressed orange juice and coffee are displayed before me. I waste no time loading my plate to the brim. Conor's judgy eyes are practically burning a hole through his black Oakley sunglasses. When he notices me scowling at him, he pretends to answer emails on his phone. *Smooth, mate.* Perhaps he is. Probably talking to Lexi—which is going to become another complication later on.

A groan escapes my lips at the thought of dealing with that. Conor lifts his head to look at me, ceremoniously dropping his phone on to the table.

"How ya feeling?" he asks, crossing his arms over his chest. *Tsk. Tsk.* He wasn't so judgy last night. *I wonder if Madison spoke to Lexi about this? She had to. That's her bestie. Rarely do they keep secrets from each other.*

"Drunk this early, *Sweetheart*?" My brother's voice sweeps in like a gust of wind. Killian struts across the teakwood in a casual pair of navy blue shorts paired with a white linen Henley t-shirt. I'm not used to seeing him look so...*relaxed.* So *casual.* A sleepy, yawning Selena is trudging along behind him, wearing a flowy peach romper and straw hat you'd see on a beach.

What a perfect, beautiful, couple. I roll my eyes at them behind my shades.

CHAPTER 22

KILLIAN

"LEAVE HIM BE, KIL," Selena admonishes as I pull out her chair for her. She takes her seat next to Conor and I take mine next to a disheveled Liam. I've seen this side of him only a handful of times. *This can't possibly be good.* You can still smell the alcohol seeping out of his pores.

The staff informed me he had fallen asleep on a lounge chair by the pool after drinking a whole bottle of whiskey. I tried to get the reason out of Conor, but he only said it had to do with Madison. Although he has loyalty to me first, Liam and him are very close. Which is why he was rather tight-lipped in the details surrounding his friend's night of binging.

Conor finishes his meal and excuses himself to his bedroom, in need of some sleep. He pulled the night shift after being sent directly here yesterday. The lad could use some much needed rest—I'm sure he's jetlagged as fuck.

Selena and I exchange concerned looks while we help ourselves to the lovely breakfast spread Lainey has prepared for us.

My fiancée is the first to break the awkward silence, addressing the elephant in the room. "Did something happen, Liam? Is Madison alright?"

My Neaderthal of a brother shoves another forkful of food into his mouth, responding in garble. "I broke things off with Madison after paying *your brother* and her a visit last night." His eyes narrow and dart to Selena, who looks horrified.

The fork I'm holding stops an inch from my mouth, as I slowly turn my head in his direction.

If looks could kill.

We didn't go through all of that with Madison for him to break things off with her the second things got a little rocky. *What the fuck is wrong with him?*

"Either I am extremely jetlagged and misheard you, or you said words I never thought I'd hear coming out of your mouth. You *broke up* with Madison?!" Anger rises inside me, prompting me to slam my fork down onto my plate. Sel jumps in her seat, quietly watching our interaction.

"I realize how selfish I've been with her. *We* were selfish with her, Kil. She doesn't deserve any of this bullshit. We should have never involved her in this world in the first place."

Pinching the bridge of my nose, I inhale sharply. "What do you mean *you paid them a visit* last night? I told you to come directly here. Geraldo and his men could be anywhere in our immediate location as we speak. How could you be so *reckless?*" My voice grows in intensity.

"Love makes you stupid and blind—*apparently.* Maddy's going through a lot emotionally. I don't blame her one bit. I do, however, blame Diego for being the cause of that. Madison has changed. And it's not that I can't love this version of her. I will always love her no matter what. But I refuse to be the one to keep her in a constant state of danger. Diego would be wise to do the same—when all of this is over. It's obvious that Madison has developed some sort of feelings for him during all of this. Even though she may still love me, she can't help but feel something for him too." He says Diego's name with such venom it makes Selena flinch.

Liam takes a sip of his coffee before continuing, "I figured now would be the best time to put an end to us. She can hate me. She *will* hate me. Eventually she'll hate him, too—and hopefully move on from us when this is all said and done."

I shake my head and let out a hefty breath. "Yer an *eejit*, Liam. What you can't grasp in all of this is that Madison chose you. She chose *you*, arsehole. It's her choice to be a part of this life. She knows damn well the risk. I know you want to protect her, because you love her, but this—" I point an index finger at him, " —this decision to let her go may have been the dumbest thing you've ever done, and I fear that you pushed her right into the arms of Diego. So that plan of yours to keep her out of this life, *will* backfire. She'll end up in this life, whether you like it or not—but not with you. You'll be forced to see her at holidays and family events—*on his arm*. Excuse me." I slide my chair back and walk over to place a kiss on Selena's head. "Stay. You need to eat, and I need to try and sort out where your uncle and his men are."

Selena pats the hand I have resting on her shoulder, before placing a sweet kiss to my palm. "Okay, baby."

SLIDING my phone out of my back pocket, I decide I should call Madison first. On the third ring she answers.

"Kil." Her voice is rough, lacking its normal charm and warmth. She mustn't have slept well last night. *Can ya blame her?*

"Are you alright, love?"

"No. I'm not," she says in a sigh.

Another female voice carries over the line.

"Madison, can we get you anything to eat? Perhaps a fruit platter? Maybe an omelette?"

Her hand covers the speaker, muffling their conversation.

"Fruit would be amazing, Eloise. Any chance you have more of those lemon tarts around?"

"Of course. I'll bring some refreshments as well."

"Thank you." More static and shuffling fills the line before Madison speaks more clearly. "I know that I'm confused and slightly unhinged, but that's not even why Liam ended this. He wants me out of this life completely. I don't know what else to do to convince him that I want to be here."

"I'll talk to him. He's...a goddamn mess right now. Lainey had to force feed him a smoothie this morning to make him puke up the bottle of whiskey he drank last night." I lean over the railing, looking out toward where *Pontus* is, wondering what Maddy is up to at the moment.

"Lainey is there?" she questions angrily. *Did I miss something?*

"Yeah, I had her fly out last night. Our head chef is sick, and I knew Lainey wouldn't mind. She could use the change of scenery. Plus, with Selena expecting, we could use a chef I am comfortable with. It always puts us at a greater risk, the more people who know."

"Well that's...perfect. *Just fucking perfect.*" *Is she mad about the baby?* I didn't think she would have taken the news this way. I was certain she was over her and I.

"Am I missing something here?" I say, picking up a lot of tension and even a hint of jealousy.

"Nope. Glad Lainey is there to lick Liam's wounds. Listen, I don't want to talk about this anymore. He made his choice. I have to accept it—even if I don't want to hear it. He's going to look back one day and realize that this was a huge mistake. The difference is, I'd rather be with him now and embrace the unknown, than to end something real and rare. And for what ? Potentially preventing bad things from happening? To give me a life I wanted before him? That changed and I'm okay with that. I'd rather know I was loved fiercely, until my last breath, than to always yearn for someone, knowing that we could have been together but chose not to."

Fuck. My mind always resorts back to the time when she was mine. The lass who is strong and unwilling to back down. The one who puts her feelings before fear and logic. The woman who would do anything to protect the ones she loves. Liam fucked up big time.

"Give him some time. Perhaps this will all blow over after Geraldo's reign ends. Speaking of, is Diego with you? I'd like to speak to him."

"He left early to meet Geraldo on the mainland. He texted me to tell me he'd be back in an hour. I'll let him know you called. Oh, and Kil?"

"Yeah?"

"Congrats. You're going to be an amazing father. You always said you wanted a family and now you'll have that."

"Thank you. That means so much. What you are doing to help end this war is commendable. You are risking a lot here... and I don't just mean Liam. Regardless of his relationship status with you, know you'll always belong in our family. You are just as much a part of the Tri-State Syndicate and the Kennedy family as Liam, Kieran, Colin, Conor or even I am. Hell, I'll even make it official if you want. You can be inducted in, get your Triskelion tattoo and say the oath just like we all did. Typically, there is a small party after. The women aren't required to get inducted in or wear the tattoo. They are usually married into this life, or are already blood. For you, and the sacrifices you've made, I want to offer you an opportunity to be recognized for that."

"I'll think about it. Thanks, Kil."

"Keep ya head up, love." I lower my voice an octave. "And keep your wits about you. Diego wants you, and I don't trust that it's with the best intentions."

She sighs heavily. "I'm a big girl, Kil. I can handle myself. I'll talk to you later."

"*Madison...*" I urge before the line disconnects.

CHAPTER 23

DIEGO

"THE ANSWER IS NO." I try my best to keep my voice level but the vitriol in my voice is hard to mask.

"Why shouldn't my men and I indulge in some fun with the girl? Yes, I gifted her to you, but my intentions were for you to marry her and knock her up. You've always been running around from one pet to the next. It's time to settle down, boy. You want the crown after me? Then you need to set yourself up for the future. Selena reuniting with Killian will not protect us from future attacks. We need Madison to solidify that. Until then, let's all have some fun. Those curves of hers and that mouth are perfect for me to slide my—"

Red hot rage works its way through my veins. I want to snap his cock right off his decrepit body and shove it down his throat to silence him. Reigning in that rage, I use the charade of playboy and uninterested to my advantage, careful not to give in to his games.

"I'll marry the girl when we return back to the States. Can a man enjoy his vacation first? You've been working me to the bone," I faux laugh, cracking my knuckles at the pun. "Besides, I have women lined up for a private show after tonight's dinner."

With a grimey chuckle, he responds, "The rest of our men

will be happy to hear that." Some of his lackeys, who are having breakfast with us, snicker and lick their lips. One bastard even grabs his crotch. "Diego, I must have a taste of *her* before you marry her. What a generous man I have been to you and your sister. I promise not to break her, I'll let you do that," he cackles sadistically. It takes every shred of willpower inside of me to not react.

He's baiting me.

So I weigh my words carefully. "I am grateful for you. I don't mind sharing my women, but I prefer my *betrothed* to remain untouched by anyone else in our organization."

"She isn't yours *officially*, a small taste wouldn't hurt anyone but your ego..." The asshole keeps pushing me.

"Then I suppose tonight we will have a larger celebration than expected," I announce, raising my drink in toast. "*A wedding.* I'll have my team organize it. Prepare for lots of drinking, dancing and women. I am *El Rompe Huesos*. My bride will remain untouched, understood?" I stand up and stare everyone down, my glare finally landing on my uncle. "If I hear of anyone even looking at her the wrong way, I will break every bone in your body—starting with your skull against my knee. *Are. We. Understood?*" Everyone nods, trepidation written across their faces. They've seen my work. None of them would dare go against my threats. My uncle on the other hand just smiles at me.

"Now we are talking. This is the type of man you need to be when *my* time is up. No mercy, take what you want, and don't let anyone disrespect you. One day, all of this will be your kingdom." Gerldo starts clapping and takes a puff of his Cuban cigar, blowing the smoke in my face. "It's a shame your lovely sister couldn't be here to watch her brother get married." He whips his phone out and places it to his ear. "Killian. I would like to speak to my niece." His eyebrows come together, detecting a lie out of whatever Killian just said. "I don't care that she is sleeping. *Wake. Her.* This is important. I think she would like to know about her brother's wedding tonight." Some of the men laugh menacingly.

Geraldo places his phone down on the table and hits speaker for all to hear. "Tío, what is this about a wedding?"

"Your brother and I are taking a nice vacation in Mykonos with the lovely Madison. We have arranged for him to prepare for his future by marrying her. Tonight, actually. The festivities will take place on *Pontus*. Being the generous man I am, I felt you and your man deserved an invitation." He looks down at his watch. "If you leave within the hour, you could be here for speeches," he coughs out another sinister laugh. "This night will end our feuding. Consider you accepting this invitation as Killian agreeing to a truce. I will talk to him about the rest of the negotiations when you arrive."

Killian answers for her, his tone firm, "We'll be there."

I FINALLY GET BACK to the yacht a few hours later with my heart slamming against my broken ribs. I had to wrap them myself last night. Madison went right to her room after our heated moment. I wanted to comfort her—well if we're being honest—I wanted to worship every inch of her, but I knew she needed space. She feels this thing between us just as intensely as I do. And now, because of my uncle being a step ahead of us, I've agreed to a wedding before even proposing. I did what I had to do in order to protect her from him.

Now, I need to make a plan with Killian and my cousin to end their pathetic lives before we say I do. The problem is that they will be expecting resistance. Geraldo may be an old fuck, but he isn't stupid. He knows Killian won't give up without a fight. Especially when it comes to Madison.

I career over the teakwood deck towards the swimming pool

and lounge chairs. My gaze lingers on the beautiful woman tanning on a float in the pool. A wide-brimmed beach hat obscures her face and a sexy black bikini wraps around her curves. Her toes wiggle along to the music blaring through the speakers. An empty Bloody Mary rests at the edge of the pool next to a half drank blood orange margarita. *Early start*—not that I'm judging, by any means. *I could use a stiff drink of my own right about now.*

Tossing my shirt on to a nearby lounge chair, and emptying my pocket of the box to a very important *gift*, I make a running start before cannon-balling right next to her. I don't even contemplate what that would do to my ribs. To say it wasn't pleasant is an understatement—*totally worth it.*

When I surface, I find Madison has flipped off the float and is swimming after her hat. "Diego!"

The heavy weight on my chest lifts instantly. She has that effect on me. It's soothing and comforting—even in her cute little moments of rage. I almost completely forget the throbbing in my ribs until she points them out.

She swims towards me and plops the wet hat on my head with a smack. We stand toe to toe in the shallow end. Her hands rest on her hips as she glares at me.

"Bet that one hurt your ribs," she says smugly, running her finger up them like a harp. Intoxicating pleasure replaces where the pain would be. Her soft hands begin tracing the tentacles of my kraken tattoo. "I forgot to help you wrap them last night... I'm sorry."

"Don't be. I managed. You needed your time alone." I keep my one hand secured in my pocket as the other comes up to wipe away the smudged mascara under her eyes. *It's fucking hot.* Reminds me of our flight here, and how I imagined Madison taking the place of the redheaded flight attendant.

"Killian wants you to call him. He asked if Geraldo was here. I just told him you were meeting him for breakfast."

I nod, staring at her plump lips, and wanting a taste of that attitude.

"You'll be seeing him and Selena later this evening."

Her brows come together in confusion. "What do you mean?"

I remove the ring from my pocket that I've had a death grip on and grab her left hand, sliding it in place on her ring finger. The three carat solitaire diamond is nestled between two pear shaped sapphires. *And damn if my ring on her hand doesn't look good there.* No matter the outcome of us after this is all over, I wanted her to always be reminded of me. What better way than to add two *'ocean eyes'* —as she likes to call them—sapphires to her ring.

"What I mean, is that you'll be my *wife* tonight. Geraldo and his men are attending a last minute wedding here on this yacht. *Our wedding.* My sister and Killian will be in attendance as well. Geraldo didn't give me much of a choice. He knows something is up, so he's playing a hard game, waiting to see when I'll break."

She gasps covering her mouth with one hand and extending the one with the ring, then she giggles as she looks up at me.

Shit. She's finally snapped, hasn't she ?

"Did you really just propose to me in a pool with a sopping wet beach hat on your head?" Her giggles explode as she bends over in hysterics. I can't help but laugh right alongside her. This moment, as tense as it is, has been lightened by the damn hat. I silently send up a thank you to mamá.

"I did. Except, I didn't propose. I'm *telling* you that you're marrying me tonight. Proposing like your... ex did... would be asking. And I'm not asking." Her smile falls a fraction at the mention of Liam.

She looks down and inspects the ring, finding her words. "Nice touch with the two blue sapphires. You just had to have me reminded of you, even in your absence, didn't you?" *Damn if this woman doesn't see right through me.*

207

"As much as I would love for this to be real, I understand you wouldn't want it to be this way. I will try my best to get this wedding called off, but in the event I can't, we can have an annulment after Geraldo is dead."

Her front teeth come down and clamp her bottom lip. "Okay."

"Okay? That's all you have to say? You aren't going to kick and scream, threaten to jump off the back of the ship like Rose from *Titanic* if I come any closer, or at the very least—curse me out?"

"Nope," she says, popping the P. She wades through the water, collects her margarita and finishes it off in one swig. Then proceeds to exit the pool, wrapping a towel tight around her center, and tossing on the designer sunglasses I purchased for her. "I guess I should get ready then." She shrugs, walking back to the main cabin.

"Madison," I say her name like a plea for my sanity. She turns back around, tightening her grip on the towel. "Thank you, and I'm sorry. Twice now, your dream proposal has been ruined. I know I threw shade at Liam for that, and here I am doing the same thing. I'm starting to think I'm not any better."

"What happens if we can't get Geraldo tonight?" She shifts her weight and grips the towel tighter, her knuckles starting to whiten.

"We make him *think* we are working on....*expanding* my bloodline. Then when he drops his guard, knowing his and my father's legacy is safe, we end him.

"First, a fake wedding. And now fake babies." She shoots me two thumbs up. "Good plan."

I sigh and take off the stupid hat, running my hands through my slickened hair. "Would it really be so bad if this were real?" The vulnerability in my voice is unnerving, and she notices.

She always notices me, the *real* me.

Shaking her head, she says, "No. It wouldn't be. But my soul belongs to Liam, so I wouldn't ever be able to give you that part of me. My heart? Yeah. I think I could give you that one day... but my soul is his and always will be." She spins on her heel and leaves me there in the pool.

Without turning around she shouts out, "Make sure you add wedding planner to the list of titles you hold with me. My captor, my protector, designer...my trainer..." She ticks off on her fingers. *The sass.* I fucking love it. Those words stung to hear but the fact that she admitted to feeling something more than lust towards me, has me feeling all sorts of fucking amazing.

"And in a few hours, your *husband*," I shout on a laugh.

She flips me the bird in her retreat, her ring gloriously sparkling in the sun.

Now, let's plan this wedding.

CHAPTER 24

MADISON

MY HANDS SHAKE as the hairstylist, Cindy, slides the last bobby pin into my hair. She has successfully completed a beautiful half-up half-down look. Full of big curls, volume, and Swarovski crystals. The bruises around my neck are barely visible with the work of these amazing makeup artists. Rita and Lucas have turned me into a freakin goddess. My eyes are lined with charcoal and smoked out just enough for that perfect bridal look.

I mean, it's all perfect. Down to the boho tulle and lace dress. It's gorgeous. Off the shoulders and patterned with lace ivy applicants on the bodice. The entire back is open, sinking down to my tail bone. I opted to go shoeless—well, *sort of*. Pearl embellished barefoot jewelry wraps around my feet. Then of course we have *the ring*. This massive, beautiful and thoughtful ring. Tears prick at my eyes. I snag a tissue from the vanity I am sitting at and dab the corner of my eyes. *No crying. This is fake, Madison. It's all fake.*

Yet, it's everything I could want for my wedding—except it's not with Liam.

And although it's all a sham, I'm still nervous as hell. Butterflies swarm in my belly with a sense of...what?

Anticipation? Guilt over Liam churns deep down. He doesn't even know. I highly doubt Killian told him, knowing damn well how he'd react. A huge part of me felt the need to tell him. Ultimately, I decided it was for the best not to.

This isn't real.

And at the end of the day, *he* broke up with me.

Nothing I say or do now will change that fact. If anything, agreeing to a fake wedding will only drive his point about my feelings for Diego further home. *Gah. What the hell is my life right now?*

The staff add their finishing touches and leave, giving me some privacy before the ceremony begins.

A gentle knock on the door grabs my attention. Selena pops her head in, shooting me a sympathetic smile. "Mind if I come in?"

"Not at all. *Please* do"

Sel makes her way over to where I am sitting at the vanity and takes a seat next to me. She grips my shaking hands tightly in hers. "I don't have to tell you that my brother has legitimate feelings for you. I think you already know that. So...these nerves may be for more than one reason. You don't have to admit it out loud to me if you don't want to, but I think, somewhere deep down, you may reciprocate those feelings. As his sister, I would be overjoyed to have you as his wife, to have you become my sister-in-law...but I've seen how you and Liam are together. Getting married to my brother doesn't have to change that. All will go back to the way it was before this mess." Her eyes raise to meet mine. Her features giving her away. Even she isn't convinced by her own statement.

A lone tear escapes the corner of my eye before I can dab at it. "Liam doesn't want me anymore. He made his choice. He ended what we had for the second time, thinking he knows what's best for me. I don't think he'll ever give me the chance to be his again. And I know it's because he loves me. That man loves me more than anything. He's doing this because he wants to give me a better shot at life, but he's wrong. My life was and is nothing without him. You're right when you said I have some sort of feelings for your brother. But it's not the same way I love Liam. It's a connection I can't describe, and I've tried to resist it. One of the fears I have is that if I marry your brother, something inside of me will break a little bit more. The part of me that put up a barrier so he couldn't ever get too close."

Sel lifts the corner of her lips into a small smile. "He's not a bad guy, my brother. His heart is really big. And between you and I—I've never seen him this way. You've enchanted him, Maddy," she says in a sigh. "I wish he never included you in this. You and Liam have a connection you could never deny. And ultimately, I think what you share is a soul connection. Two souls like yours will always find their way back. Diego might just be what you needed in this part of your life. And since you can't change the past, what if you actually embraced this?"

Another knock sounds at the door. "It's Killian. I was sent to walk you down the aisle," he says in a clipped tone from behind the door.

"Good luck. No matter how real or fake this wedding is, don't be afraid to just let yourself feel. No one but *you* needs to know what tonight means to you," Sel says in a hushed tone while giving my hand a reassuring squeeze. Killian opens the door and she pulls him in for a quick kiss before disappearing upstairs with her cousin Antonio.

Killian's eyes scan me from top to bottom as I place my veil over my face. "Fuck, Madison. You look absolutely beautiful. I'm so sorry this is how the plan is unraveling," he admits in a whisper.

"You have nothing to be sorry for. This isn't your fault, Kil. Tell me you have sorted out something with Diego. Tell me we are ending that asshole's life tonight." I search his eyes when he remains quiet.

"There's a plan, but if one thing goes astray, we are abandoning it and waiting a while. There are too many precious lives onboard. Yours, Selena's, my child's. Promise me that if shit hits the fan, you'll duck down and find a way off this yacht. Look for Conor, look for Kieran or Colin. Just get to the water. Do you hear me?"

A spike of fear paralyzes me for a second.

What are they planning?

Killian rests his palms on my shoulders and kisses my head. Where it once felt romantic, it now feels friendly and comforting. "Liam will always love you, Madison. This wedding, no matter how real or fake, could never change those feelings. You two will be together again. I know it. And he fucking knows it too."

He offers me his arm as the sound of a violin grows louder. "Ready?"

"No," I snort and roll my eyes, linking my arm around his.

IT'S a miracle we make it up those stairs to the main deck. I am shaking like a leaf. Killian rubs his thumb along my forearm, trying to calm me. I barely register his touch, my body buzzes everywhere with anxiety. The quartet is playing a beautiful rendition of *Coldplay's* A Sky Full of Stars.

All eyes are on me...one pair, specifically giving me another bout of anxiety. Geraldo's seedy black eyes lock onto me. His smug face takes in each move I make towards his nephew. I'm incredibly thankful for this veil at the moment. He can't see the absolute fear coursing through me.

Kieran and Colin are speaking in quick hushed tones before Selena slaps them with her clutch. They both chuckle before becoming stoic. My eyes continue to scan the crowd, until they meet Diego's gorgeous blues.

He looks handsome in his navy blue tuxedo. His hands are

relaxed and crossed in front of him as he watches me take baby steps down the arranged aisle. As if he's enjoying his own private joke, his lips twitch, prompting me to figure out what it is he's laughing at.

Suddenly, my anxiety goes out the window. I am already more than halfway to the flower archway they set up. The sun is setting within that archway, making it feel like I am in some parallel universe. Diego's eyes never stray from mine as I make my approach. The intensity they hold has my heart skipping a beat and my face flushing.

Killian and I make our approach, where he turns to me to lift my veil, placing a kiss on my cheek. "You've got this, love. And by the way—Kieran, Conor and Colin aren't the only ones here," he whispers.

Um. What does that mean?

Diego clasps my hand in his as Killian takes his seat next to a teary-eyed Selena. I attempt to swallow the lump in my throat. Diego raises my hand to his lips, pressing a kiss there. "You look incredible."

"Thank you," I managed to get out, over my tongue stuck on the roof of my mouth.

The officiant begins talking but I can barely make out what he's saying to the crowd. There is mostly silence and a few chuckles in response to what he said. I'm still thinking about what Killian had said, when Diego gives my hand a firm squeeze. I look up at him and then over to the officiant.

The older man hands me a black titanium wedding band, and Diego a stunning diamond eternity band. "Mr. De La Cruz, please place the ring on Madison's finger and repeat after me: I, Diego, take you Madison, to be my beloved wife. I vow to have and to hold you, to honor you, to treasure you, to be at your side through all the times of sorrow and joy, and to love and cherish you always. I promise you this until I take my last breath." He repeats each word, laying emphasis on the word love. As he slides the ring onto my finger, he blows out a silent breath. That's when I discover the moisture in his eyes.

The officiant turns towards me. "Please place the ring on Mr. De La Cruz'z finger and repeat after me. " I, Madison, take you, Diego, to be my beloved husband. I vow to have and to hold you, to honor you, to treasure you, to be at your side through all the times of sorrow and joy, and to love and cherish you always. I promise you this until I take my last breath." Stumbling, I repeat the words to a deliriously happy Diego. He can't even hide those perfect teeth of his. To any onlooker, it looks smug, but I see right past that façade. He's genuinely happy right now. Who knew the *Bone Breaker* would be such a softie for weddings.

"I now pronounce you Mr. and Mrs. De La Cruz. You may now kiss your bride, Sir."

Diego leans in, his nose and forehead touching mine. "Ask me," he demands. His minty breath and signature beachy scent overloads my senses and awakens something inside of me.

"Such an ass." I cluck my tongue. "Will you kiss me, *dear husband?*" I ask in a whisper. A hint of flirtation laces my words and it shocks me. *What does this mean for us...later? Is there going to be a later?*

He folds me into his arms and dips me as his lips come crashing down onto mine, stealing the air right out of my lungs. As if he needed it in order to survive. On a gasp at the electricity bouncing between our lips, his tongue slides in. It dances with mine as Geraldo's men hoot and holler. Some whistle. I think I hear Colin say, "Agh, for fucks sake." Fireworks explode above us, drowning out the rest of the crowd. Diego sucks my bottom lip into his mouth, grazing his teeth over it, before righting me and pulling away to stare at me. "I am nowhere near done with you, Mrs. De La Cruz. But I'd prefer not to give our guests a show." He winks.

Diego's hand snakes around my waist, holding me close to him as we make our way down the aisle. "My wife and I will be right back, we need a minute—or *twenty*. Please enjoy cocktail hour," he laughs to the crowd lightheartedly. When we reach the kitchen area, he scoops me up into his arms, and carries me downstairs to his room.

The door hasn't even had a chance to click closed before his lips are on mine again. Warm hands cup my face. He places a trail of scorching hot kisses down my neck. "Fuck, you look so good in this dress. Shame it'll end up on the floor."

"*Diego,*" I begin, but there is no conviction in my voice. His tongue slides over each of my exposed collarbones then dips down into my cleavage.

"I told you last night, the next time you asked me, you weren't going to see the side of me that held back."

"That's hardly fair..." I trail off as he pulls me closer by my ass, pressing me against his rock hard length. *Jesussss. Would it really be so horrible to want this?*

His other hand finds the zipper to my dress as his lips find mine once more. Those determined fingers lower the zipper and he slips his hand in, toying with my lace thong. "Can we just forget everything and everyone around us right now? I know you feel this too. Let go of your need for control for once. Drop that barrier and just *feel*," he says against my lips.

After a pregnant pause, I say fuck it. I grip him by his black satin lapels and unload all my frustration on him. Our lips meet again before he takes over. Little whimpers leave my mouth as he rips the veil out of my hair and backs us up to his massive bed. He slides my dress down over my hips. I grip his shoulders as he helps me step out of it. Taking a step back he admires my naked breasts and blue lace thong. I raise my hand to shield them, feeling way too exposed.

"Don't." Diego's hand gently pushes mine back down. "You're fucking perfect. Get out of your head," he insists, tapping his finger against my temple. His knuckles slowly glide over my cheek and down my neck. Goosebumps surface on my skin in

217

their wake as he moves over the swell of my breast. He squeezes my nipple between his middle and index finger, rubbing a thumb over the tip of it.

My head snaps back in pleasure. "*Mmm.*"

He leans down and picks me up by my thighs, tossing me onto the bed. "Spread those legs," he commands while tossing his tuxedo jacket onto the chair, followed by his dress shirt and tie. Diego toes off his shoes and then watches me intently as he pops the button of his pants and lowers the zipper.

I have yet to do as I was told, entirely focused on the man undressing before me. I've seen him shirtless a few times now, but nothing could prepare me for watching him drop his pants.

It's beautiful.

And I'm not joking. It's long and thick. The head of his cock already has a bead of pre-cum. He swipes at it with his thumb and then leans over me, spreading my thighs apart.

"Didn't I tell you to spread those beautiful thighs, wife?" There's a mischievous twinkle in his eyes that tells me just how excited he is to show me what I've been missing (according to him, that is). My legs fall to the sides, granting him space to lie between them. The head of his cock presses against the string of my thong. The tiny shred of fabric acting as a barrier between us. Diego presses his thumb into my mouth. "Suck, *Mariposita.*"

Swirling my tongue around his thumb, I remove the bead of cum before sucking. His cock twitches before his hips press harder into mine, sending waves of heat to my pussy. Diego removes his thumb and leans back up to standing. "Shift yourself so you are laying your head on the pillows comfortably." I do as he asks, my heart beating harder with each command. "Good girl."

He reaches into his end table and produces two fur lined, leather cuffs. Reaching up to one of the tentacles of the cast iron Kraken, he pulls down a retractable rope, like that of a dog leash.

Metal connects as the cuff slips into place. He holds out the cuff to me, waiting for my hand. "How much do you trust me?"

"Enough, or I wouldn't be here right now," I sneer playfully as he secures my hand.

He stalks around the bed and does the same with my other hand. On his way back he reaches down and grabs my veil. A look of indecision crosses his face before it's gone. Climbing up on the bed, he begins to tie the veil around my eyes so it blurs my vision. All I can see is his silhouette.

"Diego. Wait. I...I totally forgot I have my period. We can put a raincheck on this."

He straddles me, his muscular thighs caging in mine. Wet lips come down to toy with one of my nipples while his hand snakes down into my panties. I arch my back and wiggle beneath him. The throbbing between my legs is growing by the second. Each searing touch of his is heightened now that my sight has been removed and I've been restrained. "I don't give a fuck about blood, *Mariposita*. You shouldn't either," he says huskily while circling my clit with his middle finger.

"I really think we should stop—", I start to buck my hips, arching my back and pushing my breast further into his mouth. Diego growls and picks up the pace as his teeth clamp over my nipple. "*Ahh!*"

"If that's what you want..." he says, removing his hand from my panties, the elastic snapping against me, increasing my sensations.

"Ugh," I sigh. "You sure have a way of getting what you want."

"What we both want." He presses my cheeks together until my lips pucker like a fish. "That mouth of yours. I can't wait to fuck it. I *should* fuck the sass right out of it—except we are on a bit of a time crunch. My nipples harden at the visual of his vulgar words.

"Mmm. I knew you'd like that. I saw your reaction to me and Red on our flight here."

"Don't you think you should keep another woman out of the conversation while you are trying to bed your new wife?" I say bitterly.

"You're right, my apologies, Mrs. De La Cruz. In fact, I am going to show you just how sorry I am..."

CHAPTER 25

DIEGO

GRIPPING her panties with my teeth, I slide them down and over her legs. Luckily, she doesn't use this moment to kick me in the face. Sliding back up her perfect body, I settle my hips between her thighs and reach between us, teasing her clit in slow lazy circles. Her little whimpers make me harder than I ever thought imaginable. I lean over to kiss her while grabbing a few tissues from the end table. Leaving them next to me, I reach between her legs and slide my finger through her slit until I find the string. She gasps, knowing damn well my intentions. Before she has room to argue about doing it herself, I tug the string and remove her tampon, diligently wrapping it in the tissues and tossing it into the trash bin.

"Diego De La Cruz!" my wife shouts, shocked. *My wife— damn. Too bad that it will be short lived. If I could, I would make her mine forever.*

Crawling up her body, I silence her with my mouth and line the head of my cock up to her entrance. Teasingly, I inch in. Her sexy little moan against my lips lets me know she's with me. *See, that thing about trust?* She willingly gave it to me. Her trust, her need for control. Her body and mind both want this. It was Liam that always held her back, and now that he's no longer in the picture...Her pussy greedily molds around my cock and she shifts her pelvis to accommodate more of me. My little butterfly hasn't said one word or tried to buck me off her. I always knew we would both cave and give in to our temptations. Ironically enough, it's on our wedding night. With haste, I untie and remove the veil. I need to see those gorgeous brown eyes when I enter her fully.

Pressing home, she lets out a breathy moan, her eyes glued to mine as I become fully seated. *"Ocean Eyes,"* she sighs. "This feels...I've wanted to know what this felt like since you cut open my clothes on the island." Her cheeks redden, admitting to what I already knew.

A laugh escapes me at her admission. *Trust me, baby. Me too.* It feels like heaven being inside her. She's so warm and tight, and right now, she's all mine and I am hers. Reaching up, I unclasp her bindings and guide her hands around my neck. "I need to tell you something," I confess while thrusting into her at a leisurely pace. If this is the only chance I get to be intimate with her, then I damn well am going to enjoy every second of it. Madison's breathing picks up with each thrust. Her perfect tits rise and fall, pressing up against me on each inhale.

"Tell me," she whispers, bringing her hand up to cup my face. Her thumb rubs my cheek and she gives me a shy smile.

"I love you, Madison. I think I fell in love with you before I even took you captive. All the stories Selena would tell me about you, they made me crazy about you...and I didn't even know you." My pace picks up as I hook an arm under her thigh, changing the angle to get even deeper.

A tear drips down her cheek. "I *want* to love you, Diego. I just..."

"I know, baby. *Shush.* I've got you. Let me love you for as long as we have. I'll take whatever you are willing to give me in return. Because having some of you is better than not having you at all. If tomorrow never comes, I'll die happy knowing you gave me a chance."

"Whatever Liam didn't take along with him is yours. For however long that may be."

"What happened to not talking about other people we've fucked while I'm bedding you?" I smirk, throwing her words back at her.

"*Touché.*" She giggles while lifting her hips to meet mine. *Fuck me*, her pussy is gripping my cock like a vice. *I've never had this problem in the past, but I'm certain I won't last long. I've had blue balls every damn day—minus Red—which doesn't count. It wasn't the flight attendant I was getting off to, it was Madison. And let me tell ya, having the real deal? Holy fuck...*

Lowering myself over her I claim her lips. This time she takes over, opening up to me and putting equal— if not more— passion into this kiss. I thrust harder and faster as she gets closer to her climax. I'm right there with her, about to explode inside her. When her panting becomes staccato and squeaky, and her pussy clenches even tighter, I fucking lose it. I pump into her until my ribs are screaming as well as the both of us. My back stings from her nails digging into its flesh. Sweat, blood and cum stick between our bodies. Where most people would find that disgusting and even gruesome...I'd call it a beautiful mess.

Sort of like us.

Like a little blood bothers me? Psh. You remember who you're talking to? *The goddamn Bone Breaker.*

This feels like a dream. And if so, I don't want to wake up. Because in *this* dream—I actually get the girl. I collapse next to her and pull her into me, placing a kiss to her shoulder blade. "Are you okay?"

"Mhmmm. That was...*yeah*, I wasn't expecting that. I wasn't expecting to have sex with you at all, honestly."

A hum of approval slips past my lips. Jesus...I'm acting like I got laid for the first time. *Fuck, I feel amazing. Giddy, almost.*

This feeling is...incredible. She is incredible. "Which part? The part where I tied you to the bed? Or the part where I told you I loved you?"

"Both. And a few other moments in between." She scrunches her eyebrows together and nods to the trash bin. I smirk against the soft skin of her shoulder and cradle her closer to me, basking in the calmness and warmth of this moment. *The question is... how do I make it last longer?*

"Come, lets get showered and make our way back upstairs. Our guests will be waiting on us to start dinner.

On a sigh she nods, gets up, and tosses her dress onto the couch. Her eyes go wide when she sees the mess we made on my black satin sheets.

Let's call it art.

"Don't worry about that. Get out of your head, *Mariposita*. That doesn't bother me whatsoever. The staff will have that changed before we head to bed. Also, your second wedding dress is in my walk in, I tilt my head in the direction of the closet.

"Thank you," she says while making a bee-line for the shower. I can't help but enjoy the view as she waddles there, keeping her thighs squeezed together, which creates cute little dimples on each of her ass cheeks. *I want to bite them.*

I give her a minute of privacy before I join her. Coconut scented soap suds are scattered across her gorgeous breasts and toned stomach. She's straining her neck back, careful not to get her hair or face wet, still wanting to preserve it for the rest of the party. Wrapping an arm around her waist, I spin her around and pull her close to me, placing a kiss on her swollen lips.

"God willing, when Geraldo and his men are at the bottom of the Aegean Sea, and this is all over, you'll consider staying married to me.

She stays quiet while grabbing the bar of soap. Only when she starts to lather me does she look up and say, "*Diego.*"

I reach out to cup her face and kiss her again before rinsing off and leaving her to finish up. "Oh, and just so you know, you're sleeping in here from now on."

"And if I say no?" One of her eyebrows raise in playful defiance.

"Then I sleep where *you* sleep." I shrug. Because it's true. I'd sleep on the fucking floor if that's where she was. A genuine smile creeps its way to her lips as I close the bathroom door. I shake my head at the turn of events.

I may actually have a shot at keeping my wife. Hope blooms in my chest at the possibility.

But then again—you know what they say about hope, right? '*It breeds eternal misery.*'"

WE REGROUP WITH OUR GUEST, walking out onto the makeshift dance floor. I had party planners come aboard and cover the pool with plexiglass. The quartet begins playing a song I requested for our first dance. I pull my wife into me, taking her hand in mine and placing my other at her waist. The two singers, one male, one female, begin Michael Buble's *Close Your Eyes*. Madison cocks her head to the side and raises her eyebrows, recognizing the song. We float across the dance floor, ignoring the myriad of looks from the crowd. Some ranging from confused, to angry, to finding this moment downright comical—even borderline pathetic.

Fuck 'em.

Seeing Madison's reaction to the lyrics is *exactly* why I chose this song.

I lower my voice so only she can hear, bringing my lips close to her ear as we sway back and forth as the song starts to close out. "I meant what I said. After all of this, I hope you will consider staying with me. But if there is not a tomorrow for me, fly as far away from all of this as you can. Build the life *you* want.

Not your family. Not Liam. If you don't want to become a nurse. Don't. Do what makes *you* happy, baby. Life is precious. It's short."

Her delicate hands grip my shoulder blades as I back her up to the edge of the yacht. Confusion settles into her features at my change in demeanor. I spot Killian standing by the kitchen, Selena isn't with him. *Good.* He gives me a subtle nod.

I clasp her face in my hands and kiss her hard. Memorizing her scent, her lips, her heartbeat against mine. "Spread those wings, beautiful and fly." I push her over the back of the yacht as all hell breaks loose.

Gunshots go off as fireworks paint the night sky. One by one Geraldo's men drop like the annoying, blood sucking flies they are. Antonio is shuffling the remaining staff and crew to the back of the deck where they can get to safety. In our absence, I had the majority of them get on the boat we use to transport food and goods. If anyone was to ask, they were going to retrieve items for the wedding.

I take down as many fuckers as I can with my hands. Killian's men have already taken out the majority of them.

My eyes scan the crowd for my uncle. He's not on the main deck. I jog towards the main cabin, and look for him there, cursing as I come up empty. Anxiety blooms in my chest as I check the bedrooms and come up empty. *Again.*

Christ, this isn't good.

I only have a few minutes before we have to abandon this yacht. Ice runs through my veins as I climb to the upper level and not a soul is to be found.

COÑO.

That's when something, rather, *someone* catches my eye on the helipad. I jog the stairs, knowing time is certainly not on our side. With my glock out I step out onto the platform. Geraldo is there with his right hand man Mateo. Mateo has his gun trained on me as Geraldo's presses into Madison's skull.

226

The old man sneers, "I must say, you have a faithful *little wife* here. The girl came scrambling back looking like a washed up siren." He shoves Madison forward. "How fortunate I was to find her there in the stairwell."

"*Definitely* a siren with that mouth on her," Mateo contributes. I take a few cautious steps towards her.

"Diego," she cries. "I couldn't leave you. I couldn't. I'm sorry."

Geraldo raises his gun and pistol whips her. She flops over, her wet white dress clinging to her lifeless body. Blood rushes to my ears, muffling them. All I see is red. Rage boils in my chest as my finger inches closer to the trigger. I raise my gun to kill my fucking uncle when blood splatters my face and sprays Madison's dress crimson.

No.

Pain ricochetes through my body as I stumble towards her.

No. Not like this.

CHAPTER 26

MADISON

NO. *No. No.*

That bastard! How could he? I surface from the water, spluttering and treading water. Strong hands grip me by both arms and pull me over the edge of a boat.

"Calm down, lass. I've got you." It takes me a second to recognize Conor's voice. Instead of the rational thing to do, like catch my breath and relax, knowing I'm safe, I free myself and dive back into the water.

"What in the hell are ya doing, Madison?!" Conor bellows from behind me.

I swim as fast as I can in this damn dress until I reach the ladder on the hydraulic platform at the back of the yacht. Adrenaline courses through me as I arrive at the top, discovering the carnage before me. I don't recognize any as our own which gives me a brief moment of relief. The deck is a total blood bath, littered in bodies and empty shells. Bending down, I grab a pistol from one of the deceased. An eerie clanking noise fills the space around me as the gun rattles against my wedding ring. Tremor after tremor ripple through my muscles, stiffening my body.

I do a quick scan of the kitchen area, which appears empty. Holding the gun close to my chest, I pad my way up the stairs to the upper deck. As I reach the top step my breath catches in my throat when wrinkled hands grip the back of my neck.

"Drop the gun, now or your head will be blown off," Geraldo threatens.

I contemplate not listening, then think better of it and do as I'm told. I refuse to go down like this. *I'll find another way.* Another set of hands grip the back of my arms. A sweaty man with a missing pinky shoves me up the rest of the steps. I stumble a few times over my soaking dress. The man isn't having it and lifts me by my elbows, carrying me the rest of the way up. Geraldo and his henchman force me up the next set of stairs to the helipad. This time I collect my dress in a ball at my sides, careful not to trip.

Blood rushes to my ears, making me dizzy. *Calm down, Madison. You aren't of any use if you pass out.* Geraldo forces me to my knees, the metal of his gun pressing firmly against my temple.

I take a deep breath in, in an attempt to steady my breathing and try and calm the fuck down. *Focus. Look around, what is here for you to use to at least get away? Nothing. There isn't anything up here. Fuck. Those self defense lessons would have come in handy right about now.*

That's when I see *him*. In the stairwell. Those blue eyes swirl with anger and horror at the same time. The deadliest of storms brews behind them as he takes in the visual of me on my knees with his uncle's gun to my head. His finger twitches around the trigger of his own.

As if enjoying a sport, knowing he may have just won, Geraldo sneers, "I must say, you have a faithful *little wife* here. The girl came scrambling back, looking like a washed up siren." My palms smack the teakwood as I'm forced forward by the vile man. "How fortunate I was to find her there in the stairwell," he drawls.

"*Definitely* a siren with that mouth on her," his foul accomplice adds.

Diego takes a few calculated steps my way. The sight of *El Rompe Huesos* is absolutely terrifying. His posture has changed to the exact reason the underworld fears him.

I barely recognize him.

The pupils of his eyes have dilated and the Diego I know behind them has gone cold. Dark blue iris' have deepened to almost black. Ever come face to face with a shark? *Ya, me neither. But I watch a lot of Shark Week, okay?* Diego looks exactly like that.

Bloodthirsty.

He's going to go down fighting, until his last breath. There is no way in hell he'll let his uncle kill me. *Goddamnit.* He has to know if he were to die right now, that I wouldn't have ever abandoned him.

How could he think that? After all of this? He did exactly what Liam did to me. He didn't give me a choice. And he pushed me off the back of the fucking yacht! *These men! How is it okay for them to sacrifice themselves for me? But not let me do the same?*

"Diego," I cry out. "I couldn't leave you. I couldn't. I'm sorry." My voice trembles as the words leave my mouth. His eyes soften for the briefest of seconds.

My own go wide as I see a shadowy figure behind him. I don't even get the chance to warn him.

Pain and darkness engulf me.

It's becoming quite a trend with me lately.

Ugh.

CHAPTER 27

LIAM

SMOKE CURLS around the silencer of my gun as the smell of blood and gunpowder litter my nose. Of all people, *Diego De La Fucking Cruz'* blood has to splatter my face.

He stumbles forward on impact, as his uncle smacks the deck with a thud, right next to my whole world—who is currently unconscious at the moment.

Spots of blood speckle her white wedding dress. Slowly, the fabric darkens as Geraldo's pool of blood begins to dye the rest of it. The sight makes me sick to my stomach for so many other reasons than the fact that my girl has a goddamn wedding dress on. Not only that, but Diego failed to keep her safe like he promised he would. A pop goes off in my left ear as Killian takes out Mateo, Geraldo's right hand man.

Blood gushes from the wound in Diego's right shoulder. He reaches for his gun but Killian is quick to step on his injured arm. "I wouldn't try it, mate." Kil glances at his watch and then shoots me a panicked look. "Get her off this yacht. *Now.*"

"Ya better be right behind me, brother," I warn.

He nods his head in response and then squats down, getting closer to Diego. "I know that you are my future brother-in- law and all that..." He looks over at Madison's lifeless body. "And

Madison has grown rather...*fond* of you, but what got her into this mess in the first place should have never occurred. *We don't bring women into our wars, Diego.* You're no better than your father or dead uncle for that."

I gather Madison up in my arms. Her head flops backwards and her arms hang at her sides. My heart breaks seeing her like this, knowing that it isn't entirely Diego's fault. Yes, it is his fault we are on a yacht right now in the middle of the Aegean Sea. Yes, it's his fault for kidnapping my woman and plotting an entire scheme to get my brother to help him. In the end, it's mine and Killian's fault for bringing Madison into this life in the first place.

The only credit I'll give Diego is that he *tried* to protect Maddy from all of this bloodshed. I watched him push her off the back of the boat. *It's not his fault Madison is so thickheaded.*

That was the plan we all agreed on. Killian, Diego, and I. We created it just hours before the ceremony. The ceremony I had to endure in agony from a hidden door in the kitchen cabinets. There's nothing quite like watching the woman you love marrying one of the most violent and arrogant men in the underworld. Even beyond that, watching her kiss him with something more than her desire to help this assignment. *And then,* to watch your woman leave and head off to his bedroom, knowing that he'd consummate the marriage given the chance.

Killian can't find it in him to look past his future brother-in-law's actions, which is why Diego was used as collateral in killing his uncle. I personally wasn't ready to kill him just yet. But the opportunity presented itself. *Not that we had much of an option to begin with.* Geraldo had a gun pressed to my girl's head. So I made sure to choose a spot on Diego that wouldn't be fatal. It certainly was fatal for his uncle. Bullet went right through *The Bone Breaker's* shoulder and into Geraldo's heart.

When I heard about the wedding—against Killian's better judgment in telling me—I pretty much lost it. It took Colin, Con, and Kieran tackling me down to the ground on *The Triquetra* to prevent me from leaving. I was fully prepared to head into town and slaughter Geraldo and his men myself. That way, Madison would never even get the chance to marry this arsehole right here. Lowering my head I glance down at him, almost—*almost*, feeling sorry for the poor fucker.

Ya honestly can't blame him for falling for Madison. We all did. I mean who wouldn't?

Madison stirs in my arms. I tuck her in close to me, walking past Killian and towards the stairs.

"Quite frankly, I should leave you on your own yacht to be blown up to bits. I don't like you, Diego. But, my father taught me to be a fair leader, therefore I am giving you a choice."

Madison's eyes flutter open and she looks up at me, confused as fuck. "Ow," she says, rubbing her head. Diego and Killian snap their heads our way. And for a split second, I realize one thing. We are all in love with Madison. She has bewitched each of us in one way or another. It would fucking devastate her if we leave Diego on this yacht to die. She'll never forgive any of us for it. Not that I deserve her forgiveness. I broke up with her for the second time.

"*Madison,*" Kil and Diego say in unison.

She swivels her head to look at them and then to Geraldo in a pool of his own blood. "Holy shit," she rasps. Looking at me, she smiles gently. "I think I can stand."

"You were hit in the head pretty hard, love. I'd rather hold you—plus, we *really* need to get going."

Diego uses that moment to punch Killian, breaking his nose. Blood gushes over his teeth as my brother groans in agony. *The Bone Breaker* gets to his feet and rushes toward us. "Get her off this fucking yacht, Liam! Go!"

Killian get's his shit together and fires another round into Diego's thigh. He screams out, falling before us, huffing and coughing against the wood of the deck. Simultaneously, Madison screams a blood curdling scream and squirms her body until I release her.

Handing the gun to Diego, Kil says, "Your two choices are: manage to get off your yacht before it blows up, or kill yourself before then." He looks down at his watch. "You have another ten minutes to decide. Madison stumbles to Diego's side and presses her hand over his leg wound.

He hisses at the pressure. "Madison. *Don't.* You're wasting time. *Dale.* Get the fuck off this yacht. Right now!" he grits out.

"I'm staying. If that's how the two of you are going to end this, then I'm staying. We—*I* didn't just go through all of this for Diego to end up dead. He's a good man. He's just like the both of you. I know this is part of your work. It's part of war and the nature of the underworld, but you two are just like Diego. Deep down in those testosterone driven bodies are big soft hearts." She looks up at Killian. "Your future wife would never forgive you if you do this. She's like me. She *will* find out. And by some chance she didn't find out, you would end up telling her. The guilt would eat you alive, Kil."

Killian runs a hand through his hair. He's contemplating. "Your child will not forgive you for killing their uncle," Madison continues.

Diego looks at Madison in shock. "Sel is pregnant?"

"Yes." She wipes his forehead of the blood and brushes his sweat drenched hair off his face.

Kil still hasn't said a word. He's just watching the interaction between Madison and Diego.

"This isn't you, Kil," she says grilling him. Maddy turns her head my way, her eyes filled with unshed tears. "Or you," her voice cracks as she speaks. "Don't do this. Let's put this all past us. Let Diego run a brand new syndicate. Make peace with each other. You're going to be family now. A child is coming into this world with the blood that runs through all of your veins."

I look down at my watch. *Fuck.* "She's right, Killian. I'm not leaving him here. We all played a role in Madison ending up here. Let's deal with this when we get off this fucking death trap." Killian snaps out of wherever he was and scoops Madison up.

"Killian!" she screams, panic lacing her voice.

"Grab Diego, will ya?" He shakes his head, clearly wondering if Madison is right or realizing she bewitched him again. Either way, I am happy with this. I don't think I would have been able to leave Diego here to die, regardless of what my brother had wanted. Although, I don't think he would have been able to go through with it. Knowing damn well his future wife would hate him. Madison would hate him, and perhaps one day his future child would too.

I help Diego up to standing and hoist him over my shoulder. With haste, I descend the staircase. Killian and Madison are already down the second flight, leading back through the kitchen and out to the main deck. We are almost to the bottom when I slip on blood. Diego and I fall forward, sending him and I tumbling down the remaining stairs.

"Fuuuuuck," he moans out his obvious pain. I'm sure his ribs are still killing him, and he just landed on the side of his body with the bullet holes. Part of me feels satisfied knowing he's in pain. *I just hope he'll survive his wounds—for Madison's sake.*

"Come on, mate. Up ya go." I find my balance and try to hoist him back up. This time is a lot harder getting him to stand. "If you could, perhaps, move a little faster, that would be lovely," I growl.

I use all the strength I have to get him up, but he's a decent sized mother-fucker—and right now—he's pretty much dead weight. He tries walking a few steps on his own, out of pride, but stumbles. "*Fuck.* Just go, man. You don't have much time. Madison needs you. Don't waste another minute trying to save me. Give Sel a kiss for me and tell her I'm sorry."

Sweat drips down onto my watch as I check the time. We

have two minutes to get from here, across the deck and onto the boat Conor has waiting for us. We also need to get as far away from this fucking yacht as possible before the bomb goes off. The minute they said 'I do' we had Seb set the timer.

Diego knew he would only have a little bit of time to get himself off the yacht. Of course no one planned on Madison going on a suicide mission, or for Killian to change plans last minute and decide to kill Diego.

"Madison will be devastated if you don't come back with me. I can't do that to her. Cause as much as I fucking hate to admit it, you mean something to her. I won't be the reason she grieves another loss. If we go out, we go out together."

Bending over, I manage to get my arm under him and start dragging his arse across the deck. When we get to the back of the yacht, I once again toss him over my shoulder and lower myself down the ladder. Conor helps me get Diego into the boat and eases him down to the floor.

We all lose our balance as Killian takes off like a bat out of hell. I haul Madison to me and cover her and Diego with my body as the heat and power of the blast slam into us. Diego's yacht goes up in flames as we manage to escape by the skin of our teeth. Conor lets out a low whistle.

"*Jesus*. That was close," Killian murmurs, navigating us back to *The Triquetra*.

I lean back, giving Madison and Diego room to breathe. Madison looks back at the devastation and throws a hand over her mouth. Fireworks go off as the flames lick the remainder of the sinking yacht.

"Oh my God," she sobs. She doesn't allow herself to waste much time at all, refocusing her attention onto Diego. She jumps into action, grabbing me by my belt buckle and pulling me to her. She starts to undo it and my mind goes wild. So does my cock—but we aren't really in the right place to be getting naked. With a crack, she pulls the leather loose from the belt loops. Her hair whips me in the face as she drops down and uses it as a tourniquet for his leg.

"You shouldn't have come back," Diego rasps through gritted teeth. Loud enough for all of us to hear over the hum of the engine and the insane firework show.

"Agreed," Conor chimes in.

"You could have been killed," Killian says patronizingly.

"What the fuck were you thinking, baby?" I add, my voice thick with anxiety and emotion.

Madison whips her head around so fast, her fervid gaze landing on each of us. I'm not entirely sure she's even human for a moment. Her eyes hold so much heat, we are all about to go up in flames—*just like Diego's yacht.* Except this explosion—will be far worse. *Trust me.*

"Are you all serious right now? You couldn't *possibly* be serious," Madison laughs murderously. "I *chose* to be part of this life. First with Liam, then with Killian, then with Liam *again*, and now to help Diego—even if I didn't choose to be taken. Regardless. I chose to help. I chose to love and I chose to stay. For *all* of you. It's my fucking choice. If I want to face danger to protect the ones I love, then so be it. Life is about choices, and I do not for one second regret being a part of all of yours. My life was dull before all of this. I'm not saying I enjoy all the violence or my body taking a beating. But the relationships I've created and the sense of purpose I've found throughout all of this has been worth it. I finally feel like I know who I am. And I wouldn't change that for anything." When she remains silent, we all do as well. Most likely processing her words and trying to analyze them.

That speech was moreso for her than it was for us. I'm proud of the woman she's become. It makes me love her even more. This woman is fucking incredible.

She truly is.

If she is willing to stay, I wonder if she'll be willing to forgive me for being so reckless and stupid with her love? I sure as hell don't deserve it, but I desperately need it. I've needed her since the moment we met. She is and always will be the one who fought the darkness away. I've gotten so used to her light, I don't even want to imagine my life without her in it.

I thought I was doing the right thing by letting her go. *Again.*

But I was so fucking wrong.

CHAPTER 28

DIEGO

WE ARE all getting settled in on Killian's yacht. They have their medical team tending to my wounds in a guest room on the lower deck. We have decided to stay anchored, as to not immediately give ourselves away. *Pontus* is still blazing as we speak. The Greek Coast Guard has responded and is attempting to put out the fire. We made sure that there were excessive amounts of fireworks below deck. If anyone looked too deeply, they would come to realize that wedding fireworks were the most likely cause of the explosion. The type of bomb they used won't be discovered. Not after they finally manage to get the blaze under control.

Relief floods me as I am thankful to be alive. I don't know where Madison and I stand right now. And that's eating at me. I haven't seen her since we got back on their yacht. After her speech, she didn't so much as whisper another word to anyone on the way back.

Killian fucking hates me, but he' going to be my brother-in-law. So, for Selena's sake, we need to find a way to make peace. We didn't go through all of this to become enemies. If I am going to be leading my syndicate in a new direction, I want to start without any additional enemies.

Liam, well... I am incredibly thankful for him. He had no reason to help me off that yacht. *Hell, if roles were reversed, I don't know if I would have.*

Yet he did.

He did it because we are in love with the same woman. He did it to protect Madison from losing someone she cares about. I can't say *love*, because she made that clear tonight that she doesn't feel that way about me. But, there is something more than affection between us...or she wouldn't have risked her life to come back to me. Especially since I pushed her off the back of the yacht. It would be a very dangerous thing for me to hope she loved me in return.

"Sir, we are going to have to get you to a hospital. These bullet wounds are too extensive to fix here."

"I don't think that is going to be possible for a little while," I say hesitantly.

The door of the bedroom opens and my heart jumps in hopes it would be my wife.

"Oh, Diego." Selena's voice floats across the room. "Thank God you're alive," she sobs, crossing the room to wrap her arms around me.

I place a kiss on her head and pat her back with my good arm. "I have Madison and Liam to thank for that," I laugh. "When were you planning on telling me you're pregnant?" I whisper.

Her tear-stained face greets mine. A gentle smile spreads across it. "Who let the cat out of the bag?"

"*My wife.*"

"Ahh. *Your wife.* You really couldn't find any other way to get Geraldo distracted? You had to marry her? You know that it won't last, Diego. She's back where she belongs." *Ouch.* My bruised ego hurts worse than my injuries.

"I didn't have much of a choice. Geraldo forced my hand."

"Sure he did. You're *El Rompe Huesos.* You couldn't have

242

negotiated another way around a wedding?" She pinches my nose and shoots me a stern look. "We always have a choice —right?"

My sister. Just like my mother in so many ways. The thought of my mamá makes my heart crack more than my sister's words. *She's right.* Madison is back here with Liam. Geraldo is dead. I am the new leader. My time with Madison is slowly creeping to an end. I lean my head back against the pillows and close my eyes.

"You're going to be an uncle, Diego," Sel says softly, tucking her hand in mine. She'll never admit it, but she gets it. My feelings for Madison.

I squeeze her hand. "I'm happy for you, Sel. Although, I don't think your *betrothed* likes me very much." I leave out the part where he was going to leave me for dead. No use making my sister upset. Killian and I will have to have a discussion soon. I can put it behind me if he is willing to. Our two families are too entwined now to not bury the hatchet.

"He'll have to get over that. We are family," she huffs, mirroring my feelings.

I shrug and then regret it. *Fuck that hurts.* "We'll see."

His ears must have been ringing, because the Irish prick himself walks in, Madison hot on his heels. "How is everything going in here?" he addresses the team of doctors.

"We will need to move him to a local hospital to treat his injuries. The bullets caused some damage to muscle and bone, and that will need to be treated in an OR under anesthesia," the older male doctor says.

Killian crosses his arms over his chest and sighs. "I'm not sure that is possible right now."

"There has to be some way we can get him to a hospital, Killian," Madison urges. She's changed into something less macabre. Black sweatpants and an oversized hoodie hide her beautiful curves from me. I grind my teeth, holding back jealousy that they are probably Liam's. The makeup, blood and grime have been cleaned off her. Her raven colored hair is wet and tied up in a messy bun.

Stunning.

I want so badly to pull her to me and kiss her. No fucks given who's around to witness it.

She's my wife—after all.

I'd wrap her up in my arms and tuck her head under my chin. The need to hold her overwhelms me, my chest feels tight having her so close and not being able to reach out to her.

I almost lost her.

Watching Geraldo press a gun to her head awakened a fear in me I never knew existed. I've never felt pure, raw, fear the way I did watching him hold her life in his hands. I knew I wouldn't be able to get to him without her getting shot. I'd gladly have taken my uncle's bullet if I knew I wouldn't die right there. The thought haunted me, knowing if I didn't make it, there wasn't a damn thing anyone could do to help her from the same fate—or worse.

My breathtaking little butterfly has sacrificed so much for me, for my family. I'll never truly be able to thank her. But you bet your ass I'll damn well try.

"What if we make these look more like shrapnel injuries and less like bullet wounds. You can say you pulled me and Madison out of the water while heading back to your yacht?" I recommend, knowing just how badly that will hurt.

The head doctor thinks on it for a minute. "It could work. It will be extremely painful. We don't have the proper pain management here to help you."

"Do it."

"*Diego.* There must be another way," Sel reasons.

"No. This is crazy. Is there a way to keep his wounds protected and we can get on a private flight home?" Madison argues. It does make me curious as to *where* she now considers home.

"There is a greater risk of him bleeding out and infection if we go that route," the doctor sighs, walking over to me and lifting the bandages and gauze covering my thigh. He covers me with a light sheet. "The shoulder needs surgery. Luckily we were able to stop the bleeding. The wound on his leg grazed his femoral artery. Madison's quick thinking with the tourniquet saved his life."

My eyes drift to hers as the doctor continues talking. My wife is focused on the doctor, taking in every bit of information. Her brows are pushed together and she's biting the tip of her thumb nail. Both arms are crossed over her chest and her fingers are clenched into tight fists. Her rings catch my attention, glistening in the light. *She's still wearing my rings.* I'm not listening to a damn thing the doctor is saying, way too preoccupied by how adorable and concerned she looks right now.

"My apprehension would be due to the pressure on the plane. He could bleed out over the Atlantic before you even got home. It would be best to receive treatment here and recover before heading back to the States."

I catch the tail end of the conversation. "Fuck it. Let's go back. I'll take my chances."

Madison angles her body to look at me. "That's a big risk, Diego."

"How about we flip a coin. Leave it to chance. Heads we stay, tails we go."

"This isn't a fucking football coin toss, *Ocean Eyes.* This is your life." She rolls her eyes at me, her cheeks flushing with anger. Of course I noticed her flinch slightly, realizing she slipped in calling me that nickname in front of everyone. Hearing her call me that has the blood rushing below this sheet and giving me a semi.

"Who's got a coin?" I ask as my little butterfly shoots daggers at me.

I shoot her a wink just to push her buttons. She'll probably stick her tongue out at me in three..two...*There ya go.* Her tongue darts out at me as her eyes narrow. *Sassy as ever, I see.*

"I do." Liam strolls in, looking clean and refreshed as well. He reaches into his pocket and tosses it to me. I catch it with my good hand.

"Thanks." I place the coin in Madison's hand, folding her fingers around it and rest mine on top of hers. "Okay, *Mariposita.* Heads we go to the hospital. Tails we go *home*— wherever that is for you. I told you. Where you sleep, I sleep." I smirk.

Killian groans his disapproval as Liam lets out a similar sound.

"*Oh dios mío,*" Selena sighs, pinching the bridge of her nose.

Madison stares at me for a second before turning back to Killian. "Can Diego be transported back to New York to heal? Would we be able to do the surgery at home? That way, Sel can remain in the comfort and safety of her own home as he recovers?"

He contemplates a moment before nodding his head and pulling Selena close to him, wrapping his arms protectively around her stomach. Sel places a sweet kiss on his cheek.

Letting out a sigh, Madison holds the coin out between her and I, then tosses it in the air before catching it and slapping it on the top of her hand. Everyone creeps forward to take a look.

Madison's eyes go wide. She looks down at the coin and then those gorgeous brown eyes meet mine. "Tails."

I flash her a dazzling smile, making her cheeks flush for an entirely different reason. It's not enough. I need to see that beautiful smile of hers. So I decide to break out into song.

"'*Start spreadin' the news... I'm leavin' today... I want to be a part of it...*'"

Liam covers his face, mumbling, "Oh for fucks sake."

"Easy there. *New York is mine*," Killian says, actually cracking a smile.

Both Madison and Selena break out into laughter, before gripping each other and sighing. The two of them failing miserably at trying to collect themselves.

"Don't quit your day job, Diego." Madison chuckles.

CHAPTER 29

LIAM

IT'S ONLY BEEN an hour since our flight took off from Mykonos and somehow I've managed to stay sober. Alcohol is part of this lifestyle, but I tend to overindulge when shit gets heavy. It's been excruciating to say the least, watching Madison dote over Diego. The second the pilot gave the green light for us to move around the cabin, her seatbelt was off and she was in the bedroom with him. I'm not sure if it was for my sake or not, but she was gracious enough to leave the door open. The whispering and laughing is getting under my skin though.

For fucks sake he's the Bone Breaker. He'll be fine. Why is she coddling him? Perhaps she's using this as a way to avoid talking to me.

I haven't made any moves to check up on them, sitting my arse in this chair and letting Maddy come to me when she's ready. We have a lot to discuss and the flight home doesn't seem like the ideal place for that—especially since her *husband* is in the other room.

My hands find their way into my hair at the mention of the word husband. Tell me how I proposed to my woman just a few days ago—which feels like an eternity ago—and now she's married to one of the worst criminals the underworld has ever had? *Fuck.* I grip my scalp to the point of pain in an attempt to bring me back to the present moment.

Lainey, Conor, and one of Killian's doctors are taking Diego's jet home to New York with us. Killian, Selena, Colin and Kieran are taking our jet home right behind us. Diego's cousin Antonio stayed behind to make sure we didn't raise any red flags. He'll make sure to tie up any loose ends in regards to our visit.

Killian wanted to leave Conor behind as well, but I gave him hell over it. Honestly, I need my best friend around these next few weeks. *And I told him that.* Hurt flickered in his eyes before the mask came back and he just nodded in approval. My brother used to be my person the way Conor is now. After everything that happened with Madison, I think he's changed, and I'm not sure I'll ever view my brother as my best friend again. Not in the way I did before all of this.

Kil and I may be on "better" terms, but I'm still pissed at him for not putting a stop to Madison having to marry that fucker. To top it off, my brother's actions last night were uncalled for. Listen, I'll be the first to admit my hatred for Diego. Thing is, he didn't deserve to be left on that yacht. If it wasn't for Killian's weakness—*Madison*—he would have left Diego there to die.

My father, Jack Kennedy, was a tough son-of-a-bitch, but Killian is proving to be even more unforgiving when it comes to being crossed. I'm not saying the *Bone Breaker* didn't deserve the bullet in his shoulder. I was ecstatic to be the one to pull the trigger. However, Kil took it way too far. He's lucky Diego didn't bleed out right there from the damage to his femoral artery. Madison quite literally saved his goddamn life with her quick thinking in using my belt.

What we need is for Diego to establish a new version of the Cuban-Miami syndicate as well as a peaceful alliance built on trust and mutual respect. Now, more than ever, considering Selena and Killian will be married soon and expecting their first child. A child who quite possibly could be the next heir to the Tri-State Syndicate.

My head snaps away from the window to the hand that lands on my shoulder. Normally, I would have paid attention to who was moving around me, but I've been entirely lost in thought. My heart stammers in my chest and then falls when I realize it's Lainey and not Madison. Her smile is gentle as she takes a seat next to me and slides a steaming mug of black coffee across the table. I cautiously bring it to my lips, raising an eyebrow. The last time I accepted a drink from her, I puked my brains out for a solid ten minutes.

A smirk forms on her face before she takes a sip of her own frou frou latte. Licking the foam off her lips she says, "I promise this one won't make ya puke." Shooting me a wink, she takes another sip and places her hand over the one I have holding the mug. "You didn't sleep well last night. You could use it."

Tilting it back to take a sip, and hiding my smile, I see Madison over the rim. She's leaning against the threshold of the door, legs and arms crossed. Jealousy and hurt carve her usually soft features into that of someone not to be fucked with. She pushes off the wall and struts past us, not making eye contact with either of us, stopping at Diego's fancy coffee machine.

I stand up and approach her, not giving a damn about my recent thoughts about giving her space. She ignores my presence, grabbing two paper cups and pressing some buttons to produce two identical drinks. Four fucking shots of espresso each. How she doesn't get raging heartburn or an ulcer is beyond me.

Without thinking, I reach out and run my knuckles along the back of her arm. Goosebumps spring up in their wake–which should be a good sign—*until she speaks.*

"Soo...you and Lainey are a thing now, huh?" Her voice holds steady but is laced with tension.

"No." I lower my voice, not trying to hurt Lainey's feelings. "I told you we aren't like that."

Madison takes a sip of her drink, refusing to make eye contact with me. "You two sure looked rather cozy. Killian told me that she was there for you the night you broke up with me. I guess having someone within your organization is better than bringing an *outsider* in. I mean she pretty much just said you didn't get much sleep last night. So is this your way of moving on?" She sips her drink again, burning those damn taste buds right off her sharp tongue.

I lift her chin, and grasp her face between my fingers, forcing her eyes my way. "We didn't sleep together, if that's what you're insinuating. I told you we have been friends since childhood. She wasn't sleeping in my bed with me. Lainey just checked up on me when she realized that you were off sleeping in the same room as your *husband*." I can't even hold back the venom in my voice at that fucking word. Moreso *who* it's associated with.

That should be me.

Her eyes scrunch as she glares at me. "How dare you, Liam." My woman tries to pull out of my grasp only prompting me to step further into her space. I press my body flush against hers so that she's forced to place her espresso down or risk burning the both of us. On a slam, she places her cup back down and slides her hand between us. The hand that houses her wedding rings lands firmly on my chest before she gives it a good shove. *Why the fuck does she still have them on? This wedding was supposed to be a fucking sham.* As the stubborn arsehole I am, I refuse to move an inch. Instead, I lower my head until we are nose to nose.

"We need to talk, baby. Not here. Not with all these ears. Just you and me. I broke up with you. Yes, I did. I will do anything to protect you, Madison. Don't think for one fucking second I didn't break my own heart in the process. The difference between me and Killian...and now fucking Diego, is that I will *always* put your safety first. Even if you hate me for it."

"Liam. Get your hands off my wife before I break them," Diego's arrogant voice echoes from the bedroom.

Madison's eyebrows raise before falling back in place. I can't tell if it was in response to Diego's bold statement or what I just admitted. My hand loosens its grip on her face and she uses that moment to take in a steadying breath before collecting the two cups. That's when I notice the chain of my necklace peeking out under her sweatshirt. I reach for it, pulling it out and holding the black diamond raven between my fingers.

"I know I've given you whiplash, always struggling with the need to keep you safe and the need to make you mine forever. Ravens are about letting the truth set you free. I'm all in, baby. I can't do this without you and I don't want to. I almost lost you again. You are stronger than I ever gave you credit for. If you want to be in this life, I want it to be with me and not that gobshite in the other room. Just give me your truth. Is it Diego you want?"

Tears collect at her bottom lashes, threatening to spill over. "I don't know, Liam," she says, bowing her head. "I need time. This is all too much. So much has happened in such a short period of time. I don't know what I want anymore."

She sidesteps me and walks back to the bedroom to deliver Diego his coffee. I should have done it for her and spilled the damn thing all over him. Conor steps in my path as I am about to go after my woman and give Diego a piece of my mind.

"Don't, mate. Give her time." His eyes are understanding.

This fucking sucks.

WE ARE ABOUT twenty minutes from landing. Madison has remained in the bedroom with Diego the entire flight. Her food and refreshments were sent back there. This is the first time I'm seeing her. She looks frantic as she stands in the doorway with the doctor. He's talking slowly and her eyes are darting back and forth as she takes in the information being discussed. Her hand fidgets with her necklace—her little nervous habit.

Lainey is passed out with her headphones in, her head lying gently on the table. Conor makes eye contact with me, concern written across his features as I stand and start walking toward Madison.

"Everything alright back here?" I ask, placing my hand at the small of her back. Instead of moving out of my embrace, she leans into it. A small victory smile spreads across my face before it falls away at what the doctor is saying.

"Mr. De La Cruz will need immediate medevac when we land in New York. His artery has done what we feared it would and has reopened. I've made several attempts to stop the bleeding but it's been unsuccessful due to the pressure. The tourniquet will only give us enough time to reach the hospital. He needs a blood transfusion immediately and surgery to fix the artery. Another issue arising is that Mr. De La Cruz hasn't been able to shake his fever."

"Will the operating room at Killian's be sufficient enough?" Madison's voice quivers, realizing the severity of the situation at hand.

"I believe so, Ms. Marrone."

"It's *Mrs. De La Cruz*, Doc," Diego cough-laughs. Madison twitches beneath my palm, clearly affected by his words.

I roll my eyes and bite my tongue, giving a dying man some version of peace.

"This isn't a time for formalities, *Ocean Eyes*. This is serious!" Madison turns towards him.

"So am I," he growls.

The doctor interrupts their little spat. "Is anyone here B+?"

"Shit. No. I'm A+," Madison brings her hands to her lips, her rings sparkling, and her anxiety increasing by the second.

"I am," I say confidently. I may hate the situation we are in with Madison, but I refuse to have her watch him die on this goddamn plane. "Take what you need from me, Doc." I extend my arm and nod towards the older gentleman.

Maddy swivels her head back to me. Her eyes soften with appreciation. "Can you find a way to set up a medical transport back to our house?"

"Yeah, sweetheart. I can." I place a kiss on top of her head and walk back to my chair to make some calls and donate some blood. The doctor follows me with his equipment, wasting no time hooking me up to the IV.

Seb is my first contact in mind.

By now, I owe this man a vacation home.

CHAPTER 30

DIEGO

CHRIST. I am so fucking nauseous and cold. Whole body chills violently rock through me with each breath more labored than the last. My clothes cling to me like I've been in the sauna for an hour. Madison has a damp washcloth pressed to my forehead. Her other hand grips mine tightly, the cool metal of her wedding rings digging into my palm. Her delicious curves press up against me on the bed, completely unaware that she's transferring all her calming energy and heat to me.

I know she's worried. I would be lying if I said I wasn't too.

I don't want to die. *Especially* not in the arms of my girl. And definitely not 35,000 feet above the ground. We are starting to make our descent. Liam was able to arrange a medevac for when we arrive on the tarmac. No one, not even Madison, is allowed to come along. There is only room for my doctor and the rest of the medical crew. Of course, my stubborn girl tried to find a way to come along, but there physically is not enough room for her.

Liam promised to get her back to the penthouse as quickly as possible. As much as I can't stand him, I'm thankful for him. Not only is he making sure Madison remains calm during all of this, but he also saved my life last night. Even just now, he donated blood to keep me alive—*again.*

257

I'm sure he's hoping he and Madison will work it out. Can't say I blame the guy for trying. The problem will be when I recover from all of this. I'm not giving up on her.

She's my wife.

If she so much as whispers the possibility of staying that way, I will do everything in my power for it to remain so.

I love her.

I am in love with my wife, Madison De La Cruz, and I am willing to fight for her love in return.

"Sir, we will be landing in five minutes. Mrs. De La Cruz, we will be needing you to take a seat and buckle up in the front of the cabin," the co-pilot announces at the threshold of the bedroom door.

The doctor leaves us to take his own seat as the co-pilot follows him. Madison rubs her thumb over my sweaty cheek and looks back at the door briefly before kissing my lips. "Pull through this, *Ocean Eyes.* I'll be there waiting for you when you come out of surgery." She pecks my lips three more times before rubbing my cheek again and hopping off the bed.

I want to believe her, but this sense of doom is settling over my chest. If this is the last time I get to tell her, then she needs to hear it one more time. "I love you, *Mariposita.* If I don't get the chance to tell you this again, promise me you'll consider starting over. Fly away from all of this death; this chaos."

She walks back over to my bedside with tears rolling down her rosy cheeks. "Tell me that again when you wake up from surgery." She places another sweet kiss on my almost numb lips. The warmth of hers awakens mine for a few blissful seconds.

"Tell you what? That I love you?"

"Yeah, it sounds nice. I won't fly if you're around."

"And if I'm not?"

She pauses, contemplating. "Then I'll consider it."

"Good girl." It takes a hell of a lot of effort just to grab her hand and squeeze it.

I watch her leave, memorizing every inch of her.

She's fucking perfect.

THE IRRITATING BEEPING *of machines fills my senses. Intense pressure sits heavy on my chest. I'm stuck like this, unable to talk, unable to move. Everything is black around me. Bright light fills my vision. A woman approaches with a baby in a blue blanket. She reaches out and the light touches my face. Warmth and buzzing follow as the pressure slowly begins to fade.*

"My sweet boy. You've done all of this to save your sister and those innocent souls. What a beautiful sacrifice you have made. You even found the love of a woman who has softened the hardened parts of you that Basilio created."

"Mamá?" I ask, my voice sounding different than my own; younger and more childlike.

"You have a choice, Diego. We always have a choice. Do you wish to take my hand and join me and the others? Or do you wish to go back to your throne and Madison?"

Fuck. I'm dying. No. No. Not yet. I need my wife. In such a short amount of time, she's filled a place in my heart that I never thought would be open to anyone. I need her. And I'd be selfish to hope that she needs me too. My death will destroy her. I need to get back to her.

"I want to go back, Mamá."

Her hand lowers to my chest as the bright light grows even brighter. "I can give you more time, but I can't tell you how much. That's not up to me, cariño."

"I can live with that." I laugh at my own joke and the fact that I am somehow being given a second chance. I was sure my soul would have gone straight to hell or someplace similar.

"You are a good one, Diego. She wouldn't have chosen you if you weren't. Give your sister my love. Let her know I've got someone

very special here who can't wait to meet her." She rocks the baby in her arms and then her light fades away until I am left in darkness again.

The beeping increases and the pressure is back until I feel warmth spread across my hand. My eyes loosen, allowing me to force them open. The room is dimly lit. I glance around at my surroundings and discover I'm in a bedroom that looks just like a hospital room. There are a bunch of machines hooked up to me. One being a blood infusion pump. I follow the line of the IV down to my hand, the one being held by the same person who gave me the strength to come back from the dead.

My beautiful wife.

"I love you," I say groggily, remembering her request for when I was out of surgery.

She shoots me a dazzling smile and brings my hand up to place a kiss.

"We almost lost you there."

"I was given a choice, and I chose to come back to you, to my sister, and the people who need my leadership."

She gives my hand a gentle squeeze. "I'm glad you did. I wasn't quite ready to fly."

"I could always push you again," I laugh, instantly regretting it. My body feels like it's been hit by a Mack truck.

She shrugs. "'Where you sleep, I sleep.' So, I guess you'd have to come with me then." She uses my words against me. *Ahh that sass.* The things I wanna do to her right now.

Damn right I'd follow her. If she wants me, I'll follow her anywhere. I'd give up my leadership to my cousin—or my sister —if she ever wanted it.

Does this mean she is picking me? Was that what my mamá said right? My wife chose me?

"What does this mean for us, Madison?"

She stands and slowly approaches the door before opening it and then turning around to look at me. "It means that I'm willing to give our marriage a chance. Almost losing you made me question everything. I don't know who I am anymore, Diego. But what I do know, is that whoever I am now is a stronger version of myself. It's because of you. Not having you in my life will break me. I'm sure of it. That has to mean something a bit more than...infatuation with you." She smiles knowingly. She won't say the words out loud but I can feel them in the way she said them.

"Ahh...you love me, *Mariposita*."

She shakes her head from side to side while smiling. "I'm going to get your sister to tell her you're awake."

"MAMÁ WAS THERE. She was holding a baby wrapped in a blanket." Endless tears run down my sister's face and drip off her chin onto our entwined hands.

"She told me to tell you that she has someone with her who can't wait to meet you."

"Did you see what the baby looked like?" Sel sniffles.

"I didn't but...I saw the gender."

"Tell me," she demands excitedly, gripping my forearm.

"It appeared to be a boy. He was wrapped in a blue blanket."

"Oh my God!" my sister squeals. "This whole story is insane. I'm so thankful our angels were watching over you and brought you back to us."

"Mamá helped with that. I was given a choice. Come back and love Madison the way she deserves or be content with leaving this world."

"And you chose Madison," she says softly, the corner of her mouth going up an inch. She doesn't seem fully convinced our love won't end in tragedy.

"I did. And she chose me," I state proudly.

Her eyebrow raises in confusion. "What do you mean?"

"She wants to be with me. Give our marriage a real shot."

"Oh, Diego. I know you love her. I see it. I wish I could say I think this is smart. You know Madison's history with Liam. Their connection is still very much there. She's been through so much these last few weeks. I don't want to see you get hurt."

"I appreciate you trying to look out for me, Sel. I really do. You got your happily ever after. Is it so bad to want whatever version of mine Madison is willing to give?"

"No. It's not. But hope is a dangerous thing, Diego. You taught me that."

"I know."

A knock vibrates the door and Madison pops her head through the crack. "Can I come in?"

Selena stands and blows me a kiss. "I love you, hermano."

"Love you too, Sel."

My sister pulls Madison into a hug before closing the door, leaving Madison and I alone once again.

"Hi." I smile at her.

"Hi..." She leans back in her chair, sipping something that looks like an iced green tea.

I slide over as much as I can and pat the space next to me. "Join me?"

There's a moment of hesitation before she rises and curls up next to me. She lays her head on my chest as I stroke her silky hair with my good hand.

"It feels weird," I state.

"What does?" she asks nervously, her hands roaming around my body for any sign of discomfort.

I rub her arm reassuringly. "Not having anywhere to be at the moment. No enemies lurking at our backs. No flights to catch. You're here, safe in my arms. It feels weird to be so calm right now."

"It does." She nods in agreement against my chest.

"It won't last, *Mariposita*. I wish it would, but you know it

262

won't." My sister's words are circulating in my brain, making me doubt myself. "Are you sure this is what you want?"

"I could do without all the violence...and being the main target in everyone's issues...but yeah, I think this is what I want. Being with you makes me feel strong. I like the woman I've become. The woman I am when I'm with you."

I place a kiss on the top of her head and close my eyes. "I do, too. She's sexy as hell. I can't wait to train you. Then you'll feel stronger than you ever have. Plus, you'll need your endurance for the things I have planned for you," I tease while giving her ass a good slap.

"Oh yeah?" Her breathing accelerates, and her voice is raspier with lust. Like what?"

"You'll see when we get back to the island," I promise, the words coming out weaker than intended. The desire to fuck my wife and the desire to sleep are neck and neck right now.

Sleep wins, *Goddamnit.*

The last thing I feel is Madison smiling against my chest.

For the first time in my life, I feel at peace.

CHAPTER 31

LIAM

"*MADISON*. BABY, WAKE UP." I shake her gently. She looks so peaceful right now, and I am about to destroy that in the next few minutes. How badly I wish it wasn't me to do this to her. Killian even offered to do it for me, but I knew I had to be the one here when she falls apart. I will *always* be here for her when she falls apart.

I'm part of the reason she's about to.

Confused, sleep-filled eyes meet mine as she lifts her head off *his* chest. I reach out and cup her chin in my hand. "Sweetheart, I need you to get off the bed so the doctors can take a look at Diego." I keep my voice as calm and benign as possible.

Those eyebrows that hold so much emotion pinch together in confusion. That's when the severity and reality of the situation hits her. *Hard*. She glances down at a pale and bluing Diego. Luckily, his eyes are closed. Panic sets in as Madison runs her hands over his chest, feeling the chill and rigidity of his skin and the absence of a heartbeat against her palm.

My own heart stammers and starts to break, cracking right down the center watching her hyperventilate with tears springing to her widened chocolate eyes. *Baby*. I just want to hold her right now. Take all the pain away from her.

265

"No! No. No. Diego don't you fucking dare!" Her hand comes down onto his chest with a slap. She straddles him on the bed, leaning over to administer compressions. Her back heaves as she puts everything she has into getting his heart to start back up.

"How did this happen? How long has he been like this for?" she screams, turning her head around to look at me and the medical staff in the room.

I take a cautious step forward, placing my hand on her shoulder. "Mad. He's gone, baby." Thunder cracks outside and lightning illuminates the room, casting a glow on her pale face. "I need you to let the doctors move in and do what they need to do." I give her a gentle squeeze, rubbing my thumb along the top of her shoulder blade.

She glances around the room, recognizing the lack of lights lit and all of the vital monitors and IV machines unresponsive. Another clash of thunder vibrates the walls as the blue light illuminates the tears staining her face.

My heart breaks even more.

"The powers out," she states simply, void of any emotion.

I reach under her armpits, tugging her back and attempting to get her off his dead body. Her hand comes up to shove at my chest. "No. I didn't even get to say goodbye!" Lowering her head, she lays her head on his chest. "I'm not ready to fly, *Ocean Eyes*," she sniffles. "Come back."

"Mrs. De La Cruz. We understand this is a very traumatic time for you. We do need to step in now and start post mortem on your husband." The older, graying doctor from the plane places a gentle hand at her back.

Madison's shoulders vibrate with silent hysterics, an impending breakdown vast approaching. Tears spring to my own eyes hearing them call her his surname, destroying whatever was left of the strength I had walking into this room.

I attempt to get my shit together. She needs me right now. My own feelings be damned. Let her fight me, punish me with her words and fists.

Reaching past the doctor, I pull her off him. She doesn't resist like I assumed she would. Instead, Maddy spins around in my hold and circles her arms around my neck tightly, pressing her chest against mine. I adjust her, swinging her legs up and cradling her to my chest. Her head comes down and she buries her face into my shirt. A dark blanket of hair hides her face as her back shivers and the dam breaks. My shirt quickly becomes soaked in her tears.

I lead us out of the room and over to the hallway where Selena and Killian are waiting. Kil has a whimpering Selena tucked under his arm, running a soothing hand up and down her back. He removes his hand briefly, reaching out to touch Madison, but I shake my head. Reading my face, he pulls his hand back and presses a flashlight into my hand.

"We'll meet up with you in a bit," he whispers. I nod in agreement.

Taking the steps one at a time, I descend the staircase, walking us down a flight to our...to *my* bedroom...*you know what I mean*...to whatever the fuck title *the* bedroom is we once shared. Before we get to the room, I place a kiss on the top of Madison's head.

"I'm right here, baby. We are going to go to our old bedroom. There are a few things we need to talk about. Killian and Selena want us to join them—when you're ready—to discuss what to do from here."

She stays silent, nodding her head against my chest in acknowledgement. I open the door and on reflex, flick the light switch on. *The powers out, eejit.* Taking a few steps in, I kick my foot out behind me, successfully shutting the door behind us. With the glow of the flashlight, I navigate us to the bed and lower her down onto the comforter. She curls up in a little ball, turning her back to me.

Fuck.

I want to erase him from her mind. Take away this pain she's experiencing at the loss of someone she lov—cares about.

The frilly throw blanket Madison had for our bed is still at the edge of the mattress. I grab it, shake it open and cover her shaking body with it. Scanning the room, I locate the unreasonable amount of candles she had in here for us. I reach into my sweatpants pocket to grab my lighter and start lighting all the baked good scented candles. When the last candle is lit, I turn on my heel and notice the room is lit up as if we are preparing for a seance.

Too soon? Perhaps. Diego, ya arsehole, if you're here, help me soothe her. Help me get her through this. A chill runs up my spine prompting me to speed walk toward the bed. Real life monsters I can deal with. Ghosts? *Nope.*

Abso-fucking-lutely-NOT.

The mattress dips as I take a seat at the edge of it. I lift Madison's feet, placing them in my lap. My hands grip her calves and move lower to the arch in her feet. At first it's just to rub them and offer a form of comfort, eventually I find that I've fallen into my old routine of massaging them. A flash of lightning briefly brightens the room, giving me a better view of her. Even through her grief, shes still so fucking perfect. So beautiful. She lets out the smallest of sighs as another crack of thunder rumbles the penthouse.

Minutes pass. Hell, it's probably more like an hour. My hands haven't left her legs, doing what I can to comfort her and also giving her the time to process this all. The room is mostly silent —aside from her sniffles, the faint crackling of the wood wick candles, and the occasional rumble of thunder in the distance. The storm has now calmed, moving east of the city.

"How did this happen?" she whispers, her voice hoarse from crying and screaming.

"The doctors all went back to the hospital, needing to be

there. There were many accidents tonight due to the storm. They left a nurse here to do the overnight shift, but Killian had sent her home early. Her husband was involved in a serious car crash on the Long Island Expressway. He was part of a multi-car pile up caused by the decreased visibility. Kil wasn't worried, knowing you had the proper training as a nurse and hearing Diego's prognosis. The doctor and staff were coming back in only a few hours, anyway."

I look out the window as I speak, noticing the sky is not as angry as it was earlier. Pulling my phone out of my pocket, I check the time.

5:30 A.M.

With a sigh, I slide the phone back into my pocket, careful not to linger on my lock screen for too long. It's my favorite picture of us. The one taken only a few weeks ago at Madison's graduation dinner.

She just refreshed and changed here at the penthouse before heading to the restaurant. Her perfume was strong and enticing. Driving me wild like it always did. She had just doused herself in it and applied a fresh coat of lipstick to her plump lips in the mirror. I remember being envious of that beautiful dress, the one gripping her curves and making me want to skip dinner altogether.

My woman plucked my phone out of my hands as I was texting Colin to make sure the venue was clear and ready for us. She opened the camera and pulled my face close to hers so that we were cheek to cheek, fitting us both in the frame.

"Smile, Liam."

I turned my head, thinking what a fucking lucky bastard I was to be able to call this woman mine. A genuine smile formed on my face. A beautiful pink blush creeped onto hers as she noticed me staring at her through her peripheral. She turned her head and pressed her forehead to mine, then snapped the picture.

The moment she captured had me in awe.

The love we had for each other emanated through the screen.

Her doe eyes peered into mine, a stunning smile gracing her face and lighting up her beautiful features. My eyes shone brightly with the love I have for her, and the desire and devotion to do anything in the world to make her happy. My lips curved up into a smile that mirrors my woman's.

It's insane how different things are now. How fast life can change. How our actions and decisions in life have led us here. To this moment.

Warm hands wrap around my forearm, snapping me out of my painful, yet beautiful memory. She lowers her cheek to my bicep. "Why didn't the generators kick on?"

"They did, but only briefly. Long enough for everyone who noticed the power went out to be able to fall back asleep." Madison shifts, lifting my arm and tucking herself underneath it. Her own wrap around me. "I came to check on you after waking up in a panic at the thunder. When I got up, I realized the power was out. Colin and Kieran didn't realize, having been at the entrance. The main lobby of the building is lit, as well as a few other apartments. Seems our generators are not working properly." She squirms, uneasily, taking in this information. "I woke Killian first, letting him know before coming to see you. He sent me to investigate getting the power back on, giving me an out from having to see you cuddled up with him." I hang my head, knowing that it was a pussy move.

"I understand."

"Killian went upstairs and that's when he noticed you asleep and Diego not breathing. He had me come up immediately and called the doctor to come back, offering to triple his pay.

"How did he die?" Her voice is small, still in denial.

I rub her arm and tuck her head under my chin. "Blood clot, baby. Because the monitors had been shut off and they weren't switched over to the generators, no one, not even you were alerted."

"Why didn't Killian at least tell me there wasn't going to be any nurses here?"

"He said you were sleeping so peacefully, he didn't want to bother you. It was only meant to be a few hours—max."

She lifts her head, anger brewing as she goes rigid in my arms.

The lights flicker before coming back on.

Madison squints her eyes at the intrusion before sliding out of my arms and off the bed. She tosses the throw blanket around her like a cape. I stand, following her as she walks towards the bathroom.

"I'll be in here until Killian or the doctors need me," she says, turning around to look up at me. With a sigh of frustration and tears pooling in her lower lids, she clicks the bathroom door closed in my face.

CHAPTER 32

MADISON

Six months later

"AGAIN," Liam commands, holding the punching mitts out for me to strike. I bend over, bracing my hands on my knees and catch my breath as sweat drips down my nose and onto the wide planked wooden floors. I inhale deeply through my nose.

"I'm done for today, Liam."

"You're doing well, sweetheart."

I stand up straight, putting my rings back on, and walk out the doors off the living room to the balcony. The sound of the waves crashing against the shore instantly soothe my racing heart. The sun has set and the stars have begun to rise along with a stunning full moon. It cast a magnificent glow on the ocean before me. I lean against the railing, closing my eyes and inhaling the salty air. Sapphire blue eyes pop into my mind's eye, as the warmth of the breeze wraps around me in an embrace, reminding me of a different time.

It's been six months since we scattered Diego's ashes into the Atlantic Ocean, here in Miami. His cousin Antonio temporarily took over running the syndicate, until Selena and him sort out what will be best for everyone.

Diego had a vision. A new direction for the Cuban-Miami Syndicate. The whole reason Diego got all of us into this mess. It would be a disservice to him to not do everything we could to build the syndicate and leadership he wanted.

I open my eyes and stare at my wedding bands sparkling under the moonlit sky. Upon Diego's passing, Selena and I were required to sit down with his lawyer. Selena was gifted an insane amount of money for Diego's future nephew. Which, was in fact confirmed through a blood test. Selena burst into tears at her gender reveal, knowing her angels are keeping her baby boy safe.

My jaw just about hit the table we were sitting at when the lawyer then announced the rest of Diego's assets went to his wife.

The *Bone Breaker* left everything to me.

Our marriage was legitimate and not a sham—as I had once thought. Turns out, Diego De La Cruz was an insanely wealthy man. I immediately hired a lawyer to set up a trust fund for Selena's future son. He helped prepare documents in regards to Diego's private jet and the insurance money that came in on the yacht.

There was a full criminal investigation on the cause of the explosion, ultimately being closed and forgotten about. *Just like Geraldo and his lackeys.* The men we collectively left behind handled all the *minor* details that would have prevented the case from closing. The Greek government had their suspicions that Diego was to blame. At one point having authorities search for his whereabouts in Greece and at home. When they came to talk to me, I offered them his death certificate, effectively avoiding any further interrogation.

The jet remains in my name—for now. I only use it occasionally, visiting New York here and there to visit Selena and my family. Anyone in this organization is welcome to use it as long as they go through Antonio for permission. The insurance money from *Pontus* is being used to build shelters down here for women and children involved in domestic violence.

The only thing I decided to keep temporarily was the island. I transferred over the deed to Selena. She and I discussed me living here until I am ready to head back to New York. At that point, the house and jet will all be hers. Still so unsure of what my future looks like, I put a small amount of money away for emergencies.

Killian and I haven't spoken much since the night of Diego's death. I couldn't quite put aside my hatred. *And I had hated him.* If it wasn't for him, Diego never would have been shot in the back and then the thigh—ultimately leading to his untimely death. Did Liam have something to do with that as well? *Absolutely.* I haven't forgiven him either. He may have saved Diego's life twice, but it was *his* bullet that ended up leaving a hole through my husband's back. *Late husband, now.*

After the funeral, I decided to stay here on the island. It had been renovated after Killian and Diego went on their mission to retrieve me and destroyed a good amount of it. I find it extremely comforting and peaceful here. Minus the dungeon. I can barely look at that door without getting chills and flashbacks.

Diego's presence is all around here. Even his scent still lingers on his linens. I've been sleeping in his shirts and sweatpants, craving a sense of closeness to him. At night as I sleep in his bed, I can almost feel him here with me. Somehow, knowing he's there has allowed me to get the sleep I need. If not by the act of some spiritual assistance, then it's due to the pure exhaustion of sparring and training with Liam. *The man doesn't go easy on me.*

Selena and Killian came down for the memorial and stayed for a week to tie up loose ends. They went back to New York and haven't been back since. Killian needed to get back to a routine as the leader of the Tri-State Syndicate. Conor was sent back to

275

Connecticut to run *The Triskelion*. And Liam was assigned to go with him, but he fought his brother—and me—tooth and nail to stay. Killian *kindly* agreed to him dividing his time between Connecticut and Miami. Which means Liam spends the week with me. On the weekends he's back on a flight to New York, then off to the club and his own house.

So here we are. Liam currently sleeps down the hall from me in this big empty house. He originally wanted the room next to me, but I couldn't have him that close. Needless to say, he was disappointed when I told him I wanted him to sleep at the other end of the hallway. The walls are thin here. He didn't need to hear me cry myself to sleep every night. Or when I was feeling lonely and needy, cry out my orgasm, after sliding my hands under the waistband of my pajamas.

As isolating as that may seem, it's not. Antonio has some of his men surrounding the property, keeping me safe, and Killian allowed Kieran to stay behind as well. And hey, Monday's have even become game night. *That's a start, right?* Liam, Kieran and I play cards, usually poker while drinking a few beers.

About a week after the memorial, Liam presented the idea of getting all my anger and frustration, my grief, even my confusion out by training. He knows if I am going to remain in this life, I need to be able to defend myself. Diego wanted that for me too. I could almost feel him smiling and throwing some sly remark my way when I readily agreed.

It's definitely working. I can already see muscle building where it once never existed.

Sparring gives me a way to take all my anger towards Liam and Killian and dish it right back. Every hit to the bag, every jab I get in on him, everytime I defend myself, I feel empowered; stronger.

Liam and I haven't discussed 'us' or our situation since our conversation on Diego's jet to New York from Greece. The spark between us is still very much there. I've caught his eyes lingering longer than necessary when we train. He always looks ready to say something more but never does.

At night, he sits on the balcony and smokes a cigarette, usually lost in thought. Occasionally, he'll have a nightcap, having significantly cut back on his alcohol as a coping mechanism. There are so many nights I wish to join him but don't. Not wanting to confront my feelings or to give him a sense of hope.

He's given me the space where I need it, but I do find moments of missing him. His touch. The comfort his embrace brings to my whole nervous system.

The sliding door squeaks open. Liam steps out onto the balcony to join me, leaning his forearms against the railing.

"Selena's c-section is scheduled for this weekend. You barely spent any time at all with your family for the holidays. I think it would be nice to head back to New York for the New Years Eve Masquerade Gala," he announces, looking out at the reflection of the moon on the surface of the water. "Plus, Killian made me the head of the *"planning committee"*, he air quotes, laying the sarcasm on thick. "I honestly have *no* fucking clue what I'm doing. I could really use your help, love."

I turn my head to look at him. His brows have come together, clearly uncomfortable having this conversation with me. It's not like we talk much outside of our training. He tilts his head a fraction, an adorable smile creeps its way onto his face, breaking the tension between us.

"Wow. I can't believe it's been a year since...I found out about you and your involvement in the underworld." I turn and lean a hip against the railing, giving him my full attention.

He mirrors me, going as far as to take a step closer into my space. This is physically the closest we've been outside of sparring. My heart picks up at his nearness and the newfound determination igniting behind his eyes.

"So... is that a yes? If not for me, at least come home to New York to meet Selena's son. *Technically,* he's your nephew."

"Last year's party turned out *oh so well.* I can barely hold back my excitement for this year," I scoff, adding a bit of sarcasm to lessen the blow. It's become a challenge to wear this mask around him. To pretend I still don't care about Liam, when I do. Yet, so much has happened to create such a big wedge. I've had feelings towards Liam I never thought I would.

Anger. Pain. *Betrayal.*

Even if I didn't choose Diego, I'm not certain I would have gotten back with Liam. He made it clear he wanted a different life for me. In many ways Diego tried to get me to see that perspective as well. Which is why I have decided to forgive Liam.

I've been considering starting fresh, getting the hell away from all of this. But everytime I do, my heart breaks a little bit more than it already has. That would mean leaving the family I've found in all of them. Liam especially. Not seeing his handsome face or hearing his cranky ass complain about work or some college kid drama would be miserable. His stories of *Schmitty's* have lightened the energy in this house, taking me back to a simpler time.

"I promise you, you'll be safer than the Pope. If that's what you're worried about." Liam's voice breaks me out of my reverie. He takes my hand in his, his thumb tracing circles over my knuckles. "You need time away from here. As beautiful as it is, a change of scenery may be nice. Plus, there's snow up there. You love snow."

I let out a sigh, knowing damn well, I do need a change of pace. I do the same thing every day. First coffee and breakfast that I cook for Liam, Kieran and I. Then a morning full of intense training followed by reading a book or tanning on the beach. Up next is lunch, a quick dip in the pool and then sparring with Liam or Kieran. My evening ends with a healthy dinner, with or without the guys— depending on their schedule —followed by a nice bath or shower. Sometimes I'll catch up with Lexi or my sisters. Other times, I'm too tired to even keep my eyes open. Staying distracted and busy has kept my mind off of my emotions towards Liam and the grief over losing Diego.

Lifting my hand out from beneath his and tucking a strand of hair behind my ear, I nod my head. "Okay. I'm in. I'll need to get a dress."

Liam's smile widens and his chest heaves with excitement. "That can be arranged. I'll contact Rebecca and make an appointment for you and Lexi. She'll be there with Con, you know. The question is... your plane or mine?" He waggles his eyebrows playfully.

"Mine. *Definitely* mine. Yours doesn't have a fancy coffee machine. If we are going to plan an entire gala in just a few days, I am going to need some decent coffee."

He shakes his head, grinning from ear to ear. Even his mood has shifted, the dark cloud that has been hanging over him has dissipated. "Such a coffee snob," he teases as his gaze directs to the black raven necklace I still wear. *I couldn't take it off.* His lips form a thin line, probably wondering why I even bother to wear it anymore. Considering I make it a habit to still wear my wedding rings.

"You know it. What time should I set up our flight?"

"The earlier the better. Let's leave tonight."

"And where are we sleeping?" I ask, addressing the elephant in the room.

"Killian's, but we can get a hotel if you'd like," he says hesitantly. "Is that okay? I'll take the guest room, you can sleep in my room."

"Yeah. That's fine. You don't have to do that. I can sleep in the guest room. You should sleep in your own bed."

He tugs on my ponytail, "I know how much you love that

mattress. I don't mind taking the guest room if it means you sleeping in my bed again. I miss my sheets smelling like you."

I walk away, feeling flushed and needing some space between us. "I'll set it up. I'm going to go get showered and ready. I'll see you in a few, Liam." Raising my hand up I wave awkwardly before scurrying off to my room to pack.

CHAPTER 33

LIAM

"YOU LOOK INCREDIBLE, MADDY," Selena gushes, pulling her in and attempting to hug her. The lass' cute, very pregnant belly has dropped and sits between them, creating an awkward, arse out and bent forward at the hip hug. Madison blushes, taking a step back to admire Selena's rather stunning silver gown. Swarvoski crystals drip off the dress, giving it a wet effect.

"I told her the same thing when I picked her and Lexi up from the salon," I add, playfully nudging my shoulder against Maddy's. "She didn't respond as warmly as when you said it, Sel."

My little spitfire nudges me right back. "That's because I see you every day. Sel and I haven't seen each other in months! I missed you, girly."

"Missed you, too. I'm glad you came up for the New Year's Eve Gala. The baby is practically due any minute now. I'd love for you to stay and meet him if you can." She smiles gently at her best friend while resting her hand on her bare shoulder.

Emotional as ever at this reunion, both of their eyes fill with tears. Unfortunately, as of late, their relationship has been pretty strained. Sel will never know what *really* happened that night on the yacht. Killian hasn't told her and in Madison's final argument before she decided to stay on the island, he asked her and I not to either.

Personally, I can't get beyond Killian's actions that night, and quite frankly, neither can Madison. Let's not forget how he treated me when we finally got Madison back. He's changed now that he's become leader, and it's not someone Madison or I prefer to spend our time with. Because of that, it's been difficult for her to hang out with a pregnant Selena without his overbearing and looming presence.

To avoid having to come clean about why, Madison just avoids them altogether. *Christ, it fucking sucks.* I know she misses her best friends.

I'm hoping she misses me, too.

With Lexi focusing on her studies, her sister Mikayla studying abroad for her last semester, and Leah spending time with her new man, she seems to be feeling truly alone. All I want to do is take that pain from her. Of course, she has me around to keep her company, but it's been challenging keeping the line drawn between friendship and something more. *At least for me.*

There is absolutely no hiding the fact that we've regained our trust and playfulness with each other. Sparring is our new form of flirting—*some would call it therapy.* Recently, she's even shown interest in spending more time with me outside of training.

Hell, I'll take whatever I can get.

I just don't believe she's ready to come back to me yet. At least, not right now. Not when all she talks about is Diego—and how he made her feel *alive.* Everytime she says it, I feel crushed even more. I was once the man who made her feel that way.

"I wouldn't miss it for the world," Madison promises just as Killian walks up to his wife and kisses her lips, ignoring our presence the way I do my best to ignore him. It's not the easiest thing to do, considering our line of work. When I am here or in Connecticut at the club, I stick to talking about work. Any relationship outside of that, I am no longer interested in.

Not once did he try and apologize to Madison for his—*our*—role in all of this. I've just about apologized in every goddamn way possible to her. She told me she didn't want to hear it anymore and that she believed me. Even going as far as to catch me off guard one morning and tackle me to the ground.

She pressed the blade of her knife to my neck and told me if she heard 'I'm sorry' one more time, she'd give me a new scar. *It was sexy as hell.* I knew her threat wasn't fully loaded. The light in her eyes came back when she felt my pulse hammering against her hand.

Her throat bobbed as she said the words and only I could notice the tiny tremor of the blade against my skin. Madison would never physically harm me—no matter how angry she was with me. And that gives me some fucking hope.

Perhaps there is a future for us.

Tension builds and rolls off my shoulders at the thickness in the air between all of us. Keen as a horse, Madison shifts on her feet and angles her body towards me. Immediately sensing my uneasiness. Out of habit, her hand slides up the sleeve of my tux. Her fingers wrap around my bicep, giving it a warning squeeze.

Lexi breaks the tension, walking between us and handing Maddy some colorfully rimmed glass of champagne. It looks like cotton candy.

"For you, *sexy*." Her mascara coated lashes come together as she winks at her, before looking over her shoulder and shrugging. "Sorry, Kil. They were fresh out of the drink that removes the stick from out of your ass. Maybe try a laxative?"

Madison's coughs out a laugh, spraying some of that cotton candy champagne into the space between us. Those warm almond eyes of hers widen in shock, before her baby blue manicured hand comes up and covers her mouth. Conor chuckles nervously, wrapping an arm around his woman and pulling her closer to him.

I lean over and bark out a laugh to the point of tears. I look up to Sel, hoping we didn't offend her in her own home, when she also breaks out in hysterics. Her hand covers her stomach as she does so.

Killian remains stoic for a moment before the corner of his lips comes up and he shoots us all a genuine smile beneath his silver fox mask. *Did hell freeze over ?* I haven't seen a smile on my brother in quite some time.

"Good one, Lex," he says, rubbing his wife's back. The two of them had quietly married in the fall. Neither myself or Madison had been invited. Killian informed me of their marriage in passing one day and explained they will be having a larger wedding after the baby is born.

Where I am ecstatic that my brother finally got the girl he fell in love with all those years ago, I am frustrated with how he's been acting. My brother never wanted this role. He's always been the one to want a somewhat 'normal' life. He wanted the wife. The big family. I always thought out of the two of us, I was the better fit.

Killian puts his emotions into his work, which can create problems. It already has. And that's not to say that if roles were reversed, and it came to Madison, I wouldn't have let my emotions lead me. I absolutely would have. But it was how he went about seeking revenge that has me questioning if this is who he will continue to be as a leader.

We can't afford another war.

"Ohh," Sel sighs, grabbing onto her stomach. "Damn it, Lex, you made me pee myself. This baby is literally laying on my— OW." A gush of liquid splashes onto the floor from between her legs. I'm no doctor, but I can almost guarantee you that isn't pee.

Sel rubs circles around her stomach while Killian hooks and

arm around her waist. "Sel. Are you alright, love?" The concern in his voice is temporarily subduing the anger I feel towards him.

"My water just broke. Our son is ready to make his appearance, Kil."

My brother's eyes go wide and he stills. The same way you would see a new dad do in movies. I reach out to steady him and grip his shoulder.

"You've got this, Kil. You both do." I smile down at Selena and Kil breaks out of his stupor. He races over to one of the staff and asks them to grab the hospital bags, while telling another to clean up the floor.

Madison and Lexi give Sel a kiss and wish her good luck, while Killian retrieves the bags. "Do you need anything else before we leave?" he asks, turning toward his wife.

"No, baby. We have it all. Your checklist was very thorough," she giggles before pressing a sweet kiss to his cheek.

"Let's have this baby." He swings both duffle bags over his shoulder and wraps a protective arm around Sel, guiding them towards the elevator. "Colin and Ryan are coming with me," he announces before the elevator doors close.

My fingers comb through my hair, effectively messing it up, before undoing the bow tie and shoving it into my pocket. *I fucking hate dressing up.* I contemplate taking off my raven mask, but decide against it. It is a masquerade after all, and for more than one reason. There are many important people here tonight. Some political, others criminal. More than just tradition, we wear masks to help hide our identity.

From my peripheral, I see Madison smirk. "Caveman," she mumbles under her breath. I can't help but smile at her. This is the older version of Madison that is making a comeback. Not that I would change who she has become—the woman she is now is absolutely stronger than the woman who went out for a smoke at her graduation dinner.

With her training now, she could certainly take down a man

and slit his throat. She is wiser, more mature, and doesn't take shit from anyone. I admire that about her. I'm also incredibly thankful to Diego for that. He played a huge role in bringing out what was just waiting to be unleashed on the world.

And not one of us was ready for it.

Conor places a brief kiss to Lexi's lips before heading off to do a patrol. Wishing I could do the same, and saying *'fuck it'*, I pull Madison into me. My eyes devour her from head to toe, no longer hiding my intentions.

She's wearing the sexiest blue velvet dress. It has a deep V in the cleavage and a large slit running up to her hip. The way the fabric bunches—*what's the word Madison called it? Oh, yeah, ruched.* The way the fabric ruches around her arse makes it look ten times more delectable. These last few months, Madison has toned her body, really focusing on her workouts and training. Her squat game is on point. The things I would do to see her arse again in that bathing suit she wore on Valentine's Day. *Mmm.*

Keeping my hands to myself tonight is already going to be incredibly challenging. Keeping my fists from knocking out every fucker who looks at her like she's their next meal will be absolutely excruciating.

This woman was and always will be *mine.*

"Like something you see, Mr. Kennedy?" Her fingers slide up my chest and she pops the top few buttons open, revealing my raven tattoo. It's then I notice she isn't wearing her wedding rings tonight. *Hard to miss. I know. Bastard had to go all out on the damn things.* Her eyes reach mine before my gaze dips back down to her chest. And there, perched between her collarbones is the raven necklace I gave her. My heart throbs at what this could mean.

Is she ready? Did she ditch her rings and leave on my necklace to subtly tell me I can try and win back her love?

A small smile creeps on to her face as mine must look completely confused and pleased all at the same time.

I lift my mask so it sits on top of my head and lower my forehead to hers. "*Madison.* Have I told you how beautiful you look tonight?" I whisper, lust making my voice sound raspy.

"Hmm. You may have. I didn't appreciate it earlier. I should have. Hearing it again, hearing it right now, it's doing something to me, Liam. I'm breaking. I miss you." Her voice waivers and cracks as she speaks.

"I'm right here, baby." My right hand grips her hips a little tighter, pulling her in so there is not a sliver of space between us. My other comes up to cup her face, my fingers tracing the edges of her blue butterfly mask.

Sparkling, enchanting willow trees hang and wrap around us in the foyer. Faux moss, mushrooms and flowers cover the floor. There's even a fucking mini waterfall and pond to the right of us. Smoke fills the room, followed by some magical, sweet scent. Someone is playing the harp in a whimsical melody.

The moment is perfect. *Enchanting* is the right word. My woman has enchanted me. It feels like we are the only two in the room right now. Madison brings her hand up to the back of my neck, her fingers grazing my hair line. I tilt my head and our lips touch like a whisper. I need her to make that final move. She has to be the one to do it. Her breasts rise and fall against my chest. *Come on, baby.* I love you. I'm right here. Close the distance.

Cold air swirls between us as Lexi pulls Madison back, dragging her off in the direction of the outdoor bar and dancefloor. On a sigh, I lower my mask and watch them head out the back sliding doors off the kitchen to the heated tent.

Guess I'll just grab a smoke on the upstairs balcony and give those two a moment to catch up. I can be a very patient man. I'll catch Madison again—*at midnight.*

Now that's fucking enchanting.

CHAPTER 34

MADISON

I LET OUT a frustrated sigh and drain the rest of my drink, leaving the empty glass on the kitchen island. Lexi looks sternly at me as she drags me out the back door towards the heated tent. You can't even tell it's a tent. The amazing designer recreated the patio space to look like a cottage with ivy and twinkle lights, faux stone and a petrified tree stump bar. There are even some cute garden gnomes and LED lights within the ivy. *It's incredible.* This place is literally glowing, and soo freakin magical.

The energy feels magical tonight too—I can't quite place it.

Maybe it's this gorgeous dress I'm wearing. Or the Blue Monarch mask I picked up today at a costume store near Broadway. Or *maybe*, it's this renewed vibe going on between Liam and I. Where I once felt guilt for feeling something towards him again—I no longer do.

It's been replaced with feelings of peace and acceptance surrounding Diego's death.

The man the underworld spoke in whispers about was at one point in time, mine. There was some sort of energy exchange between us. Which is why I feel we bonded so well. It was more than just the situation we were in, it was a connection that went deeper than circumstance. Diego gave me some of his hardness and strength, and I in return, showed him how to be vulnerable and soft. Although, I'm not so sure who handed over their control more. That was always a struggle with us.

My mind switches back to Liam and my cheeks heat, thinking about our almost kiss in the foyer. I onced shared something incredible with Liam. It was years in the making. He wasn't always perfect—no relationship ever is. He can still be a hot head, and act on impulse at times, but it was always out of the love he had for me. To keep me safe. Liam was made to protect, I mean his damn name means protector. It's as if he was destined to take on that role since birth.

After months of mostly sitting alone with my thoughts, I realize, now, I am still very much in love with him. Diego not being here and everyone going back to a sense of "normalcy" has cleared my head a bit.

I hurt Liam.

Deeply.

The look on his face when he left *Pontus,* after recognizing the extent of my feelings for Diego, will always haunt me. I see now that him ending our relationship the way he did was to protect me from this life. From the bloodshed, the torture, the corruption and lies, the constant danger. Since day one of knowing him, he hasn't wavered from that role.

Consistency is key, right? I would have done the same if roles were reversed. Because loving someone means putting them first. As far as I'm concerned, Liam always, *always* put me first. I was just too wrapped up to see it.

The only thing preventing me from trying things again with Liam, is Diego's words in the back of my mind. He told me to fly away from all of this, just like Liam said...and I wonder if they were right. Maybe I got myself in too deep. I'm not cut out for the lies and the violence. The problem is, I can't let go.

Of Diego or Liam.

They are both so much a part of me now, that moving on, and leaving this all behind, will never truly be possible.

I will always be thinking of them.

LEXI GRABS my hand firmly in hers and drags me through the crowded dancefloor until we are right in front of the stage. A sense of déjà vu hits me. Taking me right back to last year and realizing how much has changed since then. *Amazing what a year can bring.*

My crazy bestie starts grinding her hips to the music and peddling my arms to loosen me up. I strain my neck over the lively crowd to see if I can spot Liam. Without a shadow of a doubt, that man is around. Probably in some dark corner, watching me. Waiting for the opportune moment to step in.

It's actually really comforting.

I'd be lying if I said my nerve endings weren't firing off with anticipation. A shiver runs through me as goosebumps surface on my arms.

He's around. But not the *he* I was just thinking of.

A knot of guilt forms in my stomach, disrupting the sense of peace I had tonight. Maybe it's too soon to be thinking of getting laid by my ex, when my late husband has only been dead for six months.

Conor approaches Lexi from behind, his arms circle her and pull her in close. "Hello, Beautiful." He presses a sweet kiss to her cheek. The two of them sway back and forth, wrapped up in each other. Lexi's eyes close and she releases a happy sigh.

Silently releasing a frustrated one of my own, I shout over the music to Lex, "Grabbing us a refill. Con, you need?"

"I'm alright, love. Can't stay too long, just wanted a quick dance with my woman."

I shoot him a thumbs up and navigate through the crowd towards the outdoor bar.

Which is packed.

There are definitely more people in attendance this year. Wiggling my way through the spaces between people, I manage to get to the side of the bar. I'm awkwardly standing at the corner, next to a man in a mask that looks like the skull of an elk or something of the sort. *Props to him for at least putting effort into his attire.* Many of the men here tonight have a simple black mask on. All three bartenders are busy at the other end of the bar making colorful cocktails for a large party of women.

"Here, you look like you could use this." The man next to me slides a lavender colored drink my way. It's garnished with a green sugar rim and a sprig of lavender, adding to tonight's theme. Naturally, my interest peaks. I raise an eyebrow in response. *Who is this man?* The man with such an unusual, yet familiar, baritone voice.

It's like whiskey, smooth and sensual.

I turn to look at him, unsure if I should be thankful for his generosity or worried my drink is spiked. His head still faces the bar, but his lip turns up at the corner.

"I was waiting for my date. It's not poison, I promise," he laughs, taking a small sip of it as proof.

That laugh does something to me, rolling straight through like a fucking train. My gut roils, as bile makes its way up, and my last drink threatens to surface.

As if sensing my unease, the man turns and inches his face towards mine, his blue eyes piercing mine. "As I said, I was waiting for my date," he slides the glass further towards me. "And now that she's here, I can finally do what I've been waiting to do for the last six months," he says confidently.

He stands, grips one hand at my lower back, the other cupping my cheek, and presses his lips firmly to mine.

Salt and coconut swirl around us as his minty tongue pries my lips open.

My hands come up and I push hard against his broad chest. Firmer than he had been anticipating, generating another smile from him. He looks impressed.

"*Diego.*" I say his name between clenched teeth rather than in relief. "How...*how?*" I stutter. "How is this even possible?" I lower my voice to a whisper, backing up as much as I can in the space we are in. "I watched you die!" I throw my hands up in the air dramatically before bringing them to my lips.

His fingers circle my wrist like shackles, lowering my hands back down and pulling me in closer. The Bone Breaker's lips find my ear. "Let's go somewhere more private and talk."

I'm about to agree—*because what the hell?*— when Liam comes up from behind us and tugs Diego back by the collar. "You have two seconds to leave this party before you don't leave this party at all," he growls. A few heads turn our way, others aren't impressed, used to this kind of activity by now.

I'm trying to focus but am finding it hard to even breathe. My skin prickles with goosebumps and my hands have grown clammy.

People don't just rise from the dead. I need answers and I need them now.

"Didn't mean to cause a scene, Liam," Diego responds in formality. "My wife and I were just having a discussion."

Wife. Jesus Christ.

Liam staggers a bit before collecting himself.

"The two of you, upstairs balcony by the pool, *now.*"

CHAPTER 35

DIEGO

GOD, she's fucking beautiful in that blue velvet dress. That dip in the fabric revealing her cleavage and slit running to her thigh should be illegal. Don't even get me started on that mask—*fuck*. She hasn't forgotten about me after all. The gorgeous Blue Monarch mask has my cock turning to steel in my pants. There's something about the blue, it accentuates her eyes. Dark chocolate irises with flecks of amber swirl with anger. Directed right at me.

Mariposita.

Definitely not the first response I thought I would receive from her, but then again, she thought I was dead. She watched me die.

And I did die. *Temporarily.*

Madison snatched the drink off the bar, bringing it with her as Liam lead the way up here. Unlike downstairs, this balcony doesn't protect us from the elements. And tonight is particularly chilly. A light dusting of snow is expected, adding to the cute little theme Madison created.

Steam curls in ribbons off the heated pool. If tonight goes well for us, I could bring Madison back up here tonight and show her just how sorry I am. My cock twitches and painfully presses against my zipper. *I need to calm down.* We've got things to discuss. Images of my fist cracking against a skull and blood spraying everywhere comes to mind, distracting me from how hot my wife looks tonight.

She's angled herself against the railing, grilling me and sipping her drink. Maybe the lavender will help her chill the fuck out. This conversation needs to be had when she's done fuming.

Liam walks over to her and takes his jacket off, draping it over her shoulders. His hands linger there longer than I'm comfortable with. I'm almost certain they haven't fucked. Antonio has filled me in as well as Killian and Selena. Madison has kept to herself, working on her training—which I am happy to hear—even though Liam is the one training her. I watch them, as I take a sip of my tequila neat. The burn is welcomed, bringing fire back into my veins. New York is fucking cold and I hate it.

"Liam, can I have a cigarette?" Madison's voice penetrates the silence.

"Ya, baby." The petname irritates the fuck out of me. He reaches into the pocket of his jacket and pulls out the pack of menthols. Retrieving two and slipping them between his lips, he lights both, and hands her one.

"Thank you." Her eyes linger on his, silently sending out a message. *Shit. Maybe I played dead for too long.*

She takes a long drag before walking over to me. Smoke sifts out of her lips as she speaks. "Who knows?" she spits, not trying to hide the venom in her voice.

My feet carry me until I'm inches away from her. It's then that I discover the moisture on her lashes. Her newfound strength holding the breakdown at bay. Liam closes in on us, placing a supportive hand at the base of her spine. I shouldn't allow it, but Madison instantly relaxes when he does.

Shame I'm about to ruin her faith in him.

296

"My sister, Killian, Antonio, and your man there." I nod my head in his direction.

Madison gasps and steps out of his embrace.

"What the fuck are you talking about?" Liam growls at me. He takes a step forward but her hands come up, warning us both to stop.

Taking another drag, and leaving the cigarette hanging loosely between her plump lips, she unties her mask. On bated breath, we watch as she frisbees the damn thing into the pool. It floats on the surface a few seconds before sinking to the bottom. I mirror her, flinging mine into the pool as well. Liam just lifts his own to his forehead, remaining quiet, and watching the storm brew behind Madison's eyes. *We both know that spells trouble.*

"Ya know what, I don't care. I'm so done with the lies. *The betrayal.* The fucking games. And most of all, I'm done giving my heart out....only to watch it break *again and again.*" The anguish in her voice guts me.

I reach out and grip her waist. "Listen to me, it had to be this way. Killian and I agreed this was the best course of action." Her fist snaps back before she plows it right into my brow.

Fuck. You go, baby.

That was by far the hottest thing I've ever seen her do. Surprise widens her eyes when I don't release her. Warmth oozes down my face and over my lips. *Ahh, her training definitely paid off.* I sneak a glance at Liam who is now crossing his arms over his chest and biting back a laugh.

A moment of mutual understanding before his anger returns.

"Killian only recently told Liam." I don't know why I say it. I currently may feel threatened by the prick but I'll always be grateful. He saved my life twice and then took care of the most precious thing in the world to me.

Smoke blows into the night sky as Madison releases an

aggravated cry. "You both have five minutes to explain everything. And then I'm leaving."

"Killian didn't tell me any of this," Liam snarls. Madison's eyes volley between the two of us, wondering who she can trust.

"Well that...changes things..." My brows pull together. *Why the hell wouldn't Killian tell his own brother?* "The night of my surgery, after you fell asleep on me, Killian came in with my sister. He explained to me that the authorities in Greece weren't easily convinced with our story of fireworks destroying the yacht. After we returned to the States, the Greek authorities contacted the U.S government, informing them of my role in our organization. My name was on the top of a very long list of most wanted criminals. Naturally, your name was attached—being newly married to me. Someone paid off the officiant to give up that information. My guess was Geraldo. Killian suggested I pretend to the world that I died. To help clear your name. And mine."

Madison rubs her knuckles and then takes another puff of her cigarette. The glow of the cherry illuminates the few tears gliding down her cheeks.

"Pretending to die and *actually dying* are two very different things." She blows out the smoke harshly, pinching the bridge of her nose and taking a seat on a lounge chair near the gas fire pit.

I light up the cigar I have in my pocket before taking a seat on the arm of her chair and continue. "Killian and I made a tough call. His best cardiothoracic surgeon administered a drug called adenosine. The drug has the ability to slow your heart until it stops. If lucky—only temporarily, with no other issues arising from it."

"You did NOT." Madison aggressively extinguishes her cigarette in the ashtray then spins her body around, shooting me a death glare. *Hell, I cheated death a few times in my life, but now I'm not so sure I'll survive her wrath.*

"No one planned on the severe weather knocking the power

298

out, or for the generators to go down. Killian and Selena had gone to bed, and you were still sound asleep on my chest. That's when I had Dr. Angosta inject me. It was fucking painful. The worst pain I've ever experienced. Watching your peaceful face and knowing you were safe in my arms is what helped me through it. Asystole was only supposed to last a few seconds and I would have been back. Of course, I have shit fucking luck, and reviving me wasn't an easy task. Liam wasn't even supposed to be there, but he had woken up at the perfect time. Killian had him rush in to grab you, knowing you'd need him during this. You both witnessed my 'death' as the doctors raced to get me back. It had to be real, sweetheart. All the staff, the nurses, the doctors who would later be interviewed would all say the same thing. To the world—the most dangerous criminal of the underworld had died of a cardiac episode after surgery. A surgery performed in New York where his new wife resides. There was supposed to be medical proof showing all of this, but of course the power went out. Word of mouth and hand written chart notes did the job. Authorities from both countries fell for it. Believing wedding fireworks caused the explosion and that I had died post surgery. With a little bit of outside help and Killian's hacker Seb, the case was closed. My name was now clear and so was yours. All my assets went to you and my sister."

Madison's lips hang open in the shape of an O. She's stunned to silence for a few moments. "So you...what? Rose from the dead after Liam took me out of there?"

"Precisely."

She stands abruptly and gets into my face, wafting the thick cloud of smoke obscuring her vision of me with her hand.

"How. Fucking. Dare you." She jabs her finger into my chest. "We spread your ashes! Oh God, whose ashes were those?!" Her hands come up and open wide. "Did you know that I lost my boyfriend when I was in college? That he died suddenly, and that it fucking wrecked me? Did you know what this lie would do to me?"

Deep within my chest, my heart skips a beat. *Shit.*

"No, I didn't."

"Of course you didn't," she lets out a sardonic laugh. "How could you? You don't know anything about me." She laughs again but more so to herself. "I'm so fucking stupid. This whole time, I actually thought I meant something to you. But I didn't. It was all about the sex. And I was just the perfect chess piece in your little game."

"*Madison.* I did this so that your name wouldn't be dragged all around the world and the underworld. That your attachment to me didn't bring you down with me." I reach for her hand again, but she snatches it back out of my grip.

"No. You don't get to lie to the person you claim to love. You don't put her through hell to clear your name. Even if it was to clear my name as well, you could have told me. I would have kept your secret. I would have faked the grief. We could have been together all these months." Her voice raises an octave. "Jesus, Diego. All these elaborate plans. These elaborate lies. You really didn't learn the first time, did you? How keeping people out of your plans could be detrimental? No, not detrimental. *Catastrophic*?"

She spins on her heel to face Liam. "And *you.* Her manicured index finger points his way. You're telling me the truth, that you *just* found out? Killian didn't tell you?"

His eyes fill with sadness and frustration. "No. He didn't, love. You aren't the only one who has a distant relationship with Killian. *Clearly* my brother has his own agenda." His head snaps back and he looks up at the cloudy sky threatening to snow on us. Releasing a sigh and focusing on her again, he says, "I can't fucking believe this. Trust me, baby. I would have told you, had I known. I wouldn't have kept this from you, knowing the grief you were going through and the similarities of your past."

Madison takes it all in, seemingly satisfied with his response.

"Your sister is in the hospital delivering your nephew—by the way." She faces me again, her voice void of any emotion. "Oh, but I'm sure you already knew that—considering *they* know you're alive."

"I didn't know that, but thank you for telling me. Listen, Madison, there's a lot more to discuss. I know it's a lot to take in. I did this to make sure your marriage to me didn't involve you with the law and that you would be set for life. One day in the future when the dust settled, I planned on coming back to rule my syndicate. Antonio and Selena did a good job running it with me as an absentee leader. I knew taking this would be a huge risk. But if I did come back to you, you'd be pissed but you'd be safe. And—I knew that if you couldn't possibly stand me after all this, you were free to fly. 'Til death do us part, right baby?"

With a scoff, she stands and walks towards the glass sliding doors. "We are done here. If you need anything, contact the lawyer. Don't call me, don't try and find me, don't send me anything. You wanted me to fly, and that's what I am going to do. You wanted to become a ghost to me. And now you are. Goodbye, Diego."

I sit on the edge of the chair, stunned to silence. I wasn't expecting that from her, but I deserve it. Christ, I basically trained her to do this. My heart throbs worse than it did the night I died.

This is fucking heartbreak.

Liam catches up with her and the two of them disappear behind the doors, Madison taking what's left of my heart with her.

Fly, Mariposita.

Fly.

CHAPTER 36

LIAM

HER BODY SHAKES with a mixture of being chilly in the New York air and all that just went down. I'm shocked. Never could I have prepared for what just unfolded. My poor girl, she's trembling so severely, I act on instinct and pull her to me. She doesn't resist, just wraps her arms around me and lowers her face to my shirt.

"This is so fucked up. How could they all do this to me?"

"I'm so sorry, sweetheart. I think we need to talk to Killian. And unfortunately, right now isn't ideal. I promise you tomorrow we will speak to him. I won't let Diego near you again." I press a kiss to her temple. "Come on, I'll take you to my room. I'm sure you need some time to digest all of this."

Her head lifts off my chest and her teary eyes meet mine. "I need Lexi. Can you have her meet me in there, please?" I shouldn't be hurt by her need for her best friend, but for some reason I am.

It feels like a dismissal.

Glancing down at my watch, I see that there is less than an hour until midnight. I had a sweet plan for Madison and I. *Except, that all went to shit.* She won't be interested in anything even remotely romantic now.

"Sure. But I'm not leaving you alone. I'll call Conor and have him bring her to you."

She nods, silently agreeing.

I OPEN the door to the bedroom and Madison brushes by me, taking a seat on the edge of the bed. Hesitantly, I follow her, sitting next to her and opening my arm out for her to lay on my shoulder.

She does, laying her head down as the tears drip one by one, the flow increasing steadily. Sniffling she says, "I don't think I ever got the chance to tell you, but thank you for always trying to protect me. Even when doing so hurts you too."

"You're welcome, love." My hand rubs up and down her arm in comfort. "Can...can I ask you something?" I ask nervously, afraid of her answer.

"Of course. What is it, Liam?"

"Did you and Diego...did you sleep with him?"

She jolts against my chest, giving me the answer I already knew. "Yes," she sniffles. "One time...right after the wedding."

Letting out the breath I was holding, I nod against her head pressed against me. "I figured as much."

Tilting her head, she looks up at me, her red rimmed eyes searching mine. "Are you mad at me?"

Not stopping myself from feeling everything and anything with Madison, I press a kiss to her forehead. "No. I'm not. You and Diego had something between you that I couldn't provide. Perhaps it was mixed in with your proximity and him being a safety blanket when you needed him. Regardless, you shared a special bond—no matter how mad you are with him right now. I'm not mad. Knowing you had probably consummated the marriage, the night of your wedding, I still wanted you, baby. Even then. I will *always* want you."

Her delicate hand reaches up to cup my face, her thumb tracing a line up and down my cheek. "You don't look at me differently? How could you still want me after knowing I was with someone else? The same person I'm *apparently* still married to."

The arm I have wrapped around her slides her in closer and I bring my other hand up to cup her face. My thumb skates across her lips, encouraging them to part under my touch.

I need to kiss her. I miss her so fucking much.

There is loss of warmth as her hand leaves my face and wraps around my hand on hers. She lowers it into her lap. "I love you, Liam. I do." A hint of smile pokes through her glum features. "But I need you to let me go. I can't do this anymore. Any of it. Too much has happened in such a short time. My head is spinning. There's been too much violence, too many lies, a boatload of hurt. Though this new version of me is stronger than I have ever been, it's a version of myself that I don't exactly like. I miss the version of me that wasn't always on edge. The version that was naive and ignorant to this sort of world. I miss simple. I miss being able to grab a coffee and not have to worry that someone will snatch me up."

There's a knock on the door before Lexi enters. Conor gives a two finger salute before shutting the door, giving us privacy.

Lexi runs over to Madison, taking in her disheveled appearance, and starts petting her hair. "Mad, what the hell happened? You look like you've seen a ghost."

"I have," she chuckles at her choice of words. "Diego is here."

Lexi's brows come together. "Well then." She places her hand on her hip and waves the other in the air. "Hi, Diego. If you could be so kind as to leave my friend be for the night, that would be great."

I can't help the laugh that burst from my lips. It's comical watching Lexi talk to the air as if his spirit is with us. "Alexis,

Diego is actually alive. Here in the flesh," I state, filling her in so Madison doesn't have to say the words out loud.

"*Hoooolyyyyy* shit."

Madison nods. "Liam, could you give Lexi and I a moment of privacy?"

I already don't like where this is going.

"Yeah." I stand and make my way to the door, lingering at the threshold. "I'll be right outside when you're ready."

I HAND Madison the helmet to my motorcycle then zip my oversized heated leather jacket up to her chin. Swinging my leg over the seat and sitting, I rev the engine. Madison climbs on and scooches forward, gripping my waist and laying her head on my back.

"Ready?" I ask into the speaker in my helmet.

Her beautiful voice comes through with confidence. "Ready."

I hit the throttle and we accelerate down the avenue. Once we get beyond the thickness of traffic, I open the throttle, weaving us in and out of the lanes. This is the first time having her on my bike and it'll be playing on loop in my mind. This moment. Feeling her body pressed against mine. Hearing her softly sing along to the songs on my playlist. Midnight hits and fireworks light up the city skyline.

"Wow," she sighs.

"Beautiful," I agree.

There is so much more I want to say to her. But I don't want to ruin this moment. For once, it feels like we are just a normal couple, racing down the parkway, listening to music and enjoying the feel of our bodies pressed together.

No obligations to anyone.

No distractions.

Just us.

FORTY MINUTES LATER, I'm pulling over into the drop off lane at JFK.

It's packed. New Year's Eve being one of the busiest days to travel.

Lovers and family members embrace and kiss goodbye all around us. Madison notices too, her mood shifting from peace to indecisiveness. I'll use that to my advantage. *I have to.*

"Thank you." She smiles up at me, handing me the helmet. I rest it on the seat and remove my own, placing it down next to hers. Leaning against the bike, I run a hand through my hair, smoothing it out. Madison takes off her heated jacket and hands it back to me.

"Keep it." I push her hand back.

"I don't want to deal with having to check it or carry it around." She folds the jacket and drapes it over the back of the bike.

Shaking manicured fingers pull the zipper higher on her black hoodie. She adjusts her crossbody purse and double checks for her ID and credit cards. I make a mental note to add a few thousand dollars into her account. I'm sure she won't be using Diego's money. Already refusing to use his jet. She bites her lip, driving me fucking mad. A deep crease forms between her brows as she stares down at her leather boots. Avoiding eye contact with me, she rubs her hands together and blows into them. I can't take another second of this.

I use the knuckle of my index finger to lift her chin. *There's my beautiful girl.* "You sure this is what you want?"

Tears form on her lower lash line and cascade over. She bolts forward, wrapping her arms around me and burying her face into my chest. I hold her tightly against my body, her own shaking with emotion.

"This is what I want," she whispers, her voice cracking. All that confidence she sported earlier is gone.

I am about to tell her she could always just stay—but then it really hits me. She deserves this chance at a normal life. I'd be a selfish prick to beg her to stay. *For me. For us.*

"Okay, baby." I lay my head on top of hers and we just stay there. Cars and taxis honk, trying to get us to make room for more drop offs, but I don't give a flying fuck. The president could show up in his motorcade and I *still* wouldn't move from this damn spot.

With my woman.

The other half of my soul.

She will always be that to me. No one will ever be able to fill the space that she holds.

Flurries fall from the sky and land on our faces. Madison looks up and releases a small giggle. *It's fucking adorable.* It lasts a few seconds before being replaced with gloom.

"I am going to tell you the same thing I told Diego." My body stills, knowing this is it.

The moment all the curtains Madison once opened to my soul become permanently shut.

"Don't call. Don't follow me, Liam. No gifts, no letters. No tracking me. A clean break."

She just ripped my fucking heart out and is holding it in her hands. I look around to see if anyone else is bearing witness to this.

Nope. Abso-fucking-lutely-NOT. Just more couples kissing and crying. *Lovely.*

"At least give me peace of mind that you got there safely. Wherever *there* is. A text will do."

Leaning up onto her tiptoes she places a kiss to my trembling lips.

"Goodbye, Liam."

Her voice cracks on my name but she doesn't falter. Turning on her heel, she clutches her purse close to her and walks through the automatic doors of the terminal.

And out of my life.

Forever.

CHAPTER 37

MADISON

I TURN the key and unlock the door to my new living quarters. My fingers scan the wall, feeling around for the lightswitch. With a *click*, the lights turn on, illuminating the small space. It's cozy and smells of flowers and freshly baked cookies. Bright and cheerful artwork hangs on the walls.

Comfort. That's exactly what I need right now.

Pressing a hand to the door, I close and lock it before leaning over to unzip my boots. I toe each one off and leave them at the entrance. The hardwood is cool beneath my sock-clad feet. I venture down the hall to the last door on the right. It's already open. My eyes adjust to the darkness of the room before I make my way over to the end table and switch the lamp on.

There, sitting on the desk, is a terrarium. With one beautiful Blue Monarch inside. A note sits beside it.

Mariposita,
You didn't think you could hide from the Bone Breaker, did you? I'm not writing this to worry you or intimidate you. I won't chase you. This note is to let you know I never meant to hurt you. I never wanted to lie to you. Everything I did was to protect you. To give you a

balance of the life you wanted mixed with my complicated one. My death meant we wouldn't have been on the radar anymore. We could have had a real shot at making our marriage work. I'd love to travel to Italy or France with you. Eat all the amazing food and pair it with all our favorite wines. Kiss you in front of the Eiffel Tower and make you scream my name under the stars in the countryside of Chianti. I still want that. I love you, Madison. And I understand why you chose to fly. I all but pushed you to. So when you're ready...really ready to free yourself of the past...open the cage and set her free. The climate where you are is quite pleasant for butterflies this time of year. If you change your mind or decide you want company, you know where to find me.

Your husband,
Ocean Eyes

I gently grab the terrarium and carry it to the window. Taking a deep breath in, I open the window and then the door to its enclosure. The butterfly flaps its gorgeous wings a few times, seemingly testing them out, before flying off into the early morning sky. *Time to fly, Madison.*

Emotional and physical exhaustion threaten to drop me where I stand. One final bit of strength has me reaching the bed and collapsing on top. My knees come up to my chest in the fetal position. I lay there a few moments questioning my last twenty-four hours. Then I remember my promise, and retrieve my phone from my purse. My heart pounds heavily against my ribs as I find Liam's contact.

MADISON

I'm here. I'm safe.

I don't wait for a response. Breaking my own heart, I block his number and then delete it from my phone, before tossing it onto the other end of the bed. The heaviness of my eyes is hard to ignore. I'm fucking exhausted. My eyelids flutter closed and darkness wraps me in its embrace.

Tomorrow I will get a new phone, a new number, and start a new life.

Tomorrow is a brand new day; a blank canvas.

Tomorrow everything will go back to being simple.

It has to.

....At least that's what I tell myself.

ACKNOWLEDGMENTS

Wow. As I typed out the last few words of book 2, I found myself at a loss of finding the right words to describe this feeling. This book had an entirely different path when I had first planned it out. That was, until the Bone Breaker came in. Funny how even fictional characters can grip your emotions and demand a larger role in your book. I'm not sorry about it. I enjoyed writing about Diego and Madison's connection. It was necessary for Madison's character development. Really, Diego's role affected everyone's character development. Now more than ever, I'm excited for what's to come in the last book of the trilogy. I know, I know. I left you on another cliffhanger. Don't worry. I'll be working on the last book in the series as quickly as possible. Of course, writing can become tough when a tiny human requires your attention. I'll be doing my best to carve out time to get the last book to you soon! Until then, I'd love your feedback. Are we a Diego fan? Liam fan? What about Killian? Let me know!

Now for my list of thank yous. First on the list is my husband. I know this year hasn't been easy for us, by any means, but I want you to know how much I appreciate all the love and support you show me day in and day out. Especially when it comes to supporting my books. I hope that our daughter never reads them —for obvious reasons—but she should know how much I adore her. She makes me belly laugh and smile every single day. I love you to the moon and back. Big thank you to my family and friends for reading through the book with me and offering your advice. Mom, your pride in my decision to write and desire to help fund my dream has been a huge blessing. Thank you, thank you! I would like to give a huge shout-out to my talented cover artist, as well as interior designer Emily at Quirky Circe Book Design. The series wouldn't be what it is without your artwork making it real! Seeing the cover and the interior come to life has been an incredible journey. Last, but certainly not least, to you, reading this—from the bottom of my heart, thank you for giving my books a chance. I hope you decide to ride this crazy rollercoaster—at least one more time—for the final book in the series. I'll see you there—along with a few of our favorite characters.

— *Luna Everly*

ABOUT THE AUTHOR

Luna Everly is a new indie romance author who would like to share the fantasyland she has in her mind with the world. This dream world consists of strong sarcastic men, who are grounded by their smart sassy heroines. Add a bit of suspense, impossible decisions, and amazing besties to the lives of these characters-- and you've got yourself quite the adventure to go on. Grab the tissues for emotional ups and downs and a fan for some seriously steamy moments.

As a Pisces, Luna often gets lost daydreaming. When she's not lost in thought, she's spending time with her husband, daughter, two rescue dogs, and her clingy cat Loki. Luna enjoys cooking, game nights, getting lost in a good book, self-care bubble baths, and even the occasional marathon of Call of Duty with her husband. You'll never find her far from her cup of coffee--or multiple cups for that matter.

Luna Everly is a pen name. She currently resides in New York with her family.

GET SOCIAL

authorlunaeverly.com

Facebook
https://www.facebook.com/profile.php?id=100088486166891

TikTok
https://www.tiktok.com/@authorlunaeverly

Instagram
https://instagram.com/authorlunaeverly

info@authorlunaeverly.com

* Subscribe to my newsletter to stay up to date on new releases and giveaways.

* Follow along with my blog to keep up with me and my wild adventures.